This book is dedicated to my personal "Dirty Dozen."
Justin, Heather, Samantha, Jarrod, Erin, Will, Bella-Capri,
Brittany, Mike, Ava,
and of course, the founders of the Rostron Familia,
Marilyn and Bill (William John Rostron)

ALSO BY WILLIAM JOHN ROSTRON

CAMBRIA TRILOGY (NOVELS)
Band in the Wind

Sound of Redemption

Brotherhood of Forever

CAMBRIA SERIES – STAND-ALONE NOVELS
The Other Side of the Wind

Dancing With the Lost

SHORT STORY COMPILATIONS
A Flamingo Under the Carousel

T-Rex Stole My Computer

SHORT FILMS AND VIDEOS OF STAGED PERFORMANCES
Pretty Flamingo

In the Garden of Eden

Ava's Bubble

The Fool on the Hill

The Last Chord

VIEWED AT: WWW.WILLIAMJOHNROSTRON.COM

CONTENTS

A Brief Preface   1
Time Is on My Side
Prologue   4
Where Have All the Good Times Gone?

Part I
HEY LITTLE GIRL
 1. When I Was Young   9
 2. Murder in My Heart for the Judge   13
 3. You May Be Right, I May Be Crazy   16
 4. Speak Softly   21
 5. When I Was Young (Reprise): Nicky Glue Version   25
 6. I Fought the Law   31
 7. Everybody Loves a Clown   41
 8. Brothers in Arms   45
 9. All in all, it's just another brick in the wall.   50
10. Lives in the Balance   53
11. Who Are You?   56
12. I Got the Music in Me   60
13. Slow Dancin' (Swayin' to the Music)   64
14. Hanky Panky   67
15. Long Way from Home   71

Part II
THE OTHER SIDE OF LIFE
16. We Are Family   77
17. Bad to the Bone   82
18. Human Wheels   84
19. Gimme Back My Bullets   87
20. Play With Fire   89
21. Back Door Man   93
22. Shapes of Things   96
23. Under Pressure   98
24. The Story   101
25. Whenever We Wanted To   104

26. The Good, the Bad, and the Ugly   107
27. Fountain of Sorrow   115
28. Paint it Black   120
29. The Actor   128
30. Scenes from an Italian Restaurant   133

Part III
YESTERDAY'S GONE

31. Seems Like Such a Long Time Ago   141
32. Sometimes a Fantasy   146
33. Hell Is for Children   150
34. The Thief of My Forever   154
35. Time in a Bottle   161
36. Join Together with the Band   164
37. Little Children   167
38. Never Go Home Anymore   170
39. The Way   174
40. Wasted on the Way   177
41. Lonely People   181

Part IV
THE WIND

42. A Place in the Sun   187
43. Remember Walking in the Sand   194
44. I'm Living on an Island   200
45. Sea of Heartbreak   203
46. Here in the Conch Republic   208
47. Nights in White Satin   210
48. Goodnight, Saigon   213
49. Broken Dreams   215
50. If the Sun Comes Up   219
51. Heroes and Villains in the Night   223
52. End of the Line   228
53. I've Been Lonely Too Long   232
54. Dancing with the Lost   239
55. It's My Life   246

Part V
ON THE DARK SIDE

56. With a Little Help from My Friends   251
57. Death Is Not the End   255
58. Looking for the Next Best Thing   258
59. Devil in Disguise   261
60. Bad Things   264
61. Come Alive   268
62. Showdown   274
63. Knockin' On Heaven's Door   282
64. Death of a Clown   284
65. Strangers When We Meet   290
66. I Know You're Out There Somewhere   295
67. Yesterday   298

EPILOGUE
After the Storm

Epilogue - Scene 1   305
Lola
Epilogue - Scene 2   313
Devil in Disguise (Reprise)
Epilogue - Scene 3   315
Runnin' With the Devil
Epilogue - Scene 4   319
Turn the Page

AUTHOR'S NOTES
Just a Song Before I Go

Author Note #1   327
I Was Here
Author Note #2   333
Last Words
Author Note #3   338
Live Like You Were Dying

A BRIEF PREFACE

TIME IS ON MY SIDE

"Yeah, time is on my side, yes, it is."
-Rolling Stones

1. *Dancing with the Lost* is the fifth book in the Cambria series. However, it was specifically written to be read either as that fifth book or as a stand-alone story for those who are not into long commitments.
2. For those who have read my previous books, you already know that I am obsessed with using songs and lyrics as chapter titles. This stems from the fact that I draw my inspiration from listening to the tunes of my youth. If a reader finds these lyrics distracting or time-consuming, feel free to skip them. I would if they bothered me. Life's too short.

"The end should never be the end,
That's why I always dance with the lost."

"Dancing With the Lost"
- Michael Quinn Powers

PROLOGUE

WHERE HAVE ALL THE GOOD TIMES GONE?

"Let it be like yesterday.
Please let me have happy days.
Won't you tell me,
Where have all the good times gone?"
- The Kinks

*M*aggie McAvoy had an idyllic childhood—until the age of eleven. During the summer of 1967, everything changed. Up until that point, she had the love and support of her parents, older brother, and older sisters, who pampered her. Her world was also filled with friends...and music...and dancing...and egg creams. There were plenty of egg creams and penny candies because her family owned a candy store. This blissful existence was shattered in the summer of 1967, and Maggie's life would never be the same.

Many of her happiest times revolved around the basement of her home on 221st Street in the hamlet of Cambria Heights, Queens. It was there that her brother's band practiced incessantly in their quest for stardom. Maggie and her older sisters, Aylin and Siobhan, had front-row seats at these rehearsals. They would sing and dance to the band's covers of popular songs, as well as some excellent originals.

The band members were more than just musicians to her; they were her friends and her "big brothers." Still, she had to admit to herself that they were also the objects of her childhood crushes. Primarily, she dreamed of Bracko, the group's tall and handsome lead guitar. He was so soft-spoken that it was rare to hear him interact with anyone beyond a smile or an appropriate guitar riff. Those who truly knew the enigmatic Bracko understood that a loyal and loving person was hidden beneath his quiet exterior. His long, straight, brownish-blonde hair and blue eyes made him extremely attractive; yet it was the kindness of his soul that those fortunate enough to befriend him could appreciate.

On July 5, 1967, Bracko was murdered. The object of her childhood crush and a symbol of her innocent joy was taken from Maggie in a senseless act of violence. That devastating loss was merely the opening act to the tragedies that made her world a living nightmare. Soon her father and brother suffered the same fate. The mysteries surrounding the deaths, the disappearances, and the ensuing grief would haunt her for years to come.

Yet she survived. While her mother retreated into a semi-comatose life of constant sorrow, her oldest sister, Aylin, struggled between substance abuse and rehab stints. Tragically, her other sister, Siobhan, died under unfortunate circumstances. Maggie grew tougher, refusing to let the world penetrate the shell surrounding her once sensitive exterior. She had tried to move on with her life as best she could.

Eventually, she became a widely respected therapist and lived a comfortable life. That sense of stability crumbled on a cold December night in 1989 when she began to uncover the painful truth about where all her good times...and all her good people had gone.

PART I

HEY LITTLE GIRL

"Hey, little girl, you don't have to hide nothing no more.
You ain't done nothing that hadn't been done before."
- Syndicate of Sound

December 1989

WHEN I WAS YOUNG

"When I was young,
It was more important,
Pain more painful,
Laughter much louder,
...When I was young."
- The Animals

Maggie's Memos and Memories
December 16, 1989

I buried my father, brother, and three of my friends before I was a teenager. My mother and one of my sisters passed away in the ensuing years. I was a widow shortly before turning 21. A bit depressing, don't you think? However, I will soon provide the details, as I have always been a tell-it-like-it-is kind of person.

I must mention that I reacted differently from most people to the tragedies of 1967. I don't know exactly why, but I can't shake the imagery of the Three Pigs from my mind for some reason. Yes, I am referring to *the* Three Pigs of "Big Bad Wolf" fame. I know that it may seem like a silly way for a person with a doctorate in psychology to begin her first memo. Yet, to me, it explains how I managed to survive.

My two sisters and I were *the* Three Little Pigs. My sister Aylin built her house of straw—well, she literally did start with grass—in the cannabis sense of the word. The wolf huffed and puffed and blew her house down. By that, I mean the tragedies of 1967 destroyed her mentally and physically. Aylin endured years of drug and alcohol abuse in that house of straw because she couldn't deal with "The Wolf" of our shared life story.

My sister Siobhan is dead—her house of sticks had no protection from the tragedy that befell us. She married a rock star when she was far too young—likely in an attempt to escape from our depressing home. Her husband became enamored with the whole drug and rock and roll scene and eventually couldn't resist the hard stuff. He contracted AIDS by sharing needles and then passed it on to my poor sister.

Unlike my sisters, I survived. Why? I truly don't know. I took pride in being the pig in the brick house. Perhaps I was so young—only 11 years old—that the severity of events in 1967 was beyond my comprehension. Alternatively, maybe I was just a cold-hearted, uncaring bitch incapable of feeling deeply.

Was I in denial? Or was I just numb? Was I mentally unstable? Or perhaps I am simply stronger than the others? I intend to answer these questions about myself before I address my newest patient.

Why now? That is the heart of my dilemma. What is it in this patient that provokes such self-doubt in me? I know the answer, but I suspect no one else sees the big picture.

Nicholas Toto, alias "Little Nicky Glue," was responsible for some or all of the deaths of my family and friends almost two decades ago. I want to understand him, but I also need to understand myself.

I remember that he was a part of a gang—*the* gang responsible for my downward spiral. I was a confused, emotionally unstable eleven-year-old whose dreams had been crushed by this man.

I am no longer young. However, whether I am unstable remains a question that needs to be answered. More importantly, can I deal with Toto in a professional capacity? Should I deal with him at all? I am entering into uncharted and unethical behavior. I should recuse myself; that would be the right and legal course of action. However, I seek closure. I need to know the true story of my life, even if it is being narrated from a murderer's point of view.

Here, in 1989, "Nicky Glue" Toto is believed to be complicit in the murder of a rival gang member. While it is my job to uncover the details, I really don't care about who he killed *this year*. I took the case on false pretenses. My role is to listen to his story and, with Nicky's permission, speak to the police about his potential testimony against his family's don, Guy Provenzano. To be honest, I have no interest in Nicky or his boss's guilt regarding a murder here in 1989. That death means nothing to me. Perhaps it's the cold-hearted bitch in me coming through. I only care about the deaths of my father and brother, as well as Bracko and so many others in 1967.

Am I the only one who cares about the past? Have the police and the other victims' families given up on uncovering the truth? This golden opportunity has presented itself, and I refuse to let it slip away. However, I must also dig deep into my memories to do this properly. Only then can I understand everything that happened. I can't rely solely on Nicky's account. No, I must weave his story together with mine to uncover the ultimate truth.

How can I claim to be one of the top therapists in New York City if I can't even understand myself? Therefore, I will need to explore my past as thoroughly as Nicky's. I will utilize the method I have developed, which has proven effective with most or all my patients. Will it be effective on a hardened killer? Will I be able to apply it to my own self-analysis? Analyzing myself as a patient will be a challenging task. I know I can be cold and obnoxious; so many people have told me as much. How else can you explain that I have not seen or spoken to any of my surviving family members since I left home in 1972? I know that Siobhan died in 1980—it was in all the papers because her husband was a famous guitarist. I have no idea what happened to my mother and Aylin.

But here I am...the pig in the brick house who now finds herself vulnerable.

2

MURDER IN MY HEART
FOR THE JUDGE

"I've got murder in my heart for the judge,
That old judge wouldn't budge."
- Moby Grape

Maggie's Memos and Memories
December 17, 1989

*I*t all started last week when I received a phone call from David Cooperman, a lawyer friend I once dated. It was nothing serious, just a brief connection. Since I lost my husband, nothing involving the opposite sex has ever been serious. That's another part of my story that deserves some reflection during my self-analysis.

David's still a good friend and occasionally uses me as an expert witness in some of his cases. However, this time, he offered me a slightly different task. Nicholas "Little Nicky Glue" Toto had been arrested for the murder of Desiderio Gomez, and he vehemently proclaims his innocence. Unfortunately for Nicky, an eyewitness had written down his license plate number as he drove an accomplice away from the scene.

Initially, the police had tried to leverage what they had on Nicky to identify the actual shooter. When Cooperman informed me that Toto was Mad Guy Provenzano's cousin, the implication was that Nicky might be able to testify against his cousin and link *him* to the murder. Could the DA get Nicky to testify against "the *Don* of Southeast Queens," an unindicted suspect in over a dozen murders?

With this golden opportunity, Robert Morgenthau, New York's District Attorney, stepped in and personally took over the high-profile case. He is running for mayor, and a victory in this prosecution could significantly boost his poll numbers. However, Nicky Toto immediately rejected him. Like all members of the New York organized crime family, Nicky knew that silence was not only golden but the only healthy choice. Morgenthau, frustrated and ready to send Nicky away for life, listened to a suggestion made by Cooperman. What if Nicky was kept free but allowed to talk to a therapist? A therapist who might convince him that entering a witness protection program could be a better option. Cooperman saw this as a possibility because Toto had let slip that he felt he had been set up to take the fall. His cousin Guy had something against him and was punishing him by framing him for the Gomez murder.

That's where I come into the picture. I am supposed to play on this feeling of betrayal and encourage Nicky to turn on Mad Guy Provenzano. Neither Cooperman nor Morgenthau understands that my motives for taking down "Nicky Glue" Toto and "Mad Guy" Provenzano go much deeper than punishing a crime lord. My feelings date back to 1967.

A Manhattan judge has given the authorities until June 30, 1990, to keep Nicky's case open. During that time, he will be allowed to move freely among his gang. The prosecution must proceed with its case by that date or drop the charges. Luckily, Nicky doesn't know this detail.

Damn, Judge Wilkins! Given enough time, I could manipulate Nicky Glue to reveal everything he knows. With this time constraint, I'm uncertain of my ability to do that. They want me to counsel him to discuss all his experiences. With Nicky's permission, the story will then be relayed to Cooperman, who will decide if Nicky has enough on his cousin to convict him of the Gomez murder. Hopefully, then Nicky will avoid the murder charge he faces and go into witness protection.

An added dimension to my dilemma is my mental state. Will I be able to push and prod him to reveal the past? Can I withstand the reopening of old wounds? I now realize that my tough exterior may not be as formidable as I once believed. I have an ethical and moral predicament—some of Provenzano's murders that might come to light include many of the people I loved most.

After my mother, two sisters, and I were left to pick up the pieces, I realized that they did not survive intact. Until today, I thought that I had. Was I wrong? I must pursue this further despite the nagging fear that it could backfire emotionally and legally. But hell, I didn't get this far by playing it safe.

3

YOU MAY BE RIGHT,
I MAY BE CRAZY

"Turn out the light,
Don't try to save me."
-Billy Joel

Maggie's Memos and Memories
January 4, 1990

I am ready to analyze myself. Ironically, I almost titled this the beginning of my **Self-Help Introspection Therapy**—clearly not professional. I know this is going to be an actual S.H.I.T show in every sense of the word (pun intended), but to call it that would be absurd...wouldn't it?

I've never tried this before, mainly because I never thought I needed or wanted it. However, if I am ever going to get through months of listening to a low-level hood discussing all the evil he has done, I will need something to counter it. I need to know where I've been. I need to dig deep. Okay, maybe not back-to-the-womb deep, but perhaps back to a time when I was young. Back to a time when we were a happy family of six in the 1960s…before those bastards took it all away.

My name is Dr. Maggie McAvoy Evers, and I think it has a nice ring to it. However, professionally, I only use Dr. Evers. I am very proud of my McAvoy name, but given the sadness of my family's story, I find using my married name more anonymous. I'm getting distracted by minor details. Still, since I'm writing this for myself, perhaps I should start over with my earliest emotional memories.

I loved Bracko. If someone else were reading this memo, they might ask, "What is a Bracko?" Is it some pretentious new restaurant or food choice? Or a deluxe electronic device to make my life easier? Therefore, the question is better stated as "Who was Bracko?"

The answer would be that he was the nicest, sweetest guy who just happened to play guitar in my brother's band. I fell madly in love with him as a young girl. On second thought, "love" might be too strong a word. I was eleven, and Bracko was seventeen. I guess "crush" would be a more appropriate description of my feelings. Yet, most crushes end when the reality of age and maturity sets in. That never got to happen with me because Bracko was murdered very shortly before my brother Jimmy and my father met the same fate. There was no time for childhood crushes when the three "men" you care about most are lost within weeks of each other. I grew up fast.

I had a perfect childhood until the tragedy that occurred shortly before my twelfth birthday. I grew up in a little-known hamlet on the extreme fringe of New York City called Cambria Heights. Every moment in my life felt wonderful.

How many people can say that their family owned a candy store? I was a young child and had access to the whole works: Sugar Daddies, Mary Janes, Red Hot Dollars, …and, oh, those strips of paper that had dots of sugar on them—what were they called? We also had nightly egg creams, ice cream, and a wide variety of other treats. Of course, my parents did put some restrictions on our sugar consumption.

The most ironic part of the experience was that the local dentist, Dr. Irving Shotten, rented the floor above the store. When we gorged ourselves on store products, my father opened the windows wide so that we could hear Doc Shotten's drill working away at some unfortunate patient's teeth. There were many days when I thought the connection between the dentist and the candy store was not purely coincidental.

My parents married soon after my father arrived home from his stint in the Navy during World War II. The first thing they did was rent the apartment above the very popular candy store known as Newcombe's. When Mr. Newcombe decided to retire and move to Miami, my parents got the wonderful idea to buy the store from the old man. When my brother Jimmy was born, they renamed the store Mac and Son. However, nobody in Cambria Heights embraced the name change, and it remained "Newcombe's" until our family sold it under duress in the late sixties.

With newfound prosperity, our family moved to a nice one-family home on 221st Street. This left Newcombe's upstairs space available for rent. Cambria had few vacant retail spaces, so the square footage above the store was in high demand. Nonetheless, choosing a dentist as a tenant? Hmmm…let me think on that.

In my therapy practice, clients are asked to write a brief piece about themselves or an aspect of their lives they consider significant. The session begins with a discussion focused on this written work. I then ask specific questions related to the content of the writing.

How would that work if I were to assume the roles of both the patient and the doctor?

Dr. Evers (Me) talking to myself in a bizarre voice: "So, Maggie, what do you think so far?"

ME (Maggie Evers, in normal voice): "Life was good…especially the candy!"

Bizarre Voice: "C'mon, Maggie, think deeper."

ME: "Okay, up until eleven, I was very happy…and I should have married that dreamboat, Bracko."

Bizarre Voice: "Now you are not being realistic, Maggie. You know that Bracko…"

ME: "What?… he died?… yeah, I know. But…"

Bizarre Voice: "But what?"

ME: "But I never stopped having feelings for him."

Bizarre Voice: "Go on."

ME: "He was something special. Well, so was my husband…but we're not here to talk about him…yet."

Bizarre Voice: "If you say so…"

ME: "Of course, I say so. I am the only one here talking for both of us. Which reminds me… I have a client coming in for therapy. This conversation, or should I say introspection, will have to wait."

Bizarre Voice: "Avoidance…"

ME: "Yeah, what are you going to do about it?"

Bizarre Voice: "Ouch!"

I *did* have a patient waiting on the other side of the door, so I had to end the insane conversation I was having with myself. What was that Billy Joel song from the *Glass Houses* album ten years ago—"You May

Be Right, I May Be Crazy." And let's not forget the lyric that follows—
"But it just might be a lunatic you're looking for."

I am about to meet the infamous "Little Nicky Glue" Toto. It will
be interesting to read *his* "story about himself." It is time for the "Shit
Show" to begin.

...And I just might be the lunatic *he* is looking for.

4

SPEAK SOFTLY

"Speak softly, love,
So, no one hears us but the sky."
-Theme from The Godfather (Nino Rota and Larry Kusik)

Nicky Toto's Notes #1
January 4, 1990

I was almost a ~~fucking~~ prince. Oops, I remember you said no cursing while I write down this ~~shit~~, I mean stuff. Is shit considered a curse word in your crowd? You know, with the shrink crowd.

Anyway, as I was telling you...I was almost a prince, but not of England, France, or any other place like that. Doc, do they still have princes in England and France? What the hell do I know? I quit school as soon as they let me. Actually, I think they may have asked me to leave.

No, I was almost a prince of Cambria Heights, a much more important form of royalty...at least to me. However, I could never really be a prince, a don, or a top boss because my last name was Toto, not Provenzano. Guy and Tony were Provenzanos, which made them royalty, heirs to the family throne. My mother was a Provenzano, so I was a first cousin to the princes... so close, but no cigar for Nicky Toto.

Did I suffer from feeling like crap compared to my two cousins? Well, yeah, wouldn't you? If you're going to be a member of a crime family, doesn't everyone want to be the *boss?*

This writing crap is hard, Dr. Evers. You told me I hafta write this ~~autobioga~~,...this story of my life to aid with my case...and to make me feel better. I don't write too good, so this ain't easy. However, I will do what it takes to get over feeling shitty like I have been feeling lately, and...oh yeah... maybe not go to jail forever. It's good that the nuns taught me to write neatly, or you would have trouble reading my story.

Yeah, those nun bitches were good for something. But I could've done without some of the bullshit from a few of them who taught me at Sacred Heart School. Can I get an "Amen" here if anyone has been through the same shit? I think maybe those nuns caused me to become violent. Can we use that in my defense? Nun abuse?

The two I remember most clearly (and not in a good way) were Sister "Rip-Your-Heart-Out" and "Sister Mary Nefarious." I don't even know their real names. I guess I should be thankful that their lunatic ways forced me to learn to write neatly. Yeah, the more I think about it, they might be the reason I grew up and hurt people. Then again, my friend Billy didn't hurt no one, even after he got treated worse than me.

Billy Rossini got tossed down a flight of stairs because Mary Nefarious thought he had been talking while climbing the stairs to our third-floor classroom. I watched and laughed as Billy was falsely punished for a crime he didn't even commit! It had been Larry Giaprutto, one of our young gang, who had been breaking the silence rule. However, when Larry saw the black-and-white monster turning, he quickly jumped behind stupid Billy, who was soon airborne. Luckily, Billy was caught about six steps down by his friend Greg

Santina. He coulda suffered a serious injury that no doubt would have been somehow excused and swept under the rug.

I guess the sadistic nuns will have to answer to a higher power, or maybe they did already. Who knows? For those like me, it taught us that might makes right. When I look back, I think of how we used to call them *Psychotic Lesbians*. Of course, I didn't know what those words meant at eleven. I know we hated them.

Hey, I did learn to write neatly, so they did their job. But Sister Mary Nefarious and Sister Rip-Your-Heart-Out also taught me that cruelty was a handy tool for getting your way with people.

Dr. Evers' Notes and Transcription of Interview
Session #1
January 4, 1990

I CHOSE TO OVERLOOK NICKY'S RANT ABOUT NUNS, WHICH WAS EITHER SCAPEGOATING OR AN UNCONSCIOUS EFFORT TO EVADE THE REAL ISSUES. INSTEAD, I IMMEDIATELY SHIFTED THE FOCUS TO HIS RELATIONSHIP WITH HIS COUSINS, GUY AND TONY PROVENZANO.

Dr. Evers: "So, Nicky, are you still close with your cousins?"
Nicky: "Not so much now. I was when we was growing up. I was much younger than they were, and they picked on me. Back then, I thought that was what guys did to each other. But it wasn't long before I realized that Guy was fucking crazy. Sorry, I mean, *frigging* crazy."
Dr. Evers: "Okay, Nicky, some ground rules. I don't love your language, but if it helps you to tell the story, go ahead."

Nicky smiled and continued.

Nicky: "I mean, it was no accident that everyone calls him 'Mad Guy.' I learned just a little too late just how fucking nuts he was."

Dr. Evers: "But, Nicky, if you felt that way, why did you do everything he told you to do?"

Nicky: "Are you listening to me? He was a prince. The only one higher up than Guy was his father, Dominick—*Don* Provenzano."

Dr. Evers: "So, you hated Guy?"

Nicky: "Yes and no. I hated him—but I also wanted to be him."

Dr. Evers: "When did things start to change?"

Nicky: "Doc, I don't know if I can do this?"

Dr. Evers: "But…"

Nicky: "No, I need to get the hell outta here. I need to think. I might come back. If I do, I'll write another one of your shitty little stories… and we'll see."

OUR SESSION ENDED ABRUPTLY BECAUSE NICKY WAS RELUCTANT TO DISCUSS HIS COUSIN. HOWEVER, THAT IS THE ENTIRE CRUX OF MY JOB HERE. UNDERSTANDING THE GUY/NICKY CONNECTION IS CRUCIAL TO MY MISSION. I NEED TO FIND OUT IF GUY PROVENZANO WAS INVOLVED IN THE MURDER NICKY IS ACCUSED OF. ADDITIONALLY, I NEED TO UNCOVER INFORMATION ABOUT HOW PROVENZANO WAS INVOLVED IN THE MURDERS OF ELEVEN OR MORE PEOPLE IN 1967. THAT INFORMATION IS IMPORTANT TO ME PERSONALLY!

5

WHEN I WAS YOUNG (REPRISE): NICKY GLUE VERSION

"I smoked my first cigarette at ten,
And for girls, I had a bad yen.
When I was young."
-The Animals

Nicky Toto's Notes #2
January 6, 1990

Okay, I'm back for one more try. My lawyers tell me that I don't have much choice. But I feel really smart now that I started my note by writing the lyrics of a song by The Animals from the 1960s. I got the idea because of Vinnie the Cat, a friend of mine—may he rest in peace. He was an expert on everything about music. He was always quoting the words to songs. I remembered this one in particular. It's almost like I'm a real writer or poet. ~~Fuck me~~. Oops. Dr Evers, I need to watch my language. You're a classy lady. What are you...early thirties? Probably born and raised in some swanky

Manhattan neighborhood, or one of those classy suburbs like Great Neck or Manhasset?

You know, I just realized that I think the guy singing that song was a wimp. I know I had my first cigarette at seven or eight. Let me think. Yeah, I was born in 1947, and it was in 1955 that my cousin Tony offered me my first unfiltered Camel. I know that because Tony and I were watching my cousin Guy screw Angela Salerno in a basement. The song "Love Me Tender" by Elvis Presley was playing on the radio.

"That's just what I'm gonna do to you, Angie, love you tender." Guy was smooth with the ladies, and that little who-aa fell for his line. I'm not sure of the spelling of who-aa. We watched from another room in the basement, all the while dreaming that someday we would use that line—*Love Me Tender.*

When Guy was all done, Tony tells me that after sex, we're supposed to light up cigarettes. Now, I'm pretty sure that the tradition is for the people *who actually did have sex* to light up, but I didn't argue with my cousin. In fact, I *never* argued with any of my cousins. They were older and tougher than me, and I wanted to be just like them.

Eventually, I did move up in the organization...an organization that Guy runs now because of his father's mental problems. My Uncle Dominick has ~~diment~~, ~~demeinta~~...oh, fuck, he forgets shit. Well, that's another sad story that I will tell you ~~eventoly~~...soon. But let me start with my two important cousins. First, Tony.

Tony...ah, Tony. The sensitive brother...the nice brother. However, soon after his 19th birthday, he destroyed his mind. He was huffing glue. Way too much ~~fucking~~ freaking glue. Some kids saved him before he died. To be honest, I think Tony wanted to die. He wasn't a happy person.

I believe Tony's accident was the beginning of all the bad times... all the crazy times. It was when Guy started to really, really earn the nickname "Mad Guy."

The funny thing is that some kids saved Tony's life just before it was too late. Guy didn't appreciate what they did. Guy started to hate those kids. I didn't get it. Geez, they saved his brother's life, and he holds it against them.

Guy more than once told us that he would rather have his brother dead than the retarded dumb shit he became. He never said that around the rest of the family—just us two cousins, Richie (also a half-Provenzano) and me. I know he held a grudge against those kids, which only got worse with time...which is why...which is why...

Nope, I don't want to talk about THAT yet.

However, Tony's stupidity (though the family always called it "The Accident") gave me an opportunity. Family was family. Richie would eventually become Guy's consigliere, and I would become a big shot, too. However, I had to prove myself worthy, family or no family. What I had to do to prove myself to them is why I need to see you.

Following their lead ended up giving me boatloads of money and lots of broads—not to mention a three-pack-a-day habit. But there was a downside—my conscience. Oh, and that's not to mention the 25-to-life I'm facing in a few months.

What I did in 1967 will always haunt me. Can you help me, Doc?

Dr. Evers' Pre-Interview Notes
Session #2
January 6, 1990

AFTER READING HIS STORY, I BELIEVE NICKY IS READY TO CONFRONT THE REALITY OF HIS RELATIONSHIP WITH HIS COUSIN GUY. IT IS UNUSUAL FOR A THERAPIST TO ACHIEVE A BREAKTHROUGH SO QUICKLY, THEREFORE, I MUST BE CAREFUL NOT TO PUSH HIM TOO FAST OR TOO FAR. SOME OF NICKY'S URGENCY MIGHT STEM FROM HIS MEDICAL CONDITION. I'VE REVIEWED THE DOCTOR'S REPORTS, AND ALTHOUGH ONLY IN HIS FORTIES, NICKY IS DEALING WITH THE MIDDLE STAGES OF EMPHYSEMA. HIS REVELATION ABOUT SMOKING AT A YOUNG AGE NOW CARRIES NEW SIGNIFICANCE. AN OXYGEN TANK IS A

CONSTANT COMPANION FOR HIM, AND HE APPEARS FRAIL COMPARED TO THE PHYSICALLY IMPOSING MAN HE ONCE WAS. ONE OF HIS LISTED ALIASES IS "LITTLE NICKY GLUE," A SARCASTIC REFERENCE TO HIS WELL-OVER SIX-FOOT FRAME. I DON'T RECALL HIM FROM THOSE DAYS, BUT I'VE BEEN TOLD THAT HE WAS TALL AND HANDSOME, WITH A SWARTHY COMPLEXION AND CURLY BLACK HAIR. NOW, WHAT STOOD BEFORE ME WAS A HUNCHED-OVER SHELL OF THAT PERSON WITH THINNING SALT-AND-PEPPER HAIR.

Interview Transcript
January 6, 1990

Dr. Evers*:* "So, do you want to talk about it, Nicholas?"
Nicky: "No, Doc, I'm not ready for that yet.
Dr. Evers: "You're not ready for honesty?
Nicky: "Yeah…but I ain't ready to die."
Dr. Evers: "Explain, please, Nicholas."
Nicky: "First of all, Doc, nobody in this whole goddammed world…er…stupid world calls me Nicholas. I'm Nicky…Nicky Glue to most of my friends. And many of those friends would slit my throat if they knew I was talkin' to you."
Dr. Evers: "Oh, it can't be that bad, Nicky."
Nicky: "Doc, maybe I should never have come to you. It was my lawyer's idea. I must have been outta my fu…freaking mind. I don't think you understand the price of what I am doing. I don't think you know anything about where I grew up…or how I grew up. You know nothing about my world—the streets of Queens. We were told never to be cheese-eaters…that was the worst thing you could be."
Dr. Evers: "A cheese-eater?"

Nicky: "Yeah, you know…a rat. Listen, Doc, I'm going to say one word to you, and then I am fucking out of here. But you're not Italian, so you probably aren't gonna get it. Doc, your fancy research shit ain't gonna begin to tell you about what *Omerta* means?"

Dr. Evers' Post-Interview Notes
Session #2

AND WITH THAT, HE WAS GONE. THERE WAS SO MUCH FOR ME TO PROCESS FROM THAT ONE WORD. I CAN'T STOP THINKING ABOUT NICKY'S USE OF "OMERTA." I KNOW WHAT THE WORD MEANS. AFTER ALL, WHO HASN'T SEEN ALL "THE GODFATHER" MOVIES? THIS INSCRUTABLE CODE OF HONOR FORBADE ANY MEMBER OF THE CRIME FAMILY FROM EVER "SNITCHING" ON ANOTHER. HOWEVER, WITH THE MAFIA, IT WAS MORE LIKE "SNITCHES GET STITCHES" ON STEROIDS. OMERTA CREATED A WALL OF SILENCE UNMATCHED IN THE CIVILIZED WORLD. SO WHY IS THIS PATIENT SO VITAL TO ME, MORE THAN ANY OTHER? HIS USE OF THE PHRASE "OMERTA" REMINDED ME THAT HE IS CONNECTED TO THE GANG THAT RULED MY NEIGHBORHOOD—AN ORGANIZATION THAT DEVASTATED MY LIFE. IT IS BOTH SAD AND FASCINATING HOW MY ANALYSIS OF NICKY OVERLAPS WITH MY OWN REFLECTIONS. I AGAIN ASK MYSELF—SHOULD I RECUSE MYSELF FROM HIS THERAPY SESSIONS? THE PROFESSIONAL IN ME SAYS THAT IS THE ONLY PATH TO FOLLOW. HOWEVER, THE LITTLE ELEVEN-YEAR-OLD MAGGIE IN ME FEELS DIFFERENTLY. I'LL HAVE TO NAVIGATE A FINE LINE IN MY SESSIONS WITH NICKY. I NEED TO GET HIM TO RETURN BOTH FOR PROFESSIONAL AND PERSONAL REASONS.

6

I FOUGHT THE LAW

"I fought the law,
And the law won."
- Bobby Fuller Five

Nicky Toto's Notes #3
January 10, 1990

*M*y lawyer, Cooperman, brought in the heavy guns—his partners. I think their names are Leonardo and Barlon. Doc, you know them, right? Against my better judgment, I'm back. They told me I had no choice. I have the feeling that this will be the death of me. Yeah, I know that is a ~~fucking~~ overused phrase... especially common with the broads. However, in my case, I mean it quite literally. This is ~~confidendi~~...secret, right? I mean, I know what everything I tell my lawyers... Cooperman, Leonardo, and that colored fellow...what's his name... Barlon? It can't be used against me in court. I think the same is true about you. If it isn't, I will rip this up before you ever see it.

Okay, I called my lawyers, and they say I can continue with these notes and our talks. Leonardo and Barlow (they gave me their card so I could spell their names good) say we need to know if I can mount an insanity defense. Well, I ain't ~~fucking~~ crazy…excuse me…freaking crazy. If you want to know if I can fake it, that's another question. I mean, I ain't no great actor like John Wayne or Rock Hudson, but I have seen crazy first-hand all my life. I mean, they don't call my cousin "Mad Guy" for no reason. No, I've seen plenty of his shit.

But if I don't pull off the crazy defense, then they are asking me to rat on him. As crazy as he is, I don't know if I can do that. He is my cousin and…I also don't know if I would have a long life after I opened my mouth. He is a mean, vengeful ~~motherfucker~~…kind of man.

I may have to talk to you a long, long time before I could ever do that. I may as well try the "Batshit Crazy" defense first.

Dr. Evers' Pre-Interview Notes
January 10, 1990

AFTER READING NICKY'S WORDS, I REALIZE THAT MY STRATEGY FOR THIS SESSION IS TO CREATE A DIVIDE BETWEEN NICKY AND HIS COUSIN, GUY. THE MORE I ACCOMPLISH THIS, THE MORE NICKY WILL FEEL COMFORTABLE DISCUSSING THE CRIMES HE COMMITTED FOR HIM.

Interview Transcription
January 10, 1990

Nicky: Where do you want me to start this bullshit? I'm still not sure about this."

Dr. Evers: "Okay, let's start with an easy one. Why do they call you Nicky Glue?"

Nicky: "Next question. I don't want to talk about that."

Dr. Evers: "It's a name you go through life with and accept. Come on, I want to get to know you. I need to know everything about you."

Nicky: "Bull..er...poop."

Dr. Evers: "Nicky, you can say bullshit. I was in the Navy and heard much worse."

Nicky: Now I know you're screwing with me. They don't let broads in the Navy. Besides, I was taught to respect ladies."

Dr. Evers: "So far you have called women "broads" and "who-aas" in your writing and our discussions. So cut the crap. And while we're at it—the correct word for what you are pronouncing as "who-aa" is a "whore," and you shouldn't be throwing that word around so loosely.

Nicky: "Whore? You're kidding? I never heard that word. You mean when I say that girl is a fucking *who-aa*, I am supposed to be saying a 'fucking whore?'"

Dr. Evers: No, you shouldn't be calling girls or women either one.

Nicky: "Huh?"

Dr. Evers: And while we're at it, your lawyer, Goody Barlow, is a "Black man" or an "African American." He is not a "colored."

Nicky: "I thought that was better than 'mullie' or 'ni...'"

Dr. Evers: "Stop right there. Do not even think of using the "N" word. But what the hell is a 'mullie' or shouldn't I ask?"

Nicky: "Don't ask if you don't want to know. It's short for mulanyan...Italian for eggplant. It's what we call..."

Dr. Evers: "I get it. I get it. You're a racist."

Nicky: "No more than the next guy. I mean, we have *colored*...I mean African Americans working for us...and we pay them well."

Dr Evers: "Do you let them call you *Guinea* or *Wop*?

Nicky: "Not if they want to keep living."

Dr. Evers: "So you..."

I noticed Nicky looking at his watch.

Dr. Evers: "So this conversation has all been a stalling tactic by you?"
Nicky: "I guess I'm not as stupid as you thought."
Dr. Evers: No more stalling. The Nicky 'Glue' story... now."
Nicky: "Do I have to?"
Dr. Evers: "If not...we're done here. I want the story now."
Nicky: "I am doing this under protest."
Dr. Evers: "Duly noted."
Nicky: "What does that mean?"
Dr. Evers: "Nicky, now!"
Nicky: I was twelve years old and shaving almost every day. I guess what I am saying is...I was a man... physically."
Dr. Evers: "You had reached puberty."
Nicky: "Yeah...that too."
Dr. Evers: "Go on."
Nicky: "I'm hanging out at the schoolyard with my cousins Guy, Tony, and Richie. They were older than me, so I looked up to them. They thought I was a little kid. They thought I was guvibull...they thought I was stupid. I didn't know anything yet, and I trusted them."
Dr. Evers: "I'm guessing you found out that was a mistake."
Nicky: "Yeah, I found out the hard way. I was bragging about what you said—*pubaty*...you know that I could *masticate*, no...*massabate*... the hell with it...I could, you know...*choke the chicken...cuff the carrot... turn on the sprinklers*...I'm sorry I didn't mean to be so gross."
Dr. Evers: "Oh, you mean you were *lone rangering...playing five on one... tapping your potential.* I told you, Nicky, I was in the Navy. I've heard all the euphemisms—though *cuff the carrot* was a new one. The point is, Nicky, you are still stalling."
Nicky: "Okay. So, my cousin Guy says, 'So you do know about *supersensation*...right?' Now, I should have picked up on something when I took a quick look at Tony and Richie, and they looked confused. However, I was so excited that my big cousins were letting me in on their secrets of manhood that I went along."

Dr. Evers: "Supersensation?"

Nicky: "Doc, it's not a real thing. Guy was pulling a joke on me."

Dr. Evers: "Oh."

Nicky: "We walked along Linden Boulevard to A-to-Z Hardware. Guy goes in alone. He tells me that it's a secret formula, which the store sells out of the back room if you know the password. Our family business sold lots of stuff out of back rooms, so what he is saying is not suspicious. He goes in and a little while later comes out with a bag."

Dr. Evers: "What was in it?"

Nicky: "I'll get to that soon enough. First, Guy tells me that we need to go to the Garden of Eden. Yeah, I know you have no idea what that means because you've never been to Cambria Heights. It was a garden in the schoolyard that was so overgrown with bushes and weeds that you could do just about anything in there. And so somewhere along the line, it became the place where guys would go to get high. They named it the Garden of Eden."

Dr. Evers: "So, what happened?"

Nicky: "So, Guy pulls out a tube of something and keeps it in the bag so I can't see. He tells me to pull down my pants so that I can feel what the *supersensation* does to an ordinary jerk off. I tell him, 'In front of you guys?' Guy laughs and says, 'I saw your *peesche* before you even knew you had one, you dumb shit.'"

Dr. Evers: "*Peesche?*"

Nicky: "It's what Italians call a dick—especially when a boy is very young."

Dr. Evers: "So, what happened?"

Nicky: "So, Guy tells me to put out the palm of my hand and then gives directions. 'It loses its potency as soon as it comes out of the tube. When I put it in your palm, go over there and enjoy yourself. I promise we won't watch.' I did as he said. I was twelve, and he was my older cousin. I didn't expect the cruelty that I got...not from my own blood. But I know now that Guy was that absolute fucking nuts...and I am not apologizing for that word."

Dr. Evers: "There was no supersensation?"

Nicky: "It was glue."

Dr. Evers: "Oh, shit!"

Nicky: "Luckily, it was winter, so I had a coat on which covered my hand and crotch as I ran home…all the while hearing Guy's vicious laugh. I don't think my other cousins found it funny because I vaguely remember them calling him an *asshole*."

Dr. Evers: "So, then what?"

Nicky: "I was too embarrassed to tell my parents or a doctor or anyone. I used whatever crap I could find to get the glue off. Layers of skin also came off. Doc, I don't think it…my…peesche was ever the same. It might be why I never had any kids! It took weeks for the physical pain to go away, but the…but the shame…it never left. The first time I arrived at the schoolyard after weeks of staying in my room, I just wanted to forget the whole thing had happened."

Dr. Evers: "And Guy reminded you?"

Nicky: "No, he said nothing when I came back to the schoolyard the first time after his big joke on me. He even smiled at me, and I thought maybe I could put the whole thing behind me. The guys welcomed me back."

'Nicky, good to see you.'

'Nicky, welcome, stranger…been too busy for your old gang?'

'Nicky, long time no see.'

"And then it came out. Joey Pasco, that bastard, says, 'We missed you, Nicky…er…Nicky Glue.' Everyone let out the laughs they had been holding in. Guy had told the whole gang what happened in the Garden of Eden. Only Tony and Richie didn't laugh."

Dr. Evers: "But wasn't Tony…"

Nicky: "Retarded?"

Dr. Evers: "We don't use that word."

Nicky: "Well, we do. But to answer your question, this is long before Tony had his 'accident.'"

Dr. Evers: "Back to you. How'd you deal with it?"

Nicky: "What do you think? I sucked it up and went on with my life…

and my new name. Remember, Guy was a prince, who, by the way, is now the king. There was nothing I could do. While his father ruled the crime family, young Guy ruled over us. But that didn't stop me from hating the goddam motherfucker the rest of my life...sorry Doc, for the language, but sometimes there are no other words."

I saw my chance for a breakthrough. I had reached the core of Nicky's hatred for his cousin. I pushed on, assuming he was vulnerable at this point.

Dr. Evers: "So, why did you kill Gomez for him? I mean, if you despised your cousin, why would you follow his orders?"
Nicky: "I didn't. I did many things through the years because Guy was the boss, and that was my path to riches. But...I didn't kill Gomez. I swear to God, I didn't even know that he was going to get whacked. Joey Pasco tells me that Guy wants us to do a routine errand. I guess my definition of 'routine' and Guy's were very different.

"Therefore, I drove Pasco to Mauro's, an Italian food place near the Cross Island Parkway. Before I know it, he pulls out a mask for his face, takes out a gun, and goes inside. Then I hear gunshots, and Pasco is running out. I panic and drive us to safety in Elmont. He told me to park the car, and we went into Broadway Sherwood Diner. We had some ice cream and acted like nothing ever happened. Joey Pasco was the second-worst cold-hearted bastard in the world...next to Guy."
Dr. Evers: "And?"
Nicky: "Honestly, I didn't know that he was going to do that. Otherwise, I wouldn't have used my car."
Dr. Evers: "So, you had no qualms about the hit. It was just using your car that bothered you?"
Nicky: "You have to understand me when I tell you that no one, I mean no one, disagrees with or questions Mad Guy...ever."

Dr. Evers: "How'd that work out for you?"

Nicky: "The next day, the cops are at my door. A witness had seen my plates. I knew then that Guy had set me up to take the rap."

Dr. Evers: "Why?"

Nicky: "We'll get to that some other time."

Dr. Evers: "Bullshit! We're doing this now. What do you mean you were set up? Why do you think that?"

Nicky: "To be honest, I was not a great criminal. I screwed up so many times through the years that Guy wanted me dead."

Dr. Evers: "If that's true, how are you still alive?"

Nicky: "On more than one occasion, my cousin Richie…Richie Shea saved me and protected me. He was the only one on my side. However, even he will desert me if I testify."

Dr. Evers: "But…are you now ready to testify against Mad Guy?"

Nicky: "Yeah, I think I am. Talking to you makes me realize I owe that son-of-a-bitch nothing. He's been an asshole to me my whole life. I think I'm ready to talk about the Gomez murder…and maybe much more."

Dr. Evers: "I want to get this straight. You only claim to have unknowingly driven the getaway car?"

Nicky: "That's right."

Dr. Evers: "If I understand you correctly, you are saying that you are not a murderer?"

Nicky: "Well, now I didn't say that…did I?"

Dr. Evers' Post-Interview Notes
Session #3
January 10, 1990

IT WAS AN AMAZING SESSION WITH NICKY TOTO. AFTER HEARING ABOUT THE CRUELTY OF THE GLUE INCIDENT, I WILL NEVER USE THAT VILE NICKNAME AGAIN. THERE ARE SEVERAL KEY POINTS TO BE

TAKEN AWAY FROM OUR WORK TOGETHER.

NICKY HAS NO IDEA THAT I WAS BORN AND RAISED IN CAMBRIA HEIGHTS, SO HE SHARES DETAILS IN HIS STORY THAT HE DOESN'T REALIZE I ALREADY KNOW. YET, I MUST REMEMBER THAT I WAS ONLY 11 WHEN MOST OF THE CHAOS HAPPENED. THE NEW YORK POST BRANDED EVENTS AS THE "CARNAGE IN CAMBRIA," AND THE DAILY NEWS CALLED IT THE "HOLOCAUST IN THE HEIGHTS." THERE WERE SO MANY DEATHS THAT WERE NEVER CONNECTED. TO BE HONEST, I NEVER KNEW OR WANTED TO SEE THE EXTENT OF THE PROVENZANO FAMILY'S CULPABILITY. I SUPPOSE I WAS HIDING FROM REALITY...FROM THE TRUTH. IN THE END, I COULDN'T HIDE FROM THE FACT THAT MY FATHER AND BROTHER DIED...AND BRACKO. DO I NEED TO KNOW MORE? FOR MOST OF MY LIFE, I DIDN'T. NOW I DO!

I HAVE ONLY BEEN TASKED WITH DISCUSSING THE 1989 GOMEZ MURDER WITH NICKY, BUT "LITTLE MAGGIE" NEEDS TO KNOW THE DETAILS OF 1967. I NEED TO HEAR WHAT HAPPENED TO MY FAMILY FROM NICKY'S MOUTH. THIS COURSE MAY LEAD ME INTO AN ETHICALLY GRAY AREA, BUT STILL, I MUST SEEK OUT THE TRUTH, EVEN IF IT HURTS.

DID HIS FINAL COMMENT ("I DIDN'T SAY THAT NOW... DID I?") MEAN THAT HE HAD MURDERED IN 1967?

I HAVE SUCCESSFULLY NEGOTIATED A PLEA DEAL WITH NICKY. FINALLY, JUSTICE WILL BE SERVED ON MAD GUY PROVENZANO, WHO WILL BE PROSECUTED FOR THE MURDER HE WAS RESPONSIBLE FOR IN 1989. MAYBE THIS WILL BE A MODICUM OF SATISFACTION FOR THE YOUNG NICKY, WHO SUFFERED EMOTIONAL AND PHYSICAL ABUSE AT THE HANDS OF HIS COUSIN.

BUT WILL THERE EVER BE JUSTICE FOR NICKY

BUT WILL THERE EVER BE JUSTICE FOR NOEL
MCAVOY, JIMMY MCAVOY, BRACKO, AND THE REST?
I DON'T KNOW IF I AM NOW "ANALYZING" MYSELF,
ANALYZING NICKY, OR JUST DIGGING INTO A LONG-
AGO TRAGEDY. I WILL GO AS FAR AS I CAN GO. I
NEED TO PIECE TOGETHER THE REST OF THE STORY.

7

EVERYBODY LOVES A CLOWN

"Everybody loves a clown,
So why can't you?
A clown has feelings too."
- Gary Lewis and the Playboys

Maggie's Memos and Memories
March 11, 1990

*M*aybe it's a sign of age that I no longer have patience for idiots. The DA seems to be stalling, and I had no idea why. However, today, after more than six weeks, I found out why the delay, ...and that was the least surprising moment of the day!

I am not a lawyer. Indeed, I know very little about the law. I realized this truth abruptly today. After waiting over two months for a pat on the back or some acknowledgment of my hard work in getting Nicky to admit to his role in the Desiderio Gomez murder, I received nothing. Instead, I was summoned to a meeting at the law offices of Leonardo, Barlow, and Cooperman.

It was my first trip to their plush Twin Tower offices, and indeed, it would be the first time I would meet Leonardo and Barlow in person. Coop had prepared me, explaining that both of his partners were real characters. They are both disabled Vietnam War veterans who had put themselves through law school on the G.I. Bill. He warned me to be ready for their razor-sharp, but sometimes corny, wit. When I asked him what that meant, he replied, "You'll see...you'll see."

I arrived around 11 a.m. after a rather unpleasant drive from my office in Astoria. Coop met me at the bottom of Tower Two of the World Trade Center, and we took the elevator up to the 82nd floor. He didn't say much but had a shit-eating grin that suggested that I had no idea what I was in for.

Exiting the elevator, we bypassed the busy receptionist, who simply smiled and pointed to the room on the right side of the offices. As we entered, I found Leonardo and Barlow seated behind large desks. They made no effort to rise and greet me. I am not a big believer in strict protocols, but I usually expect a handshake or some acknowledgment when meeting new colleagues. Instead, both just sat, sporting ear-to-ear smiles. Noticing my confusion, Coop spoke up.

"Oh, Maggie, we don't...*stand* on tradition here," Coop chuckled, and attempted to introduce his partners, but was cut off by Barlow, who was trying to suppress laughter.

I was confused.

"Very good, Coop, you're getting the hang of our gimp humor," Barlow snickered.

I was even more bewildered.

"Well, I'll *see* about that," Leonardo responded, only to be met with a chorus of raspberries from Coop and Barlow.

I gave up trying to understand their little game and took a seat across from them.

"Leo, that's an embarrassment. I know you can do better. Though I must tell you, she looks remarkably like Denny's wife—just as beautiful," Coop commented.

"I don't...*see*...the resemblance to her at all," Leonardo replied.

With that, both Coop and Barlow let out muffled laughs. I, however, grew angry as they spoke about me in such an unprofessional way. I was ready to get up and walk out when Coop turned to me with a small smile, motioning for me to stay a bit longer.

"Oh, Leo, that was better," smirked Barlow,

"Enough with the orientation," complained Coop, "Maggie is starting to think you two are nuts."

Just starting? I was well past that.

"They like to loosen people up so...so... they don't feel put off...or feel pity," Coop explained. "They want you to get past their handicaps."

Huh!

"I don't '*stand on protocol*' because I don't stand for many things," murmured Barlow. He casually lifted his detached prosthetic leg and placed it on the desk. "I usually have this on; however, from 11 a.m. to noon each day, I give my stump some fresh air."

Meanwhile, Leonardo's stare bore into me, and I thought it was some form of misogynistic voyeurism until Coop saw me looking uncomfortable.

"Leo is as blind as a bat. Get it? That's why he couldn't '*see your resemblance*' to Denny's wife," he said.

Leo raised a hand to quiet the room. It worked, and for the first time, a serious demeanor was evident among us.

"I'm sorry if we upset you or offended you. We didn't mean to. We are so comfortable using self-deprecating humor without considering how it might affect others."

"It's okay. I get it," I mumbled, thinking of my own analogy of the three pigs. *I suppose we all find different ways to build our brick walls for protection.*

Then Goody Barlow spoke, and the situation suddenly got very real.

"The DA has rejected our plea deal. Based on Nicky Toto's

testimony, they would lose if they tried to prosecute Guy Provenzano. Provenzano never talked to Nicky directly but rather used Joey Pasco as an intermediary. Provenzano can deny everything, and in legal terms, Nicky's testimony is considered hearsay. They might give Nicky a slight reduction in sentencing for testifying against Pasco, but that is about it."

"You know Nicky wouldn't last a week in prison after testifying against Pasco," I countered.

"We're aware of that," responded Barlow.

"So?" I was eager to see where this was leading.

Leo Leonardo, who had let his partner do most of the talking so far, now took over the conversation with a passion I hadn't anticipated.

"We're going after Mad Guy Provenzano for the crimes of 1967. And we're going to hang that bastard by his nuts. You can take that to the bank. With me...it's personal."

Me too, I thought, but I didn't say it out loud.

"I'm going to share our story with you. You might not understand some of what I say because it is connected to Cambria Heights, life there, and the gangs that exist. You see, Goody and I are both from that area. It was no accident that Nicky became our client. Nicky and I were childhood friends, and we both belonged to the Provenzano gang.

I am not keeping this a secret, but it seems that no one knows I am Maggie McAvoy Evers, and I know a great deal about the story.

8

BROTHERS IN ARMS

"And though we were hurt so bad,
In the fear and alarm.
You did not desert me,
My brothers in arms."
- Dire Straits

Maggie's Memos and Memories (continued)

I looked into the silent depths of Jack "Leo" Leonardo's eyes as he spoke. His expression never wavered as he stared at me with unseeing stillness, his entire demeanor betraying no emotion. He was determined to tell his story as factually and unemotionally as possible. Yet I could tell that emotion was brewing under the surface of that calm exterior.

"In a little while, a friend of ours will walk through that door. He has dedicated his life to investigating the Provenzano empire, particularly as it relates to events that occurred in the 1960s. We use the code name "Denny" in this office to protect his real identity from the outside world. He is a famous writer and if it got out that he was meeting with us, it would not be long before it would get back to Guy Provenzano.

"He has been personally involved for decades, and during that time his research has remained secretive. I hope you will respect that. He has pieced together as much of the narrative as possible from various sources. Believe it or not, when the DA—that publicity-hungry mongrel—mentioned publicizing our upcoming victory (which he sees as HIS victory) over the Provenzano gang, we knew just who to involve. Denny would be happy to recount the story of the downfall of Mad Guy Provenzano. In truth, he has been trying to uncover it since he was a teenager himself.

"Of course, Morgenthau aims to become the hero of the tale, thus boosting his chances of being elected mayor of New York. Our friend, Denny, sees a great story, even if it is hijacked for political purposes. Goody and I just want to see the bastard go down because he killed people and destroyed our neighborhood. Of course, we want to save our client, Nicky, from the death penalty. We are strange bedfellows— the defense attorneys, the DA, the writer…and you, Nicky's therapist."

And I want the Provenzano gang to go down. Indeed, I care more for the destruction of the criminal empire than I do for Nicky's safety. Am I wrong to think this way?

"It's a long story, but I'll try to keep it brief. I used to be a member of Guy Provenzano's gang. I was his handball partner and his friend. That all changed the day I stood up to him when he was bullying a young Black kid who had the misfortune to encounter Guy in the schoolyard."

"My people, thank you," mumbled Goody Barlow as an aside. Leo ignored him and continued.

"In response, Guy held a gun to my head in front of everyone in the schoolyard and pulled the trigger."

What?

"It turned out to be a water gun. I realized this too late, as my own "water" soaked my pants. I could never show my face in the yard again. But maybe that was for the best. I turned away from what could have been an ugly life...a bad life. My future would have dead-ended right there if I had stayed a member of the gang. Instead, I joined the army in a misguided attempt to gain honor or at least restore my self-image."

"And there he met me," Goody interrupted. "I didn't know much about Provenzano then, but I saw the effects he had on the neighborhood. There had always been a tension between the Black and white residents of Cambria Heights, but it might not have escalated had not that asshole and his gang stoked the fires of racism in every way possible."

Where was this going?

Goody Barlow continued.

"One day, I witnessed a white boy being beaten by five of my so-called 'friends.' I didn't intend to be a hero, but I entered the fray, distracting the gang while the boy escaped."

"My people, thank you," Leonardo jokingly mocked his partner.

"For my efforts, I became an outcast in my community—a traitor to my race. I was labeled as a 'goody-two-shoes,' an old-fashioned term used in place of the more fashionable 'Uncle Tom.' The name stuck. Eventually, after joining the army and meeting this joker—*he pointed at Leonardo who didn't notice*—I grew proud of my actions and the nickname I had earned. I embraced it."

"So, you joined the army to escape, just like Leo?" I interjected, intrigued by stories of events in Cambria Heights, which had occurred while I was still young and naïve.

"Oh, no, joining the army was always my plan. I saw it as my only path to having the funds needed to go to college and law school."

"I guess that the country at least owed you that, after..."

"Our sacrifice? Is that the phrase you are searching for?"

"Yeah...exactly."

"Our sacrifice was nothing compared to—" Barlow began but was abruptly cut off by Leonardo.

"Chinx and Junior, our buddies, died in the same incident that injured us. They made the real sacrifice," Leonardo, his voice filled with raw emotion that I hadn't anticipated, with a deep-seated emotion that I didn't see coming. Somehow, his unseeing eyes seemed to pierce right into mine.

"Calm down," soothed Coop, who I had forgotten was even in the room.

"Goody and Junior—that's Davis 'Junior' Jones—were in those jungles because Guy's actions provoked the racism that drove them there. Chinx and I found ourselves in the situation because the madman's direct actions forced us to escape in the only way we knew how.

Greg "Chinx" Cincotta lost his life saving both Goody and me, and he would not even have been in that hellhole if he had given in to Guy's wishes and killed that kid."

"What kid?" I questioned.

"You'll get the whole story from Denny—at least as much as we can piece together. It was all part of a vendetta that Guy was obsessed with. You'll understand after you read Denny's book notes. And we are hoping Nicky Toto's testimony may be the final piece of the puzzle."

"Humor me. What kid?" I asked again.

"He was in a band, and every single one of the members of that band ended up either dead or missing and presumed dead. Chinx knew the story first-hand and shared it with me on his deathbed. Unfortunately, due to my prior experiences with Guy, I was unable to testify against him. Any jury would assume I was seeking revenge for the whole water gun incident."

"What was his name?" I repeated, but Leonardo continued with his thoughts.

"And Goody couldn't testify either because he was zonked out on painkillers after his leg amputation.

"What was his name?" I insisted.

"Not that it will mean much to you, but he was the bass guitarist in a group called Those Born Free. His name was John Cippitelli, but they called him Johnny Cipp. If Chinx...er...Greg agreed to find and kill this Johnny character; Mad Guy would then use his political influence (Translation: bribed officials) to keep Chinx out of the army. But Greg or Chinx, as we called him, had no interest in murdering an innocent boy—or anyone, for that matter. He refused, and he ended up in the army...and died in Vietnam."

Oh God, Those Born Free was my brother Jimmy's band. This whole process has become all the more real for me.

9

ALL IN ALL, IT'S JUST ANOTHER BRICK IN THE WALL.

- Pink Floyd

Maggie's Memos and Memories – (continued)

I had previously worried that my involvement in the case might be a conflict of interest. Well, screw that. Nicky's lawyers are at least as invested in the outcome as I am. It could have been a problem if their desires had influenced their advice to Nicky. However, what's best for Nicky also aligns with the best outcome for their (*our?*) case.

I am genuinely curious about what this Denny guy has to offer. How could he be involved with Those Born Free, and I didn't know about him? I was there, after all. Admittedly, I was only eleven and did not understand everything around me. I do remember that Johnny Cipp and Gio DeAngelis from the band went missing after the deaths of the other three members. Looking back, I realize they must have seen the writing on the wall and fled.

I realize that I would have been more knowledgeable if I had stayed in contact with my family, but I haven't. I have not seen or spoken to my sister, Aylin, or my mother since I left home to join the Navy in 1972—almost two decades ago! I suppose it's mostly my fault. It is just another brick in the wall that I built around myself to protect my sanity.

From 1967 onward, our home was a depressing wreck, and I blamed Aylin and my mother. My mother suffered from severe depression and barely functioned on a daily basis. She often spent hours in our basement listening to tapes the band had made, hoping to catch a moment of my father or brother speaking on them.

Aylin was another story. Almost immediately after the deaths, her personality changed. The vibrant, exuberant 16-year-old turned into a morose drunk and eventual addict. Her lifestyle led to her near-death on more than one occasion. After one such incident at Woodstock, she went into a lengthy rehab program. The cost of that rehab and her subsequent rehabs ultimately cost us the family store and our house. I give her credit for trying, but there always seemed to be more to the story that I was too young to understand.

I remember she had a friend, possibly a boyfriend, named DJ, who helped her at the time. I knew him, but not well, because he was always at the band practices held in our basement. He contributed by writing songs for Those Born Free. He eventually became famous as a songwriter, author, and founding member of the supergroup Chris Delaney and the Brotherhood Blues Band. I have seen him in the papers and on TV.

I know he had a crush on my sister, but I don't think anything came of it. They lost contact after the deaths of the band members. Later, I sort of remember them reconnecting. He tried so hard to get her off the drugs. He even wrote a hit song that I believe was about my sister. I don't think many people are aware of that. It was called "I Could Love You If You Live." Still, his frustration with her is evident in the following line, "But that doesn't seem to be." Maybe if he had tried harder, she wouldn't have been in such bad shape—and perhaps I wouldn't have left.

Something happened in 1970, and Aylin disappeared. My mother and the parish priest told everyone who would listen that she had become a nun. I knew Aylin, and I knew that wasn't true. So why lie to me? Disgusted by the deceit and chaos, I left home in 1972 and never looked back.

I often thought of contacting them, especially Siobhan, who had taken care of our mom in our absence, both Aylin's and mine. Then I heard of Siobhan's death in 1980, and I never thought of my family again. My brick house became impenetrable. By then, I cared about no one.

1 0

LIVES IN THE BALANCE

"And there are lives in the balance,
There are people under fire."
- Jackson Brown

Maggie's Memos and Memories (continued)

Coop brought me back to reality.

"Earth to Maggie...are you there?"

"Yeah, yeah, I'm just thinking. So, this Denny guy was somehow able to reconstruct the complete story of the Provenzano crime family...and they haven't killed him yet?"

"It's a very convoluted story, but the short answer is no," whispered Goody, as if speaking out loud would somehow alert Mad Guy Provenzano to our plot to dethrone him.

"So far, he has managed to escape detection by claiming to his publisher and the public that he is working on a novel about a fictional crime family. He even has created duplicate copies of the book, one with the actual names and one with fictional substitutes. Of course, all the conversations attributed to the real people can't be verified, but Denny believes that they are reasonable recreations of what would have been said."

"But isn't the whole thing merely supposition?" I interjected.

"Yes and no," Leo replied. "We have used multiple sources to uncover the truth. It would help if you remembered that I was close to Guy for quite a while, and Greg Cincotta shared his powerful tale just before he passed away. Then, there are others." He stopped speaking and looked at me with a severe stare from his unseeing eyes. I am guessing he has perfected this intimidating method since becoming blind.

"Yes?" I murmured.

"You must swear to keep this secret. There are lives at stake."

"I swear." *I would swear to anything to hear the story finally.*

"We have my story. We have Greg Cincotta's story. We also have police reports on what we believe was Mad Guy's first kill—a hobby shop owner named Harry Rothstein. However, our most concrete evidence of the death of one of those band members at the hands of a Provenzano gang member comes from two sources.

"First is Charlie Catalano, father of Vinnie 'The Cat' Catalano. Vinnie was also a childhood friend of mine," Leo said, his voice tinged with sadness as he relayed this information. "Vinnie was a good guy who never engaged in the nasty stuff. He advised Provenzano on musical topics and helped him set up dance clubs—nothing more sinister. However, he made one fatal mistake and became the madman's second victim. His father knows all the details leading up to his death, and he shared them with us."

"But what did he know about the band members' deaths?" I spoke a bit too anxiously.

"Well, as a bartender in a Provenzano-owned bar, he overheard a great deal. More than that, he knows exactly who took out one of the Provenzano hitmen. As his revenge for the death of his son Vinnie, he never disclosed to Provenzano that he knew who had killed Sammy Crespo, the murderer of Jimmy 'Mac' McAvoy."

They didn't see the tears in my eyes because there was a knock on the door, and their attention all went in that direction. Before I even had a chance to mourn my brother, I heard Goody say, "Come in, Denny."

11

WHO ARE YOU?

"Who are you?
I really wanna know."
- The Who

Maggie's Memos and Memories (continued)

I was in a trance, shocked by the revelation of who killed my brother. I was pulled back to reality by the sight of an all too familiar face walking in the door...and in the distance, the voice of Goody now addressing me.

"Okay, I guess the cat's out of the bag. Our "Denny" code name is no longer necessary. You now know that our 'secret writer' is none other than the Grammy-Award winning songwriter and Pulitzer Prize author..."

I didn't let Goody finish his sentence when I screamed, "DJ?"

"So, I guess you keep up with your celebrities," responded Goody. He was not surprised that I knew who had walked through the door.

Everyone in the world knew who DJ Spinelli was. However, he was blown away by DJ's response.

"Hi, Maggie...or 'Little Miss Maggie' as Bracko called you," DJ Spinelli chirped as the shocked faces of Coop, Leo, and Goody looked on. He continued, "Your sister Aylin misses you."

"How would you know that?" I answered, almost offended.

"Because she's my wife...has been for almost twenty years." Then, looking at the faces of the three lawyers, he laughed and said, "Tell me that you three geniuses didn't know this is Maggie McAvoy?"

The three lawyers discussed details and made plans while DJ and I stared at each other awkwardly. Leo led the strategy session, and when they had finalized the next steps, they drew the two of us back into the conversation.

"So, in the interest of security, Maggie, you leave first. Go home and get some rest. Soon, the assistant DA will arrive. He will probably tell us that Nicky is toast, to which we will hold him to the June 30 deadline the judge gave us. We will tell him that you are making excellent progress and that with Nicky's help and full immunity, your patient and our client will be able to make the case against Guy Provenzano by early June."

It was now Goody's turn.

"At that point, Leo and I will argue intensely with ADA Drossel, but Coop will intervene. He will emphasize the point that waiting until June 30 doesn't hurt anyone. Drossel respects Coop more than he does us because of our partner's Harvard Law Degree. Leo and I are seen as inferior City College dirtbags to him. We've heard that Drossel refers to our law firm as 'The Black, the Blind, and the Blueblood.'"

"You know, I've spoken to him about how offensive that is," murmured Coop angrily.

"No, let him think like that. We always want to be underestimated."

Returning to the agenda, Leo explained that DJ would leave *after* the meeting. He would, therefore, note everything that had taken place. DJ chuckled.

"I don't think Drossel is going to like it when 'The Black, the Blind, and the Blueblood' description is attributed to him in the book," smirked DJ. Leo and Goody both smiled, and Goody continued with the plan.

"The next step is for DJ to turn over the pertinent pages of the book to you, Maggie."

"They are at my house. I never let the originals leave a safe in my home. I suggest you discreetly come out tomorrow, and I can give you copies," instructed DJ, adding, "Is that a problem? We do live north of the Long Island Expressway at exit 68. It's probably a good two hours from here."

I didn't answer, and he knew why. Distance wasn't my problem with the trip to his house.

"Aylin?"

"DJ, what will I say to her? I deserted her, and Mom, and Siobhan…"

"Your mom and Siobhan are gone…"

"I know," I whispered. I started to cry. The floodgates opened as seventeen years of pent-up emotion flowed from the deepest recesses of my soul. DJ pulled me into his arms. It seemed like an eternity that he held me tightly. I had not been held that way in a very long time. I had let no one into my brick house…ever. And then DJ spoke.

"Aylin is a different person…she has been for quite a while. She will welcome you with open arms."

I just nodded. There was nothing more that I could say. After DJ wrote his address on paper, giving me a time, I left. I had so much to think about. Memories of those yesterdays flooded my head as I made my way home. I never slept that night but scribbled notes furiously, trying to recollect as much of my childhood as possible. The next day, I would start my journey to Aylin…and a return to my past.

I couldn't help but think of a *quote* I heard in college by the Chinese philosopher Lao Tzu…

WHO ARE YOU?

The past is history,
The present is a gift,
And the future is a mystery.

12

I GOT THE MUSIC IN ME

"Ain't got no trouble in my life,
No foolish dream to make me cry.
I'm never frightened or worried,
I know I'll always get by."
- Kiki Dee

Maggie's Memos and Memories
March 12, 1990

*I*t is going to be hard to meet Aylin—my only living relative. If things had not gotten so chaotic in 1967, we would probably have had a great Christmas dinner three months ago. Mom and Dad would have been closing in on their eighties, yet I believe they would still be around. Siobhan would have been 36. Instead, Aylin and I are all that is left.

Would there be grandchildren around my parents' feet? Would I have settled down and started a family if I hadn't joined the Navy?

Would I ever have thought of joining the Navy? Would Siobhan still be alive?

I've been thinking a lot about those years, about what could have been if life hadn't taken such a tragic turn. I wonder if Aylin feels the same way. The conversations we'll have when we meet again after all this time—I can only imagine. Will she remember the same streets we played on, the same echoes of laughter that used to fill our neighborhood? Or has time softened those sharp edges of childhood memory as it has for me? Now, we're heading for an awkward reunion. All I have are fading memories.

Aylin, Siobhan, and I did so many things together. We spent hours with the other neighborhood kids playing city games like running bases, red light/green light, Potsie, Skelsey, and many more. I know our family tragedy ended those games for us, but why don't I see kids playing them anymore?

These thoughts all come back to me, yet nothing meant so much to me as music in those days. Music still sharpens my memories and fills my heart. I still religiously listen to 1950s Doo-Wop, British Invasion, and Garage Band groups of the 1960s. I get quite a bit of ridicule from my contemporaries who are more into Bon Jovi, Madonna, and New Kids on the Block. Those performers are okay, but to quote Bob Seger, "Today's music ain't got the same soul; I like that old-time rock 'n' roll."

As far back as I can remember, I was surrounded by music. My older sisters would take me to the Triboro Music store on Linden Boulevard to buy the latest records that we had seen played on American Bandstand (4 p.m. on ABC). Each day, the show would feature some newly released songs, and certain audience members would be asked to rate what they had heard. Our purchases showed a distinct preference for the music the reviewers determined was a "10," including the almost automatic codicil, "because we can dance to it."

We would run home, put the week's choice on an old Victrola, and dance until we dropped. I could fill this whole sheet with my wonderful memories of dancing with my sisters. The Twist, the Mashed Potato, the Hully Gully, the Pony, and Hitchhike, to mention a few. However, one dance is seared into my mind more than any other – The Stroll.

I started dancing with my sisters when I was as young as three (they were five and seven years old). There are no detailed memories except that we would be in a circle in the basement, moving to the music. We got better. We learned all the current dances. We laughed a lot, and I will never forget those times when the McAvoy girls had nothing but great things ahead of us and no care in the world. We thought.

Music was the glue holding everything together back then. Music wasn't just entertainment but a way of life, a backdrop to our joys and heartaches. And when tragedy struck, music helped me find solace, even if only briefly.

In 1965, a new dimension was added to our dancing and our lives. Jimmy, our older brother, was also into music—playing it. I may be prejudiced, but he may have been the best damn drummer around. He started with two guys named Johnny and Gio, and the cast of characters surrounding those three changed for a while, with all kinds of people coming and going until the final version of the band came together. Being nine at the time, I didn't remember much except that we now danced to live music. What a sensation of uncontrolled joy dancing the Monkey to…obviously, the band's cover of the Miracles' "Mickey's Monkey."

However, the advent of live music also meant something else. Not all the music played was fast, danceable music. There were slow songs, too. Growing up and dancing to records, we would occasionally buy slow songs, especially if we thought the singer was handsome (think Fabian, Frankie Avalon, Bobby Vee, Bobby Rydell, et al.)

Looking back with the benefit of hindsight, I realize that American Bandstand had a profound influence on us. We were inordinately invested in white singers who often covered versions of songs originally done (better) by black artists. We were too interested in our singers being in our potential dating pool to care. (I was nine!)

But now we had real-life musicians to fantasize about. Jimmy was our brother, so he was out, and so was his best friend Johnny because he had a steady girl, Maria, who sometimes came to practices and even danced with us. However, that left Gio, Joey the Tinman, and my favorite, Bracko. Yes, I have come full circle to Bracko and my crush.

Rocco "Bracko" Brackowski received his nickname because someone with a disability (Tony Provenzano, I later discovered) was unable to remember or pronounce Rocco Brackowski, and Tony's mangled attempts came out as "Bracko." It was the only name I ever heard him called.

He was tall, with the dreamiest blue eyes resting on an angelic face that was surrounded by long, straight blonde or light brown hair. However, that beautiful face was often covered with black and blue marks. Later, Aylin would explain to me that Bracko was the victim of physical abuse by his father.

Bracko never spoke of it. Realistically, Bracko very seldom spoke of anything. It was a lot if he said a handful of words during an entire practice. Though the band loved and accepted him, he always stood as an outsider to the world as a whole...except me. Bracko and I became friends...and it all began with a slow song.

13

SLOW DANCIN' (SWAYIN' TO THE MUSIC)

"Slow dancin'
Swayin' to the music.
Slow dancin'
Just me and my girl."
- Johnny Rivers

Maggie's Memos and Memories
March 12, 1990 (continued)

*W*hen we were very young, we always did the "Stroll" to slow songs. That dance was a prehistoric remnant of the 1950s and was done as what we would call a line dance today. The three of us would "stroll" to the rhythm of the slow beat.

However, by 1966, our world had changed. Aylin was now 15, and Siobhan was 13. They were preparing to "come out" and go to their first real dances...with boys. Granted, it would be in the church basement under the watchful eye of the circulating nuns who would remind them to leave "room for the Holy Ghost" between the boys and them. Yet it would be real boys, and they had to practice their slow dancing. So, when the band played a slow song, they took turns taking the lead and simulated being at a dance.

Three minus two leaves one...as in one little girl named Maggie with no one to dance with. I did everything I could to hold back the tears. They were leaving me out and alone.

The band played a medley of '50s and '60s songs that were so similar that they used the same chords and beats, simply changing the lyrics. The kids at the dance would love this because they would have a chance to get up close and personal with the opposite sex for quite an extended period. They ran through "In the Still of the Night," "Angel Baby," "That's My Desire," and "Daddy's Home." Musically, this was no challenge, with the only significant achievement being the beautiful harmonizing of Gio, Joey, and my brother Jimmy. Bracko had so little to do that he went for a bathroom break mid-medley.

As Bracko came back down the stairs, he picked up his guitar to do a romantic guitar solo. He then looked down at me and saw the tears in my eyes. He removed his guitar and walked toward me. He bowed, and the black and blue tint surrounding his left eye came into my view. However, I paid very little attention as he finally spoke to me.

"Miss Maggie, could I have this dance?"

To this day, I try to remember who was most stunned by Bracko's act of kindness...the band...my sisters...me..., or perhaps even Bracko himself. In total shock, I nodded yes, and he took both my hands as the band played on. Bracko was always a gentleman, so he not only left room for the Holy Ghost (as the nuns would have required at a church basement dance) but also left room for Jesus Christ himself and all of the apostles. Yet as I looked up at him (the foot and a half he was taller than me), he smiled. I melted.

"I've never danced with a boy before," I stammered.

"Well then, I am proud to be the first," he answered, winking at me.

I realized I was dancing with a boy, and my older sisters had yet to reach that lofty achievement. I stuck my tongue out at them.

"Thank you," I mumbled as I looked up at Bracko.

"No thanks are necessary. People should always dance with people they care about. And I think of you as the little sister I never had."

I looked over at Aylin and Siobhan, who were now so jealous that I could almost see steam coming out of their ears.

"Yeah, them too...they are my other little sisters. But you don't have to let them know I said that any time soon if you want some payback." For one of the very few times in his life, Bracko laughed at something he had said.

The song ended and, with it, the most magical moment of my life. As he picked up his guitar, Bracko turned to me and whispered, "Thank you, Miss Maggie."

It was not whispered softly enough, as the rest of the band heard, and in unison, they echoed a mocking version of "Thank you, Miss Maggie."

HANKY PANKY

"My baby does the hanky-panky.
My baby does the hanky-panky,
Yeah."
- Tommy James and the Shondells

Maggie's Memos and Memories

*B*racko had left a lasting impression that night, one that would carry me through so many of the bad times to come. The band played for hours, each song weaving itself into the fabric of my memory. Bracko, Gio, Johnny, Jimmy, and Tinman—each of them had their individual quirks and moments of brilliance. I remember watching them, hoping that I would always be a part of their world.

Aylin and Siobhan were never far from me during those practices. They hummed along, tapping their feet to the rhythm, and sometimes teased me for being so utterly starstruck by the band. But I didn't care. To me, those five were larger than life. Their music, their camaraderie, the way they treated me like their own kid sister—it all created a sanctuary for me, a little world apart from everything else.

One night, Bracko stopped mid-rehearsal and pointed at me with mock seriousness. "Hey, Miss Maggie, what should our next song be?"

I blinked, startled, and then blurted out the first thing that came to mind: "A happy song."

"Happy, it is," Bracko grinned as he strummed his guitar and yelled to the rest of the band, "Miss Maggie wants happy." He started to play and sing "Do You Believe in Magic" by the Lovin' Spoonful.

Do you believe in magic in a young girl's heart?
How music can free her whenever it starts
And it's magic if the music is groovy.
It makes you feel happy, like in an old-time movie.

After it was over, their laughter filled the room, and for a moment, it felt as though nothing bad could ever touch us, as if time itself had paused just to let that one perfect evening stretch on forever. Little did I know of the fragility of it all, like the notes of their music floating away into the night, life would not always be "happy."

———

So many memories...so many feelings. Aylin, Siobhan, and I spent hours sitting on the stairs listening to the band. At one practice, the band started singing a song I didn't understand.

"My baby does the Hanky Panky," sang Gio... and my sisters giggled.

"What's 'Hanky Panky'?" I innocently questioned, and they rolled their eyes and laughed at me. I got angry. Aylin hugged me and whispered, "Maggie, it's not a bad word, but you'll understand when you're older."

"But, Aylin, you said the same thing about 'Wooly Bully'...and you never told me what that means. And you know that part in 'Wild

Thing' when Gio sings 'Wild Thing, you make my thing ping.' What 'thing' is pinging?" (I was fourteen before I realized that the words to the song were actually 'Wild Thing, you make my heart sing'...and Gio was just being gross with his version.)

Aylin never explained anything that day... or ever, because shortly after, things became crazy. Yet, I never forgot the hugs from both her and Siobhan. They were my rocks...along with...the band. Those five...Those Born Free...my older *brothers*. They promised to always be there for me. But they weren't. They all died. Aylin went off the deep end and was lost to drugs for a very long time. Siobhan took care of our grieving mother.

That is when I began to isolate myself—when I began my role as the pig in the brick house. I built that protective house around me and became a cold-hearted bitch in order to survive. I am not entirely like that now, and a lot has to do with my husband. He comes along later in my story. Yet, I wouldn't have accepted him or anyone into my life if it hadn't been for Bracko during my early years. It was the person he was. He helped me be warm and cozy inside that brick house.

It all started with our slow dance. It became our thing. As a trained therapist, I must analyze the situation intelligently and professionally. Did I see anything weird about a 17-year-old guy dancing with an 11-year-old girl?

I realized that I knew Bracko. He was always a friend, a gentleman. I have tried for years to see if perhaps I was naïve. But no, I realized there were boundaries, and he always made sure to be just a friend. It was funny because 11-year-old me fantasized about him as my boyfriend or even husband. Once, I even voiced that to him.

After that first dance, he whispered to me very seriously, "Think of me as one of your five brothers...and next to your real brother Jimmy...your favorite."

I chuckled and responded, "Only one thing wrong with that... you're easily way ahead of Jimmy as my favorite. He wouldn't share his dessert with me last night."

He smiled at me and replied, "It's an honor."

He then returned to playing with the band, and something weird happened. While using his thumb and index finger to hold his pick and play the guitar, his pinkie and ring finger were making unusual motions on the body of his guitar. They moved to the beat of the music. It was like they were...dancing. He nodded to me to follow suit, so I took my index finger and middle finger and made the same dancing motion on the stairstep beside where I sat.

He mouthed to me, "Always keep dancing."

After practice, I spoke to Bracko and thanked him for creating our special dance.

"Oh, Miss Maggie, I'm not smart enough to make up something like that. Two very special people taught it to me."

At first, I was jealous that I was sharing Bracko with anyone. Yet Bracko had taught me so much about kindness that I would not be surprised if anyone he chose to interact with were special.

Our ritual of dancing fingers occurred at least once during every practice until Bracko's death in July 1967. Now and then, I find my fingers dancing on my desk alongside reams of paperwork. Sometimes, I imagine they are dancing with Bracko, and many times, they are dancing with my husband (whom I had taught the finger dancing tradition).

But also, my fingers danced with Michael. Yes, Michael, the eight-year-old boy who Bracko brought to practice so his mother could deal with her illness. Michael, who would become my best childhood friend. Michael, who always finger-danced with me during the practices. Michael, who disappeared in November 1967.

Often, my fingers still dance on my desk consciously and unconsciously. Sometimes they move to a song on my CD player, and at other times only to a tune playing in my head. But...now...my fingers are now always dancing all alone.

15

LONG WAY FROM HOME

"And you think
That you need no one to guide you,
But you're still a long way from home."
- The Kinks

Maggie's Memos and Memories

J was correct in telling me they lived far out on Long Island. After all the commotion they had gone through in their lives, they had chosen to retreat to a home in a little rural town known as Ridge, seventy miles east of Manhattan.

After leaving the Long Island Expressway at Exit 68, I traveled about six miles north on the William Floyd Parkway. I then exited that road onto something called Middle Country Road. I laughed. This same road began in Manhattan and eventually evolved into a twelve-lane highway known as Queens Boulevard before transitioning into a slightly narrower thoroughfare named Jamaica Avenue. Then, when it crossed into Nassau County, it became Jericho

Turnpike. Zillions of cars traveled those roads, yet here in Suffolk County, a mere 70 miles from the city, it took on the name of Middle Country Road and did not have a person on it. Indeed, commercial and residential buildings were extremely scarce as I proceeded toward DJ and Aylin's home. Trees were abundant on this main road, and I imagined they created a bucolic scene on spring and summer days. I truly was a long way from the city.

I realized that my observation was not just about my physical location but also my mental state. For years, perhaps since my husband died, I had lived in a very closed world. I let very few people in and did not like many of those I did. Now, I would see one of the few people in the world I had truly loved. But how would she react to me?

I nervously knocked on the door. DJ answered and hugged me warmly. It made me realize I had more family than just Aylin. I had a brother-in-law who seemed caring. Although DJ had attended my brother's band practices, I have already mentioned that I don't remember much about him. I believe he liked my sister even back then. But I'll need to hear how that led to marriage. This felt like a whole new world, far from home.

"Aylin's not here," DJ announced, but quickly noticed the disappointment on my face.

"Oh," I mumbled and looked at my feet.

"Oh, oh no, she can't wait to see you. She had to run into Nassau to bring something to our son, Roberto. He's only in town today before completing his tour with his group. She'll be back in a few hours, and you can spend the rest of your lives catching up."

"So, I have a nephew named Roberto. Do you have other children? Do I have other nieces and nephews?" I was excited at the prospect of an even larger extended family. However, now he looked away, a sadness encroaching on the moment.

"Yes...and no," he sighed. "Yes, you have a nephew...Roberto Mac..."

"Roberto Mac, the outstanding guitarist of the Chris Delaney and the Brotherhood Blues Band, is my nephew? Holy shit, I never realized there was talent in the family." I gushed, failing to notice DJ's sober mood.

"He took the name Roberto Mac because he is indeed half McAvoy...but he's not our biological son. He was born to Siobhan. When she and her husband both passed away, we adopted him. We have loved him as much as anyone can love a child. My sadness is because Aylin cannot have children."

"Oh..."

"Aylin suffered a devastating injury during a pregnancy, and it left her..."

It was my turn to console him with a hug. He quickly pulled away.

"No, this reunion will be joyous as long as it can. After you know and understand everything you came here to find out, there will be time for tears."

"What do you mean?"

"There is so much more to the story of the Provenzano gang and Those Born Free that even your lawyer friends do not know...and never will. Aylin will have to tell you most of it. Some secrets will never be written down by me."

Now, I was confused.

"I will give you the transcript and then put you in a quiet spot to read. Remember, it is written as a novel, for now. You will read the copy that uses real names because you need to understand the context. In reality, I could never know how the actual conversations took place. However, I knew what went on. Therefore, I reconstructed the most likely sequence of events.

"There were enough witnesses and resources that I feel it is as close to reality as is humanly possible. As I mentioned before, we have resources available, including Charlie Catalano, Greg Cincotta, and Leo Leonardo, all of whom were connected to the gang during that time. We have police reports to flesh out some details. And...

"And... what?"

"And be kind to Aylin and the person she became in 1967. She knows more than she has ever told anyone in the world besides me."

"What?"

"It's a very, very long story that has never come out... and it never will as long as Mad Guy has the power to destroy those who oppose him." He just held up his hand as if to dismiss me and end my further probing. I looked at him, confused.

"Eventually, you will have the complete story...well, as much as we know."

"No, DJ, you will need more to make a case...and to get to the truth. I will get you more from Nicky, even if I have to beat it out of him—figuratively, of course."

"I don't care if it is literally," he laughed.

"I probably could. Although Nicky is physically large, he is very ill. His heart and lungs are like those of a man twice his age. He relies on oxygen constantly and is very weak right now."

"After you read this," he glowered, "You will understand why I have no sympathy for the bastard."

There were no more words, and I went off to the den, sat by a blazing fire, and started to read.

PART II

THE OTHER SIDE OF LIFE

"The lovers and the fighters, and the risks they take,
Are on the other side of life tonight.
Let's lose our way,
Go completely astray."
- Moody Blues

1960 to 1990

16

WE ARE FAMILY

"High hopes we have for the future
And our goal's in sight
We are family.
I have all my sisters and me."
- Sister Sledge

Excerpt from the book *Empire of the Mad* by DJ Spinelli

*D*ominick Provenzano, also known as "Dom the Pro," "Don" Provenzano, and "The King of Cambria," struggled to keep up with his expanding crime syndicate in southeast Queens. To maintain control, he needed more top-level managers.

Provenzano's first choice was to use family. That had always been the plan. He had envisioned a pyramid of power with him at the top, with the second tier comprising his sons, Guy and Tony. The third tier would be their cousins Richie, Joey, Frankie, and Nicky. That plan was shot to shit with Tony's "accidental" overdose of glue sniffing.

Dom would always call what happened to his son an accident,

even though it had been explained to him many times that his huffing excessive glue was either an attempt at escape from reality...or a suicide attempt. Dom would not concede either of those scenarios. How would Tony fit into either category? As the son of a rich *don,* he had everything money could buy. Dominick *could* not see...and now *would* never see, inside a mind that rejected all the violence required of him.

Dominick Provenzano was now forced to reorganize. Fortunately, he had two sisters, Graciela and Rose, and each had two sons. However, even that situation was screwed up. Graciela, or Grace as she was called, had married a big, strong, red-headed Irish boy from Hell's Kitchen named Joe Shea. Dominick, of course, had opposed the marriage because Joseph Shea was goddammed "*Mic.*" He had done everything to dissuade Grace from marrying "that piece of shit," as he referred to his prospective brother-in-law. It didn't matter to Grace, who defied her brother and married Joseph anyway.

Grace's dream was fulfilled with the birth of her sons, Joseph Jr. and Richard. Her husband, Joseph Sr., a New York City policeman, bullied his wife and allowed limited contact with Grace's "connected" family, which upset the family-oriented Dominick Provenzano.

Joseph Shea, Sr., unfortunately, was killed in the line of duty while breaking up a knife fight in Hell's Kitchen. The perpetrators were never caught, and there were even rumors on the street that it had been a setup. However, this version of the truth never reached Grace's ears. Either that, or she ignored what she heard because she now needed the support of her brother. Living together in the large house, Guy and Tony accepted their cousins Joey and Richie as their brothers. Dominick, for his part, now happily envisioned the next generation of leadership.

That dream was crushed when his nephew, Joey Jr., joined the Marines and was rarely seen by the family again. His nephew Richie followed in his father's footsteps and joined the New York City Police Department at the youngest age possible. When his son Tony became a "vegetable" in his father's eyes, Dominick had to rely on his son Guy. However, Dominick was astute enough to know that many called his lone remaining offspring "Mad Guy," and it was a label that he understood was probably accurate for his sadistic son.

Throughout 1966, the "King of Cambria" sought a plan to strengthen his management team.

Don Provenzano's other sister, Rose's two sons, were full-blooded Italian; therefore, Dominick had high hopes for them. The only roadblock was that both were as dumb as shit. Frankie Toto showed a bit of promise when he graduated from high school—a task way beyond his younger brother Nicky's capabilities. Then, he defied both his father and his Uncle Dom and joined the seminary. Where the hell did that come from? How could he use him? Maybe the kid could pray for his uncle's soul. Who the hell cared about that? Maybe he could pray for Dominick's continued success. Yeah, that wasn't going to happen. If Dom Provenzano was going to keep his empire all in the family, he would need to pull some rabbits out of a hat. First, he had to curb his son Guy's tendency to overdo everything he did, especially his tendency to get angry.

His second task was somewhat more challenging. He had to lure his nephew Richie Shea back to his family. Perhaps this might even work out better. Imagine having a family cop on the inside. It would not be easy. He would start by buying him a new car—one that would cost more than the kid's yearly salary.

"Uncle Dom, this is too much."

"Nothing is too much for my other son."

"Thank you...and thank you for thinking of me that way."

"Only the best for my family...Oh, bullshit."

"Huh?"

"I was going to go slow. You know...ease into what I have to say. But fuck it."

DANCING WITH THE LOST

"Uncle, what are you talking about?"

"You make what? 5K a year?"

"Well, I'm glad you did your research. That's the starting pay for a patrolman. You forget I am a detective and make..."

"$7,656 per annum."

"Yeah, but I'm up for..."

"A promotion?"

"Yeah, but how did you know?"

"You think I got this far without me having connections?"

"What do you mean?"

"I can make your promotion happen tomorrow...Or I can prevent it from ever happening."

"You wouldn't."

Dominick didn't answer that question but merely smiled an all-knowing smile.

"You wouldn't," repeated Richie

"Here me out. $50,000 a year to start. Then, I pay for law school at night. We need a lawyer in the family anyway. And you know that ain't going to be your cousin Nicky."

"But I'd be a dirty cop. What would my father think?"

"Let's get this straight. You're worried about what your father would think? Hey, numbnuts, he's dead. That's what being a clean, honest cop got him. Do you get it? He's dead! And your family had to come and live with your Aunt Carmela and me. So, please don't look down your nose at what I am offering you. I am giving you financial security forever. Better yet, I'm giving you physical security forever—not that you'll ever need it. You're not getting hurt like your father. That will never happen to you. You'll have so many promotions that you'll be safe and sound behind your gold detective shield."

"But I'll know...I'll know that I'm a dirty cop."

"No, that's the beauty of it. You only act as an insider and give us a heads up when something is happening that concerns us...and only us. The rest of the time, you be the straightest, most honest cop you can be. And you'll be able to do a lot as you move up the line with the promotions...that I will arrange."

"Well…"

"And you can take your pension at twenty years and then come and openly work for Guy and me as our consigliere."

Richie Shea thought of his career, his safety…and most importantly, his shiny new car, and begrudgingly nodded to his uncle.

Richie Shea started on his path to power and riches in the family business.

17

BAD TO THE BONE

"On the day I was born,
The head nurse spoke up,
And she said, 'Leave this one alone.'
She could tell right away,
That I was bad to the bone."
- George Thorogood and the Delaware Destroyers

Empire of the Mad (continued)

With Guy as his second-in-command and Richie, an insider embedded with the police, Dominick considered his nephew, Nicky Toto. Though not very smart, Nicky was tough and physically imposing. Ironically, due to his large size, he was often called "Little Nicky Glue." Dominick needed to know if Nicky had the guts for the role he envisioned as supervisor of enforcement. He planned to give him a crew to intimidate anyone necessary.

Under the guiding hand of Guy, Richie, and Nicky, this crew

would crush anyone or anything that stood in their way. Nicky would be the leader of enforcement because he was family. But he had heard good things about three kids, Joey Pasco, Sammy Crespo, and Sal Timpani.

Yet, Dominick and Guy had one other weapon at their disposal—a character who was known only as "The Actor," a hired killer without equal. He was not a part of their family, or any family for that matter, but could be called upon to do the dirty jobs—and do them well. Nobody knew his real name or what he even looked like. The Actor could disguise himself as anyone.

There were even rumors that he had once posed as a sexy woman to stick a stiletto in some unsuspecting jerk's heart. He could and would do anything to get close enough to kill. The Actor would remain Dom and Guy's secret weapon, known to no one, not even their closest family members.

Dominick Provenzano had a feeling that he would need the Actor again. After all, he had done such a good job "taking care of" his sister's husband, Joe Shea.

The years 1966 and 1967 would be a testing period for Nicky and his band of enforcers. Could they get the job done?

18

HUMAN WHEELS

"Human wheels spin round and round,
While the clock keeps the pace."
- John Mellencamp

Empire of the Mad (continued)

*N*icky Toto had dropped out of school as soon as they let him. In reality, school officials encouraged his departure. Unfortunately, there were few job opportunities available to dropouts. He had wanted to be an electrician, but he had been rejected due to his lack of education. He considered becoming a cop but knew he wouldn't pass the test. Yet, with his brother becoming a priest, the family needed some income to supplement what his lazy, and not too bright, father made. The apple did not fall too far from the tree. Nicky had inherited stupidity from dear old Dad.

In his wildest dreams, he never thought there would be a place for him in the Provenzano family business. The way Guy had treated him his whole life was proof that he would not be welcome. Therefore, he was shocked when his Uncle Dom and cousin Guy laid out their plans for his future.

But only if he proved himself worthy.

Nicky's first task was quite simple and not violent at all. He discovered he had the ability and patience to tail anyone whom Guy required information on. Nicky was a natural-born stalker. As his first test, Nicky was assigned to work with a Provenzano associate known as Vinnie "the Cat" Catalano. This job assignment developed from a wild scheme (wild, at least to the traditional mob) that Guy had convinced his father to pursue.

The younger Provenzano wanted to set up a series of music and dance clubs to cater to their growing popularity among the young. Old-school Dominick did not understand where his son was heading with this curious plan but told him he could pursue it — or at least research it.

Guy's first act was to contact his old school buddy, Vinnie Catalano. "Vinnie the Cat," as he was known, was a wiz when it came to music. He knew what was truly current with the younger generation (which at this point was only about five years younger than Guy himself). Besides being psychotic, Guy was also out of touch with every cultural norm. At least he had the sense to know this about himself. Therefore, he left it up to Vinnie the Cat to make all the musical decisions.

Vinnie was now on the path to achieving the music career he had always dreamed of. After a year of scouting talent, he identified several groups with the potential to attract large audiences to Guy's future business. It was at this point that Nicky became involved.

Vinnie delegated Nicky Glue to research some of the potential "stars" to be used in Guy's venture. To his credit, Nicky did discover some valuable information: The lead singer of The Creatures had a bad drug addiction, and The Shaggy Boys' drummer was related to the leader of a Puerto Rican gang that was giving the Provenzano family some grief. Other than that, most of the groups chosen by Vinnie were cleared.

Vinnie had a special surprise in store for Guy—a piece of information uncovered by Nicky. The best of the bands was a local group featuring five young men from their hometown of Cambria Heights, and three of them were the same individuals who had saved Guy's brother's life during the tragic glue-sniffing incident.

Unfortunately, Vinnie was unaware that Guy felt immense embarrassment over his brother's diminished mental abilities, which prevented Guy from viewing this situation positively. Had he known who they were, Guy might have dismissed them entirely out of sheer hatred.

As it was, Vinnie toiled under the false premise that he was pleasing his boss. Nicky Toto, in turn, was instructed to assist Vinnie with whatever he requested. Vinnie asked Nicky to research every member of any band that he was going to employ full-time. Nicky, like a good soldier and grateful employee, did his research. He tailed each member of every band. He secretly listened to their practices, assessed their appearance (considered necessary by Vinnie), and ensured that they didn't have bad habits like gambling or drug use.

What Nicky never checked out was that the band members were not legally old enough to play in clubs that served alcohol. Vinnie had never instructed Nicky to research this factor, and Nicky had never thought to do it on his own. Ultimately, Vinnie paid the price for this mistake with his life. Nicky didn't. After all, Nicky was family, even if he was stupid.

19

GIMME BACK MY BULLETS

"Gimme back my bullets."
Put them back where they belong."
- Lynyrd Skynyrd

Empire of the Mad (continued)

*Y*et snooping was not Nicky's only charge in life. Weapons were also under his command. Unmarked vans cruised both sides of the racial divide in Cambria Heights. The business of these vans made a killing (literally and figuratively) for the Provenzano empire. The selling of knives, brass knuckles, and even guns to those who could afford them intensified the level of combat in Cambria.

Nicky's primary responsibility was picking the junior members of the crime family to sell to the wannabe street fighters. It was not a particularly tough task since no one would even think of skimming anything off the top and thereby cheating the Provenzano family. Punishment would be quick and devastating for anyone caught double-crossing Dominick and Guy. Nicky knew this but realized that there was a certain finesse required in dealing with both sides of a raging battle.

He also had to make his underlings understand that this was one of the few Provenzano business ventures that did *not* come with bought and paid protection from the police. Gratuities would not influence the decision of police officers regarding the purchase of weapons. Weapons could potentially be used in situations involving law enforcement. The guns sold did not include instructions specifying who could be shot.

Nicky Toto took pride in supplying weapons to his troubled childhood neighborhood but avoided being present during the destruction they caused. He knew he couldn't stomach violence, a liability for an enforcer in a crime family. He kept his squeamishness hidden.

This all changed when Nicky was called upon to "take care of" Harry Rothstein, the owner of the Men-at-Arms Hobby Shoppe. Little Nicky Glue realized he had a problem. In the world of the Provenzanos, everyone knew what "taking care of" something meant.

20

PLAY WITH FIRE

"Don't play with me,
Cause you're playing with fire."
- Rolling Stones

Empire of the Mad (continued)

*N*icky did not want to seem hesitant about committing his first murder. However, he was. He tried very hard to convince his cousin Guy that, for some reason, he was not the right man for the job. He was unsuccessful. From Guy's point of view, there was no one else. This would also be Guy's first ordered kill, and he felt that it had to be done by a member of his real family. Only someone related could be trusted not to talk if he was caught.

Nicky knew that Guy's desire for this particular act of murder was the result of an event that was set in motion in October 1966...his brother Tony's "accident."

One Indian Summer evening, Tony Provenzano was provoked by his brother to beat an innocent boy who had accidentally hit him with a rubber ball. Two boys had been playing stickball when one hit a foul ball directly at Tony's head. Tony initially pushed the boy as punishment; however, after his brother's taunts, he escalated his violence against the boy, causing him serious harm.

Guy laughed with psychotic glee as the boy was sent to the hospital. However, Tony was not like his brother. He had hurt the boy only to gain the admiration of the appropriately named "Mad Guy." Before the dust had settled on the asphalt of the schoolyard, Tony had left. His anger and remorse for his actions led him to make a tragic mistake.

Looking to hide from his self-loathing, Tony sought escape. This led him to purchase glue from a hobby shop in Nassau County and find a secluded section of the local schoolyard. There, he inhaled excessive amounts of Duco cement glue. He quickly fell unconscious and would have died had not three younger boys accidentally happened upon the scene.

Johnny Cipp and his best friend, Gio DeAngelis, had scaled the fence into the Garden of Eden, as this enclosed section of overgrown weeds was sarcastically called. They were in search of a spaldeen that had cleared the fence during their stickball game. Rocco Brackowski had been playing the guitar in an isolated corner of the same garden. Though they did not know each other at the time, Rocco and the two stickball players combined to save the dying Tony Provenzano.

Though Tony lived, he suffered severe brain trauma because of a lack of oxygen to his brain. This damage left him with the mental abilities of a young child. The three teenagers who had saved Tony's life were hailed as heroes by Carmela Provenzano, Tony's mother. If she had her way, the boys would immediately be considered for sainthood by the Roman Catholic Church.

Dominick and Guy Provenzano disagreed. If Tony could not be himself, he should have had the good sense to die. His diminished state was detrimental to the tough-guy image the Provenzanos wanted to present to the world. Guy blamed the three boys for the situation and vowed to deal with them when his mother was no longer a factor.

However, there was one person who could be taken care of immediately—the man who had sold Tony the glue. And so, Nicky was given his first hit job—Harry Rothstein, owner of The Men-at-Arms Hobby Shop.

It was a task Nicky did not want to complete. Yet, he knew that his future with the Provenzano gang depended on his ability to produce. For a long time, he believed that monitoring people would be sufficient. Then, he thought that they could not overlook his value as the primary arms dealer for the gang. He was wrong. When you are the "Enforcer," you need to live up to your name.

Nicky delayed taking out Harry Rothstein by claiming he needed time for surveillance, a tactic supported by Guy, who wanted the hit to look accidental. Seeing this as a chance to postpone the task, Nicky next asked for an assistant. Although Guy hesitated, his growing mental instability led him to agree when Nicky argued that backup would make the job safer.

Nicky was miffed when he learned who was to accompany him on his first job. He hated Joey Pasco. They had grown up together and seemed opposites when it came to temperament. While Nicky was quiet and reserved. Joey was (by all insider reports) a loud-mouthed, egotistical prick. What's more, he was supremely jealous of Nicky's birthright. Joey correctly assumed that Nicky had passed him by in the gang hierarchy simply because the latter was related to Guy. Everyone who knew Joey conceded this fact.

Yet, ultimately, it was the team of Little Nicky Glue and Joey "The Back Door Man" Pasco that would commit the first known murder attributed to Mad Guy Provenzano.

On a cold December night in 1966, Harry Rothstein was busy doing inventory in the back room of his hobby shop. The Christmas rush was upon him, and he wanted to ensure that he could fulfill all the orders for the model cars, boats, and more that he sold. If Harry had not been partially deaf, he might have heard the lock of his front door being picked by Nicky Toto and Joey Pasco. He might also have been aware of the clatter caused by Nicky and Joey piling up boxes, in order to prevent any attempt at escape through the back door. Harry Rothstein heard nothing.

Nicky and Joey spread gallons of acetone paint thinner near other extremely flammable products on the shelves. Nicky had done his research and knew that this product was sold in small quantities in the store. If the Nassau County police had had an arson squad at the time, it would have been apparent that the amount of acetone was completely disproportionate to what should reasonably be found in a hobby shop.

BACK DOOR MAN

"I am, the Back Door Man.
The men don't know,
But the little girls understand."
- The Doors (by way of the Blues Project)

Empire of the Mad (continued)

"*N*icky, let's light this shithole up and get the hell out of here."

"Joey...um...maybe we should...ya know...ah...open the back door."

"Are you crazy? You know what we need to fuckin' do. Your cousin was clear that this fucker had to die for what he did to Tony."

"But...but...he didn't do it on purpose."

"Nicky, are you a pussy?"

"Joey, we could let the guy escape and say we think he learned his lesson."

"Do you really have Provenzano blood in your veins? On second thought, you do...Tony's chickenshit blood. The word is that he was such a wimp that he cried after he beat up that McCarthy kid. Some of the guys told me he left the schoolyard whimpering like a baby and..."

Nicky's roundhouse punch sent Joey to the floor.

"You wanna talk shit about me, I can chalk it up to you being a first-class asshole. But don't you ever say a word about Tony...ever."

"Are you fuckin' nuts? We're in the middle of whacking a guy—our first real hit... and you're sucker-punching me. Are you crazy?"

"Just say another word about Tony, and you'll see just how crazy I am."

"He tried to kill himself, you idiot!"

Nicky was going to say something like, "Take that back," or "Screw you," or "You don't know nothing,'" but Nicky couldn't think that fast, so he used a left hook to send Joey to the ground...again.

"Because we have been friends since we were little kids, I'm going to make believe you didn't just sucker punch me...again. But you need to get your fuckin' act together if you're going to survive in this world."

In reality, Joey knew two things as facts. First, he would never come out looking good to Mad Guy if he bad-mouthed any of his cousins. Second, Nicky, though dull of mind, could beat the shit out of him any day of the week. Joey's anger and hatred of Nicky grew exponentially that day. Yet, he needed to play the game. After all, his gang nickname wasn't "The Back Door Man" for no reason. He was always conniving and sneaking behind people's backs. He accepted this title only because it had a second connotation...his prowess with the ladies, even those who "belonged" to other gang members. Joey would never forget this moment.

The loud commotion in the front room was heard by partially deaf Harry Rothstein. With Joey on the floor and Nicky standing over him, he walked out from the back room.

"What are you two doing here?" were the first words out of his mouth. He then smelled the overwhelming odor of the acetone and figured out what exactly was happening. As Harry and Nicky stood staring at each other, Joey scrambled from the floor and grabbed a nearby crowbar that Harry had used to open wooden crates of merchandise. In one swift motion, he struck Harry with a blow to the head that knocked him unconscious.

"What do we do now?" questioned the very confused Nicky.

"No matter how many times you hit me, you are still going to be a moron. He's seen your face…what do you think we have to do?"

With that, Nicky took out his lighter, struck a flame…and wavered again. Joey looked at him like he was crazy.

"If you use your lighter, the flames are going to catch onto you as you lower it to ignite the acetone. Then, you will drop the goddammed thing…you know, the one with your initials on it. into the fire. You idiot, the police will then have evidence against you. You are not too bright." (*Nicky wasn't*)

Nicky looked at him as if he would throw another punch but said nothing. He looked at Harry Rothstein on the floor. Still, he stood frozen.

"What an ass," mumbled Joey in a disgusted voice and took a book of matches from his coat pocket. He lit one and then looked at Nicky.

"It's your honor," taunted Joey, but Nicky shook his head in disagreement.

Joey used the one match to light the entire matchbook and then threw it into the puddle of acetone. In seconds, the entire Men-at-Arms building became an inferno. Nicky and Joey exited onto the street, but not before they watched billowing flames engulf the rear of the store.

As they ran to the car, Joey Pasco cackled hysterically with joy. He was now on the right track to being a "made man."

"That was fun…I mean real fun," chortled Joey.

Nicky wasn't laughing. He didn't think it was fun. Indeed, he did everything he could to keep from puking.

SHAPES OF THINGS

"Shapes of things before my eyes,
Just teach me to despise.
Will time make men more wise?"
- The Yardbirds

Empire of the Mad (continued)

*M*aggie had read enough. *Although DJ's book continued with more details, she didn't need to read it. She needed to speak with Nicky. She now had leverage to force him to tell the complete story. Her pleas for more information would be off the record...at least at first. If it proved helpful to his case, she would tell Leo, Goody, and Cooperman.*

Nicky could never have suspected that Greg Cincotta, on his deathbed, had divulged all the details of the Rothstein incident to Leo Leonardo. Not only that, but the story had additional verification. Joey Pasco was not always in control when he drank. On one occasion, bartender Charlie Catalano was listening. While trying to impress his latest female conquest,

Joey Pasco revealed the story of the Men-at-Arms Hobby Shoppe arson within earshot of Catalano.

DJ also flushed out several details on his own, but it was all still legally "hearsay." Unfortunately, even some of the "hearsay" witnesses were deceased. Provenzano's next victim was Vinnie "The Cat" Catalano, Charlie's son. Wouldn't a skilled defense attorney challenge Charlie Catalano's testimony against Joey and Nicky as biased?

And then, the murders of Bracko...and her father...and her brother...and more. Who would give solid testimony if not an insider like Nicky? Yeah, Nicky was going to talk to Maggie, or she was going to blow up his world, if necessary. Her fury fueled her resolve—the hell with confidentiality—the hell with legalities—the hell with professionalism...and especially, the hell with conflict of interest. Maggie was out for blood and damn anyone who got in her way.

23

UNDER PRESSURE

"It's the terror of knowing what the world is all about,
Watching some good friends say, 'Let me out.'"
- David Bowie and Queen

Maggie's Memos and Memories

I needed to see Nicky as soon as possible. Nothing else mattered. This thought hit home when DJ interrupted me as I was about to walk out the door without even saying goodbye.

"Aylin will be here in less than an hour. Can't you wait?"

"I've been a bitch to her and everyone else. She deserves so much better."

"Maggie, Aylin will take you any way she can get you."

"DJ, I'm going to see Nicky, and I'm getting the whole damn story out of him...no matter what I have to do to get it. I'll cross any line of what is professionally or ethically right or wrong. I don't give a shit anymore."

"But what do I say to Aylin?"

"Seeing her again will be the highlight of my otherwise fucked up life. But I want to do it right...when my head is on straight. It isn't right now. Perhaps, in a couple of days, after I have this whole thing sorted out in my mind."

"Maggie, you forgot one thing. You are going to hear the story from Nicky's point of view...and only Nicky's point of view. From him, you are not going to hear about all the good times or all the good people who loved you in your eleven-year-old world."

"But they are not around anymore...are they? Do you understand that? They aren't around, and Nicky knows why."

"That doesn't change what we lived through...or who we loved... or who we lost. Are all the good people and good times less important to the final story?"

"DJ, I'll leave the storytelling to you, and I'll get the justice needed...or maybe just revenge."

"But..."

"Tell Aylin that I will be back...and that...and goddammit, I love her, and I am sorry."

The long ride back to the city seemed to pass quickly. My mind swirled in confusion. My final decision was to go full speed ahead and damn the consequences. As soon as I got home, I called Nicky and asked, scratch that...I demanded that he see me in my office at ten the next morning. I then instructed my secretary, Vanessa, to cancel all my appointments for the day. I was not going to have a typical session with Nicky. I was going to spend the day with him.

If I needed to go down into the gutter myself to get the truth, well, so be it. If going to the dark side was required, I didn't even care if I had a flashlight.

I was there at ten, but Nicky was not. To my annoyance, he drifted in at about 10:40, and I didn't hesitate to lay into him.

"What the hell? I thought you weren't coming. Do you realize the importance of this meeting? Your whole future could be at stake. What was so crucial that you couldn't get here?"

Meekly, he handed me a piece of paper.

"After I shit, shaved, and showered, I remembered that I had to do my homework. You know, write something that we could talk about."

I almost laughed. I was going to take our relationship and discussions to a whole new level. However, I had never told Nicky that. He came with his prepared writing, which I took from him and tried to pretend I cared.

Then I read it, and I did.

Nicky's Notes March 14, 1990

"Hey Doc, I know that you have this thing about me writing parts of my story down before we meet. I have three problems with that. First, I am a shitty writer. Second, I can't think good while I'm busy trying to write. Third, I am putting in writing all my bad shit. I am discriminating myself. Nope, that's wrong. I am incriminating myself. I'm confessing. And I ain't got no deal yet. So, this note is real short and sweet. If you want to know more, my lawyers need to get me a deal in writing.

P.S. No names...no details...and I will deny it if anyone asks. But just to freakin' tease ya. Me and the boys did away with 15 people...that I remember."

24

THE STORY

"All of these lines across my face,
Tell you the story of who I am.
So many stories of where I've been,
And how I got to where I am."
- Brandi Carlile

Maggie's Memos and Memories

Nicky was a step ahead of me, so I had to pivot on the spot.

"Okay, Nicky, let's keep this informal. How about you and I go for a very unofficial field trip to…let's say…a bar. There, you can tell me your story, and because it is not in the office, it doesn't mean anything.

Okay, the location doesn't change anything, but Nicky didn't know that. Of course, everything he told me was confidential anyway, but going to a bar made him loosen up.

"I guess it's okay. Are we going on a date, Doc?"

"Wrong, Nicky," I answered emphatically, but gave him a smile out of the side of my mouth. He was so damn dumb.

As I opened the door, I was surprised to see one of my other patients sitting in the waiting room. I felt a pang of guilt as I thought of all my regulars that I had been neglecting in the passion of dealing with Nicky.

I had a wide variety of people who needed my help. My patients included at least a dozen women and children who were victims of abuse. Then there were those with classic mental problems... schizophrenia, paranoia, anxiety, PTSD, depression, and substance use disorder.

Josef Stern was different. He has touched my heart since he became my patient a little over two months ago. That is not supposed to happen. His story was so compelling that I felt privileged to be his therapist.

Josef was a Holocaust survivor. His deep-rooted problem was survivor's guilt. He could not understand why he had lived while all his friends and relatives had not. Realistically, I knew why. Josef had played the violin for his Nazi captors, and they had spared him for their own prurient enjoyment. Knowing this reality did not ease his feelings. He came to me with two goals. To find some peace of mind in his otherwise tragic life.

His second goal is to play the violin again. Though he carried the instrument in its well-worn case everywhere he went, he had not opened the case or played the instrument since his rescue from Buchenwald Concentration Camp over four decades ago.

Now, he looked at me with puppy dog eyes that revealed his real debilitating sadness. What was I doing? Didn't my patients, especially Josef, need me? Shouldn't that be more important than my all-consuming quest for revenge? I had to face the fact that perhaps I truly did need counseling...and not *from myself*, but from a real professional. I would get to it...later. Isn't that what I always said?

I told Nicky to go ahead to a corner bar called Bamboozlers and that I would catch up with him. I sat with Josef.

"I tink I vill go nah. I huhp I din't cause any problems."

"Josef, you could never be a problem. I will call you as soon as possible."

I looked at him, and he gave me a brief, almost invisible, smile. He went to get up and leave, but I put my hand on his shoulder.

"You rest here as long as you want. Let yourself out. I will see you soon."

I had to deal with Nicky, and now I had a guilt trip to contend with. Yet, looking at Josef and his deep malaise calmed down the intense anger. Seeing this kindly old man made me realize that evil had always been a part of the world. It was the job of the good people to deal with that evil. I felt better equipped to deal with Nicky.

25

WHENEVER WE WANTED TO

"We just did what we did,
Yeah, we did what we did,
Whenever we wanted to."
- John Mellencamp

Maggie's Memos and Memories – The Conversation with Nicky

My encounter with Josef had calmed the rage that had been building in me for months. It gave me a whole new attitude and approach as I entered Bamboozlers Pub. I had frequented this little neighborhood watering hole on the rare occasion when I felt like a drink. I found Nicky sitting at the bar but signaled for him to join me in a little corner booth where we could have some privacy.

As he sat across from me, I saw him in a different light. He wasn't a murderer or a member of the hated Provenzano gang. He was just a person with a story to tell me. Perhaps I would not feel the same after we talked. However, at that very moment, I saw a person who had been screwed and used by everyone who knew him. True, he had done some terrible things, but I had to keep asking myself why. Was he used as a pawn because of his obvious dullness? Is stupidity an excuse for murder? I decided I wouldn't push the issue. Instead, I would sit back and see what he had to say. If I didn't get answers, I would push and push hard.

Of all the things *I* could have said to him, I don't think he ever expected it to be, "So what are you drinking?" Nicky was confused. My idea was not to get him drunk, but a little loosening up wouldn't hurt. It knocked him off guard when I ordered a vodka tonic. He surprised me when he told the waitress to make that two. He had struck me as a Scotch sort of guy.

"Doc, are you allowed to drink while you are on duty?"

"Nicky, I think you have me confused with being a cop."

"Well, as far as I know, you are all on the same side."

"Not really. I am your therapist. I am on your side."

Okay, that wouldn't be the first or last time I lied to him.

"Oh."

"No, Nicky, we are here instead of in my office, so this is completely unofficial." -*Lie #2*

"Then why *are* we here?"

"As your friend, I just want to make it clear where you stand." *Friend?—Lie #3*

As he quickly downed *his* vodka tonic, I ordered him another.

"Do you mind if I smoke?"

"Yes, I fucking mind! Not only do I abhor smoke, but you have a goddammed oxygen tank at your side. Didn't anyone warn you that oxygen is highly flammable?"

"No, and Doc, I never heard you use those words."

"That's because we are in a bar and not in my office. We're about to get real here, and I don't want you igniting your oxygen tank and destroying this place. Are we clear?"

"Okay, but I am really craving..."

"Cut the crap. Do you realize what you have already done to your heart and lungs?"

"Yeah, so maybe none of this will matter. Maybe I should take what is coming and make everyone happy and just die."

"Everyone? You mean like your cousin. You honestly want to make him happy?"

He shrugged. It was time to hit him with my best shot.

"How about Harry Rothstein's family in 1966? Or the others in 1967?"

Though I had shocked him with the use of Rothstein's name, I was bluffing about who else he had been involved in killing. It was better not to be specific than to make a mistake and show him I didn't have the details of who did what. He was speechless. After a long silence, I used my final card.

"Greg Cincotta implicated you on his deathbed."

I didn't say what Cincotta implied Nicky had done, but it seemed to work.

"Okay, Doc, you got me. In for a dollar, in for a penny."

I didn't correct him that it is "In for a dollar, in for a dime." I didn't want to slow the momentum. I ordered his third drink.

26

THE GOOD, THE BAD, AND THE UGLY

"Let go, let go, let go the power."
- Ennio Morricone

Maggie's Memos and Memories – The Conversation with Nicky

"The don, my Uncle Dominick, was a big movie guy, and a movie had just come out with Lee Marvin. It was called the "Dirty Dozen." He always laughed when he called us *his* "Dirty Dozen" because there were twelve of us who were his regulars in the organization. We had a stranglehold on the neighborhood, and we squeezed every penny we could out of it. We thought we were invincible. We just followed orders and did whatever we wanted, whenever we wanted. No one dared stand in our way. We had money, cars, and girls — lots of girls. But our reign of terror did not last long. In reality, there are only five of us still around in the gang."

He downed the third drink with great ease, and he was perfectly calm now as if deciding to speak was the hardest thing he had ever done...now he was relaxed. He seemed relieved to finally tell his story.

"When the boss man wasn't around, we laughed at his 'Dirty Dozen' name. We knew where everyone stood in the gang, and it was Richie who renamed us behind his Uncle Dom's back. After all, we all knew that Richie was much, much smarter than dear old Uncle Dom. In fact, he still is the smartest guy I know...and my cousin and best friend. He doesn't care that I am not as smart as him."

"Nicky, you're stalling again."

"But, Doc, it's important that you understand how Richie is the brains of the operation. Everything bad that happened was because Guy didn't take Richie's advice when he should have."

"Okay, but what's this got to do with what happened in 1967? Nicky, c'mon."

"Richie knew exactly who we were and what we were capable of. If you want to understand the gang, look at us through Richie's eyes."

"Okay, I'll bite. Tell me what your cousin said."

"So, this one night we're at a bar, just like you and me are now, and Richie says, 'We ain't a fucking Dirty Dozen. That would mean we were all equal. You know we're not. It would also mean that we were all equally evil, and you know we are not that either. Would you do all the things that Guy or Joey Pasco would do? No. I think that we are more like that Clint Eastwood movie."

"Nicky, where is all this going?"

"Richie nailed it. He explained that there was another movie out at the same time that better described our gang— "The Good, The Bad, and the Ugly."

Huh?

"You see, there were different levels of responsibility, as well as different levels of badass among us. Three different levels of evil. Richie saw it, and he explained it to me over drinks. Speaking of that…"

He ordered a fourth vodka and tonic.

"He really did hit it on the nose. Richie had his shit together, and we all knew he would someday rule the gang."

"The Good, the Bad, and the Ugly? I don't get it."

He grinned, took a napkin and a pen from his pocket, and proceeded to draw. At the top was Dominick Provenzano and then coming down from him were three separate groups, much like a flow chart of a corporate structure, which was precisely what it was. In each of the three boxes, there were four names. I recognized most of them. The police in 1967 could have greatly benefited from this design. I looked at the drawn chart as Nicky pointed and spoke.

"The top name was the leader of each group."

"The Good"

Richie Shea
Greg "Chinx" Cincotta
Vinnie "The Cat" Catalano
Jack "Leo" Leonardo

"The Bad"

Little Nicky Glue Toto (me)
Sammy Crespo
Sal Timpani
Frankie "The Roach" Resch

"The Ugly"

Mad Guy Provenzano
Tony Provenzano
Joey Pasco
"The Actor"

"So, what did these labels indicate?"

I was now fascinated.

"Just how little you cared about anyone but yourself...what level of evil would you get involved in. But to get this straight, only those on "The Good" list didn't hurt anyone."

"Or kill?"

"Yeah, everyone on the 'The Bad' and 'The Ugly' lists killed. It was just that those on the 'The Ugly' list enjoyed it."

"Oh yeah, me, Sammy, Sal, and Frankie committed acts of … well…. you know. But to us, it was just a job.

"You think that made it okay?"

"It is what it is. It was what it was. But it isn't anymore. The whole strength of the gang started to collapse because of one night in October 1967."

"Go on."

He ordered a fifth vodka tonic. I would have worried that he would pass out, but "Little" Nicky had the bulk to consume these drinks, and he seemed very experienced at doing it.

"I remember it was still warm out when Leo and Guy played handball against two…er…color…Black kids. Leo was the best handball player around, but Guy blamed him for the unexpected loss. If you looked in a dictionary for the words "sore loser," it would probably have the name "Mad Guy Provenzano."

After the game, my cousin proceeded to beat and torture his two opponents. I mean, physically beat them. Many of the gang held them while Guy administered a lesson: *You should not win a handball match if a madman is your opponent.* Only Leo didn't participate. He didn't laugh. Instead, he tried to reason with Guy…he tried to stop the beatings. It was a mistake.

"Mistake number two came when Leo physically interrupted Guy's attack. Guy not only embarrassed Leo but also threw him out of the gang."

(12 minus 1 = 11 in the gang? No more Dirty Dozen—perhaps they were now the "Evil Eleven." I had been distracted by the story or by my stupid math analogy. It was then that I realized he was referring to Leo Leonardo, who was now one of his lawyers.

"Still angry *at* Leo, Guy's fury led him to bully his brother Tony into pummeling a young, innocent white boy over a minor incident. Later that night, Tony was so guilty about what he had done to the boy that he needed an escape. He went to the Garden of Eden and…"

Nicky got choked up, showing emotion I had never seen before in him. From DJ's book, I knew what had happened to Tony. I said nothing and waited for Nicky to regain his composure.

"Tony used way, way too much glue to get high. He would have died had he not been saved by three boys who were there. I lost my cousin and best friend that night."

This is where the story begins for me.

"So, what did Guy think about those three kids who saved his brother?"

"He hated them. Guy always said he would rather his brother had died than become the...the...person he became."

So far, Nicky's tale followed the words that DJ had written.

"What do you mean?" I prodded.

"Tony's brain was damaged. His body recovered, but his brain never did. He had the thoughts and mental abilities of a small child."

"So that's why Guy had those three kids killed?"

"Absolutely not! But it was the beginning of the end. Everything that happened after that night was the direct result of Tony's accident. We weren't allowed to call it anything else."

"I don't get it."

"Without Tony as his conscience, Mad Guy truly earned his name. And everything went to shit after that."

He pointed to the "Good" list. He crossed out Leo's name...and then emphatically Greg Cincotta's.

"Greg Cincotta, who was always a nice guy, was the first casualty. Guy asked Greg to look after the now childish Tony one night. Tony wanted to see a band play music. While at the dance, someone started to make fun of Tony for being retarded. Greg beat the shit out of the guy for picking on Tony."

"Nicky, we don't use the word retarded anymore."

"Why not? That's what Tony is."

I gave up trying to teach Nicky social correctness.

"Anyhow, the judge offered Greg jail or joining the army. Greg chose the army. He died in Vietnam—he died serving his country."

(12 minus 2 = 10)

111

"He was so brave, and here I am just being a cheese-eater…a rat. Of all the Dirty Dozen, I'm one of the few still around, and now I am turning on them. But, Doc, you gotta understand…the day I killed Harry Rothstein, I lost my soul. And it was all bullshit. We had to take care of him to make Guy happy. The poor, old guy was just running his store. But one by one, we all paid the price for Guy's insanity. Frankie Resch and Sammy Crespo ended up in jail. Frankie died there—a shiv to the gut."

Numbers are dwindling for the Dirty Dozen.

"And then Guy murdered Vinnie the Cat."

What! No wonder Charlie Catalano was so helpful in telling DJ the story.

"Why?"

"It was that whole band fiasco."

I pretended to be ignorant, but I was finally going to get the story.

"Guy wanted to become a big shot. He got permission from the bosses to set up ten clubs for dancing and drinking. Those clubs would be lucrative on their own, but the drugs and prostitution under the table were the real money makers. To set up these clubs, he needed a musical act to draw in the crowds. Therefore, he had Vinnie the Cat scout the area for a year while the clubs were being designed and equipped."

"He found two groups, *The Mellotones* and *Those Born Free,* and had them audition head-to-head. *Those Born Free* won… and *The Mellotones* ended up dead. Actually, so did *Those Born Free* come to think of it."

I wanted to reach across the table and strangle him for the glibness with which he spoke of my brother and father's deaths. However, he continued.

"They were good kids, but they caused their own deaths. They lied about their ages, and the club was raided as a result. Guy found out that *The Mellotones,* realizing they lost the audition, called the cops—a goddamned stupid mistake. I hear they all died in a…ahem…mysterious house explosion."

The body count was mounting, but I still didn't know if there was any evidence to suggest who was to blame.

"Guy's entire dance club plan collapsed because of Vinnie's miscalculation, and Guy was made the laughing stock of the New

York mob. If he wasn't insane before, he was now. Vinnie the Cat, who had hired the kids without checking their ages, was the first to go."

"Yeah, but Nicky, who was committing these murders?"

"Oh, Guy killed Vinnie himself; the night the club was raided, he bashed Vinnie's skull in."

"Were there witnesses?"

"Yeah, Sal Timpani and Sammy Crespo. But Sal is in jail for life, and he ain't talking because Guy is taking care of his family forever. Sammy, now, was another story. Some skank broad put a high heel through Sammy's eye into his brain. He died instantly."

"What do you mean?"

"According to Charlie Catalano, who was tending bar at the time, this blond broad played up to Sammy and lured him to a room with the promise of…well, you know."

"And then?"

"The fuckin' broad puts a stiletto in his eye…and I don't mean the knife. They found Sammy with her shoe's three-inch heel in his brain. Charlie gave a great description of the murderer, but Guy never found her."

"What a shame," I said sarcastically, but I don't think Nicky picked up on my attitude.

"Yeah, rest in peace."

"What about the other murders? It seems as if there are not many people left in the Dirty Dozen to have committed them."

He took the napkin on which he had written and now drew lines through specific names.

"The Good"

Richie Shea

~~Greg "Chinx" Cincotta~~ **R.I.P**

~~Vinnie "The Cat" Catalano~~ **R.I.P**

~~Jack "Leo" Leonardo~~ **Gone straight and now a cripple**

"The Bad"

Little Nicky Glue Toto (me)
~~Sammy Crespo~~ R.I.P.
~~Sal Timpani~~ (Life in Sing-Sing)
~~Frankie "The Roach" Resch~~ R.I.P.

"The Ugly"

Mad Guy Provenzano
~~Tony Provenzano~~ **Retarded**
Joey Pasco
"The Actor"

"Do you see the pattern? What did Billy Joel sing? 'Only the Good Die Young'"

I saw his point. Only five of the original Dirty Dozen were still in action, and three of the five were from "The Ugly," those on the really evil list. Only Richie and Nicky survived outside that list, and no one doubted that it was because they were Guy's cousins.

However, I still needed to know who committed each murder

2 7

FOUNTAIN OF SORROW

"Fountain of sorrow, fountain of light
You've known that hollow sound of your own steps in flight
You've had to struggle, you've had to fight
To keep understanding and compassion in sight."
- Jackson Browne

Maggie's Memos and Memories – The Conversation with Nicky

kay, Nicky, time to shit or get off the pot. Who killed all those people you mentioned before?"

"How do I do this?"

"Okay, I'll say a name, and you fill in the killer...for the record."

Damn, did this feel heartless, but I was tired of beating around the bush.

"Harry Rothstein?"

"Joey Pasco and me."

"Vinnie Catalano?"

"Guy, with Sammy and Sal there."

Did I have the nerve? Can I bear to hear his answer?

"Who killed the members of *Those Born Free?*"

"Four different people killed the four different members of the group."

"But there were five members of *Those Born Free*. The math doesn't add up."

"Yeah, due to a mix-up, the police only arrested four members of the band that night. By the time Guy figured out that *five* guys had caused him problems, one of them had disappeared."

"One? As far as we all knew, two had disappeared, Johnny Cipp and Gio DeAngelis."

"Who says that two survived?"

Damn, I forgot Nicky doesn't know that I knew the band and was related to Jimmy.

"Umm, the case files list only three dead. Rocco "Bracko" Brackowski, "Jimmy Mac" McAvoy, and Joey "The Tin Man" Tinley.

"They don't mention that Tinley's parents were killed, too?"

"No!"

"Frankie 'The Roach' Resch took care of the lining of the brakes on their car. They were getting too snoopy about the death of their son. Guy ordered that they be 'taken care of.' That's how he always stated it."

Oh shit, no one even made that connection about Joey the Tinman's parents.

"So, who was killed that people don't know about?"

"Oh, Guy killed Gio DeAngelis, strangled him with a rope. Timpani and Crespo were there again. He did what he called a "schoolyard lynching." He was trying to get the DeAngelis kid to tell him where Cipp was. However, Johnny Cipp was never found. Lucky for him. Right?"

I said nothing. This entire conversation was destroying me inside. Nicky was talking about my family and friends. He wasn't gloating but instead stated facts and provided details as if he were announcing sports scores from a Yankees game the night before.

"In those years, Mad Guy truly earned his name. I need you to understand that my cousin was and still is a raving lunatic. On his 40th

birthday, he gave himself a 'present.' He went and killed Gio DeAngelis' parents just for the sport of it. He came back to the gang that night laughing and screaming, 'Vendetta, vendetta, vendetta.' He was insanely singing 'Happy Birthday to me.' He was nuts, but nobody had the balls to tell him so or do anything about it."

"And...the drummer...Jimmy?"

"Oh, that was Timpani and Crespo...and boy did they botch that job. They never got caught, but Guy was so pissed at them that I thought that he was going to whack the two of them himself!"

I knew the story as told to me by my mom, but with very few details. I'm not even sure if there was an official story. The police merely said the two of them died in a robbery attempt. The only specific detail was that my father and brother fought back. Case closed.

"Nicky, tell me how they died."

I guess he sensed something in either my tone or behavior.

"You, okay...Doc?"

"Just tell me the fucking details." With that, the floodgates opened. I was an emotional wreck, but I tried not to show it to Nicky. The bricks in the third little pig's house were rapidly collapsing. Yet, I knew I had to get through my questioning for the sake of all those depending upon me—I had to get through it for my sanity.

Nicky didn't know what to do or say.

"Tell me, Nicky, tell me! How the hell did my father and brother die?"

"Your father? Your brother? I don't..."

"Nicky, my name is Maggie McAvoy. My father, Noel, and my brother, Jimmy, were killed that day, and I want to know every goddamn detail."

"I'm...I'm so sorry, Doc. I didn't know that you were family. I'd tell you anything you want to know, but I wasn't there. Still, everyone in the gang knew what happened. Guy made Sammy and Sal tell the story. He wanted to embarrass them. He encouraged the guys to laugh at them. Doc, are you really, really sure that you want to hear this?"

"Every fucking detail."

"You really want to hear it?"

"Isn't that what I said, Nicky *Glue?*" I emphasized the odious nickname I swore I would never use.

"Sammy and Sal entered the family candy store...*your* family store with their faces covered in ski masks. However, they were such assholes that they didn't cut the holes for their eyes very well. Your father was prepared to let the store be robbed. He couldn't know that they were sent to murder Jimmy, and nothing he could have done would have changed that. They were not there for robbery.

"Because of their stupid masks that covered up their vision, they didn't see the kid...er...your brother come from the side and swing a baseball bat right into Sammy Crespo's face. Sammy fell to the floor, tearing the mask from his face to get more air. Sal..."

"Sal...what?"

"Sal put two shots in your brother's chest. Your father jumped over the counter, caught Sal by surprise, and beat him relentlessly. He would have killed Sal, but Sammy recovered enough to look through the blood streaming down his swollen face to put a bullet in your father. Before they left, they found Jimmy's girlfriend Diane hiding in the back office and made sure that there were no witnesses."

Though torn apart inside, I never shed a tear. It wasn't because I was being professional, but rather because I hadn't shed a tear in the last fifteen years. That did not mean I did not feel anger, sadness, loss, and a thousand other emotions. I just didn't show what I was feeling as I tried to get the rest of the story out of Nicky.

"Who killed Joey, 'The Tinman,' Tinley? Who killed The Mellotones?"

Nicky looked at me as if to ask "How are you still here? How are you still asking questions?"

"The same person who is going to kill me if you don't get me protection real soon...The Actor. He is Guy's secret weapon, and Guy pays him to do jobs that no one else can or will do. I don't think that even Guy knows what he looks like. He only meets with Guy while he is in disguise. He killed Joey Tinley while disguised as a strait-laced college kid. He killed the Mellotones while they were at practice. For that hit, he was a fat repairman with a butt crack showing. He "adjusted" the gas lines in the house where they practiced. After the band took a break and lit up their smokes, well...very few pieces of the band were found after the total implosion of the basement."

I was speechless.

"The Actor could be at the table right next to us, and we would never know. He's that good at what he does. He scares the shit out of me."

With that, a loud beeping sound emitted from Nicky's side.

"Damn! I'm almost out of oxygen. That's my warning alarm. I gotta go real soon."

Usually, I would have thought of something; I could have driven him somewhere to get what he needed or taken some sort of action. I was emotionally and physically drained and, therefore, slow to respond. I knew I didn't have much time.

"Nicky, so far, you have mentioned more than ten people that Guy was responsible for killing, but not one case where there is a witness who can finger him. Not one person can testify in court against him. It's all stuff you heard but didn't see."

"Except for the one person that he personally directed *me* to kill. Is that good enough to tell you about?"

"So, did you kill someone on his direct orders?"

Nicky nodded his head.

"Who?" I screamed out so loud that people at adjoining tables again looked up. However, I didn't need to wait for his answer. I knew who. In all our morbid talk of death, there was one name unaccounted for. There was one name I dreaded hearing him say.

"I killed a kid named Bracko...and there was a witness."

2 8

PAINT IT BLACK

"I see a red door,
And I want it painted black."
- Rolling Stones

Maggie's Memos and Memories – The Conversation with Nicky

I don't know how, but I knew that it was coming. Still, I sat there shocked as Nicky admitted to killing Bracko. I guess I knew we would reach the point when Nicky's misdeeds would be laid bare. I was numb from the revelation of the circumstances of the deaths of my brother and father. Yet, the fact that Nicky had killed Bracko had particularly disturbed me. Nicky, this person that I had come to know through our discussions, was not just there when Bracko died, but single-handedly had committed the act. I almost didn't want it to be true because Nicky had started to be a sympathetic character to me. I *almost* liked him. Yet, I knew this was the first breakthrough that could be used legally. I knew that was a good thing for Nicky and his lawyers. He could now go into witness protection. Yet, all I could think of was Bracko looking down at me and smiling.

You finally got the truth, Miss Maggie.

"Nicky, you do understand that you just admitted to a second murder?"

"Yeah, I know, and it feels good to get it off my chest because killing Bracko was the only time that I considered myself a murderer."

"But Nicky, you already admitted to killing Harry Rothstein. How is this different?"

"Joey Pasco lit the match."

"I call bullshit on you, Nicky. You know you are just as responsible for Rothstein's death. You can't spin it any other way."

He sat there in stunned silence, and I endeavored to determine whether this was the moment he first grasped the implications of his actions. Could he have been in a state of denial all these years?

"Nicky, if you didn't think that you were responsible for Harry Rothstein's death, was all the guilt for Bracko?"

"I was there for the end of Harry, but I don't know if I would have done anything if Joey wasn't there. I hated Joey, and Joey hated me. I think Joey was jealous of me. Joey was tougher, and he was a cruel bastard. He was everything Guy admired in a follower. However, there was one thing he didn't have that I did—Provenzano blood. And that bothered the hell out of him. Therefore, he mocked me as a coward after the whole Rothstein fiasco. And maybe he was right. Or maybe I just wasn't cut out to be a killer. But I needed to be just that. Guy had no place for me in the organization if I wasn't tough enough to pull my weight. I had nowhere to go if I wasn't in the Provenzano gang. I was nothing without Guy."

"Nicky, you don't think you could have done something else with your life."

"No, I was in my early twenties, and I had just gotten married to Lucia. Without the gang, I was nothing. I couldn't support her and the family we wanted to start. I had nothing without Mad Guy, and he pulled me aside after the Rothstein thing to let me know just that."

"I don't get it."

"You don't get it because it's not your world. Guy got me alone in Brookville Park in Rosedale, and he beat the shit out of me."

"Why?"

"He wanted to tell a story about how we got jumped in that park by five guys, and the two of us sent them all to the hospital. He was trying to save my honor. I'll never forget what he said to me, 'You ever fucking dishonor me and our family again like this Rothstein shit, I'll tell everyone the next time that *eight* strangers jumped us, and you just couldn't handle it. The truth is you'll be dead because I will have killed you with my bare hands. At least, people will think you died being brave.'

"Nicky, what did you do?"

"I asked Guy how I could make it right. After the whole Driftwood screwup destroyed his reputation with the mob, he needed to act quickly to redeem his honor. Rothstein was first because he had sold Tony the glue. Then, in a fit of rage, he killed Vinnie the Cat.

"However, Guy had some sense. He knew his revenge against the band had to be done with a level head. Their murders had to look like accidents. I was given the job of being the first *to take care of* one of the band members, He *suggested* Bracko because he was a loner.

"I had been doing my research for months. I followed the kid and the rest of the band around night and day to truly understand them and know what made each of them tick. I was going to make my cousin proud."

"Nicky, I call bullshit...again. There were only three weeks between the raid at the Driftwood Club and the death of Bracko. How do you explain that?"

"Yes, but I had been following them for nearly a year. My job was to gather info for Vinnie the Cat, who wanted to know if the band had potential secrets that could affect the gang. I worked exclusively for Vinnie, so I did not make the connection between the guys my cousin hated and the guys in the band."

"That makes no sense. You watched the band for almost a year and never knew they were the same guys your cousin hated...or that they were underage?"

"I only did what I was told, and no one asked me to check birth certificates. Besides, I didn't know you had to be eighteen to play in a club. When I was fifteen, they let me drink at the gang hangout, the Dew Drop Inn. That was supposed to be Vinnie's expertise and…"

"And what?"

"He died for getting it wrong. He never checked proof of age or any other identification. According to Crespo and Timpani, Guy never said anything after the raid. But, instead, went to the bar at midnight to confront Vinnie."

"How did Vinnie try to explain the mistake?"

"Vinnie never got a word out. Guy jumped over the bar, grabbed the nearest bottle, and smashed it over his head. Vinnie was already unconscious when he repeated the bottle smashing two more times."

"And there was no blowback on you?"

"No, Vinnie was a good guy, and he probably wouldn't have thrown me under the bus by telling Guy that it was me who had been doing the research. In the end, I'll never know. Vinnie was dead in a matter of minutes."

"Oh, Shit!"

"Yet, things worked out well for me. I was given the job of…of…of eliminating one of them and knew everything about them already."

"Everything…really?"

"I thought that my research would make them less like people. It didn't work. I…I…got to know Bracko just a little too well. More than that, I got to like and respect him. I mean, the fact that Bracko took time to help his neighbor and her little boy still haunts me. The sick mom and the kid had no one in this world besides Bracko…and I took him away. I didn't want to do that."

This brought back many memories from those days.

"You selfish bastard. You didn't want to do it? But you did it just so you could please Mad Guy,"

"No, I did it so that I could stay alive! Cousin or not, I was running out of chances. And in the end, I was too much of a coward to cross Mad Guy."

"What are you saying?"

123

"I liked them all. I mean the band and those who hung around them. Maria...the three McAvoy sisters. Oh yeah, which one were you?"

"I am the youngest."

"And I liked Michael, who came to the practices."

"Michael? You knew Michael? How?"

"I told you I was obsessed with knowing everything about them. At first, I was doing it for Vinnie. Then, I was doing it to..."

"What were you going to say? To be able to murder one or more of them?"

"Yeah, but then I got to know them all, especially Bracko. I know you will never understand how good he was...and what the hell I robbed the world of when I killed him. And how I felt that I was robbing that kid, Michael, of Bracko's help and friendship."

"Nicky, I do. If you followed him as much as you say, you'll remember a little girl who came to visit Michael sometimes? That was me. I was that little girl. I knew Bracko better than you ever could. And Michael was my best friend."

"Oh God, Doc, I'm so sorry. I'm so, so sorry. I know you won't believe this, but I haven't been the same since that day...and, and Michael..."

I sensed he wanted to say more; however, in my growing anger, I grew impatient.

"Tell me every detail," I responded to him coldly, wondering how he would sound while giving his testimony at Mad Guy's trial. Inwardly, I wasn't sure if I could bear hearing the details.

"I followed Bracko around for weeks and got to know his routine. The band had not met up since the raid. So, he went to work with some old brick mason, returned home, and either played the guitar in his basement or went next door to help the woman living there. I think she was very sick. Sometimes, he would sit on the stoop with Michael and a little girl...I mean you."

"You saw me?"

"Yeah. I was always watching Bracko once Guy gave me my...er... job. I found out that the one consistent habit of the two of them was to drink huge amounts of orange juice daily—the father, because he was in the AA program to recover from alcoholism, and the son, because he was thirsty after doing backbreaking work all day."

"I remember that."

"When they were both out of the house, I snuck in and spiked all the orange juice with a heavy sedative. The father came home and, according to plan, drank the juice and was unconscious on the couch when Bracko came in. I assumed that Bracko would drink the orange juice before going to his basement room to play the guitar. I couldn't know that he broke the pattern for one reason or another.

"I snuck into the house, poured gasoline all over the living room, and then lit it. I knew the police would never check that out because they had been bought and paid for. As the fire spread through the house, I still heard the strings of Bracko's guitar wailing down the basement. He was unaware that the flames were starting to block his exit from his basement room. But he would soon...and try to escape. I realized this and I ran into the burning house to lock the basement door. Earlier, I had seen the deadbolt that the father had placed on that door. I guess it had been part of the father's discipline code. I locked it.

Bracko was now trapped in the basement, waiting for the all-consuming flames to bring the house down on him. As I escaped from the inferno, the little boy from next door had been watching events and knew that I had been inside."

"Please save Bracko," he cried desperately. "He's my friend and the only person who helps me."

"I just tried," I lied. I had doomed this little boy's best friend and protector to a horrible death by locking the door.

"But he's still alive...listen."

"It was then that I heard the sound that would haunt me the rest of my life—the strains of Bracko's guitar cut through the roaring fire and touched me. I wanted to undo what I had done, but I realized it was too late. As the guitar playing slowed down and then died out, Bracko knew he was a dead man and went out his way...playing the guitar."

"Please, mister, try," yelled the boy, now sobbing.

"I did go in one more time. However, it was not to save Bracko but rather myself. I realized that the firemen, who had not been bribed, would notice the bolted and locked door and have questions. This loose end might come back to haunt me...and, likewise, my cousin Guy."

"I went into the blazing building once more, this time to unlock the basement. Perhaps in the back of my mind, unlocking the door might give Bracko a chance. I was too late. No sounds came from the basement as I undid the bolt and ran out. By now, crowds had formed, and the little boy was yelling, 'He tried to save Bracko! He tried to save Bracko!'"

I was choking on my emotions—thinking of Bracko dying and Michael screaming.

"I was deemed a hero, but Mad Guy did not look kindly on the news headlines my actions had created. I had done the job he requested, but he was furious. I think that he wanted to exact some sort of punishment on me, but our cousin Richie intervened. I was sent away to a place where the gang had interests, but it was not near New York. I was never asked to kill again...but that was of little consequence because no matter how far away I went, I was still haunted by the little boy's...Michael's... cries, and the sound of Bracko's guitar."

"So, there you have it. Your case against Mad Guy Provenzano. However, I don't want to see you again until you have arranged for me to be in witness protection."

"Will anyone be going with you...into witness protection?"

"No, my wife is long gone...and there is no one else who cares enough."

"I'll talk to your lawyers and the DA and get it going."

"Don't take long?"

"I understand your concern."

"Do you?"

"Huh?"

"You see that fat, bald man at the third table from the door?"

"Yeah."

"Do you see that 80-something-year-old guy three tables to our left?"

"Yeah."

"Do you see that sexy broad...er...excuse me, the woman sitting alone at the bar?

"Yeah, what's your point?"

"Any one of them could be 'The Actor,' and I could be dead the minute I walk out the door. So, work fast, Doc."

I watched Nicky as he slowly drifted away, constantly looking around. I knew I would not see him again until the deal was done and possibly not until the trial. I hoped he was wrong about The Actor, yet I found myself analyzing every person I passed on the way to my car.

29

THE ACTOR

"The curtain rises on the scene,
With someone shouting to be free.
The play unfolds before my eyes,
There stands The Actor, who is me."
- Moody Blues

The Actor's Script

$\mathcal{I}$ am an actor. I play parts. I always play parts...I mean, always. You will never see the real me, and I like it that way. I want absolutely no one to uncover the person who lies beneath the characters I create. He is probably ugly—at least on the inside. But I enjoy my work. The deception, the hunt, and...of course, the final prize.

Oh...didn't I tell you? Besides being a disguise artist, I am also a first-class sadist. I just love to inflict pain. I relish those moments when I see the *fear of God* in others' eyes. No, that was wrong. I enjoy immensely seeing the *fear of Me* in the eyes of others.

Do you want to know my story? Now, think before you answer. I allow no one to know the real me. If you read this, I might just have to kill you.

My first memories were of my mom crying. I guess I was about five, and my father wasn't there anymore. Did he die...or did he run away? Momma was never very clear on that point. I am not even sure if the man I called "Dad" was my father. In reality, I was probably a bastard. But, I prefer the term 'Actor' better than "Bastard." If the years afterward were the same as the years before, there would have been many, many candidates to consider for my Father's Day cards.

Yet those were just the ones Momma liked. I am not including those who paid her to "like" them. That's bullshit, pinko talk for the fact that she was a fucking whore. But she cared for me, and I loved her. Why else would I commit my first murder at age eight...just because of her?

This one fine gentleman had decided not to pay her. That happens on occasion when you are freelancing and don't have a pimp. When Momma spoke up, this guy took a few shots at her face, thus damaging her ability to make a living...and pissing me off.

I don't know if I planned it or if it was spontaneous, but I ran up to the roof of our apartment building. I was there before he even made his way down to the street. From my location, way above the front door, I often threw small, light objects down to the street below. It was never more than an annoyance to those passing by, and I enjoyed their smug anger at my actions.

I spent a great deal of time on that roof because being in a one-bedroom apartment with a hooker mom is not a great deal of fun. Often, when I was bored, I scraped away at the grout that held together the low brick wall at the top of the roof. Was this premeditation for some act I had not yet planned?

As the asshole emerged onto the street below me, the bricks *somehow* dislodged from the wall and tumbled downward. They didn't all hit him. But one did, and from that height, one was more than enough to make sure he never hit my mom (or anyone else) again. Interestingly, I remember looking down at the blood splattered on the ground and having no feelings at all.

I don't think Momma ever figured out how nuts her son had become, and she fawned all over me. She always told me how handsome I was. Occasionally, she used a descriptive word that I didn't understand—WASPY. Everyone in our part of Queens looked like a stereotype of some nationality. But not me. I didn't look like any one group. This isn't something you want to tell a kid who's trying to fit in.

At that young age, I thought I had a solution. Whenever my mom had over someone (very often more than once a day), I listened and watched. No, I was not a voyeur of the sex but rather the man himself, you know, the flavor of the day. I studied their facial mannerisms and their appearances. I observed how they walked, talked, and moved.

By eleven years old, I was getting into my mother's makeup and trying to recreate a look. If the guy had gray hair, I would throw some talcum powder in my hair and then prance in front of the mirror, acting old. One day, Mom walked in while I was putting on heavy, heavy makeup, trying to recreate some swarthy kind of guy.

"What are you...a faggot?" yelled my surprised mother. She followed it very quickly with, "I never would have thought it, but if that's what you want, go with it."

I had to explain my fascination with adopting others' personas. My mom understood, and from that point on, she helped me. She even took me to all kinds of costume stores, and we got professional help from acting classes.

I had no friends, so I roamed the streets and people watched. Sometimes, I would be a Middle Eastern teenager and go to order falafel from a restaurant that thought I was getting some home cooking. Italian was easy. I would slightly darken my pale skin, darken my mousy hair, and use just the right kind of hand and face gestures.

It didn't always work. I got my ass kicked by more than one ethnic group who thought I was making fun of them. That made me get better. A few times, I pretended to be a girl. Nothing sexual about it. I just had to make sure that my cast of characters was well-rounded. This practice continued for a few years before I found a practical application for my talents.

Shoplifting and pickpocketing are easier if targets feel comfortable around you. Momma loved our increased income and often repeated the phrase, "Momma loves her little actor." To me, that was as good as her saying, "I love you," words I had never heard too often from her mouth.

I don't know how long I would have kept up that lifestyle if tragedy hadn't struck when I was sixteen. I came home from a very successful day as an elderly Asian gentleman in Chinatown. The Chinese always show great respect to their elders (even make-believe ones), so the pickpocketing was exceptional. I was thinking about doing it again the next day when I saw a man running out of our apartment. As he passed me on the staircase, he pushed me aside, making some kind of comment that told me two things. First, he had a German accent, and second, he obviously did not respect his elders like the men of Chinatown.

As I entered through the open door, I saw Momma crumpled on the floor. Blood was streaming from her head. As I approached, I knew that it was serious and that I had to call for an ambulance. That was the only reason that I did not either pursue my mom's attacker or head to the roof for another impromptu science lesson in gravity.

Of course, the EMTs who arrived on the scene looked at me a little sideways because I had only partially taken off my disguise. After their best efforts, they got her breathing, but not conscious. In fact, she never regained consciousness...ever.

I visited the hospital every day, hoping for a miracle and knowing it wouldn't happen. Her life was out of my control. Yet, while life and death were topics beyond The Actor's abilities, revenge was not. I scoured the immediate neighborhood, searching for the broad-shouldered balding man with a German accent. I found him.

Horst Schillenheim was a butcher. Why I didn't figure that out sooner is a mystery to me. Now I had him. He had no idea what I looked like. As far as he knew, the only witness to his crime was a myopic Asian on his last legs. Many men (which I already considered myself) would have rushed in and confronted him. Some people might have called the police. But I was "The Actor" (not to mention a sadist). What is the old saying? "Revenge is a dish best served cold." How about real cold...like in a butcher's freezer with a whole lot of bloody meat, to screw up the crime scene technicians.

I learned a bit of German before putting on my best European immigrant disguise. I immediately told him that my wife insisted that we only speak English. I was proficient in languages, but not yet fluent enough to speak a language other than English consistently. Being a cheap bastard, he hired me as an assistant when I offered to work at one-third of the minimum wage "in order to learn from a master like him." (Yeah, he was a sucker for blowing smoke up his ass.) I was there for a week when I got my chance.

"I vill show you how you cut da meat in de proper vay," he proudly boasted and had me hold the entire torso of the cow. He struck hard with the cleaver into the meat, and I realized that those same muscular arms had given my petite mother a devastating blow.

"Now you vill try." Music to my ears. As he held the cow and encouraged me to strike as hard as I could...I did. I separated his right hand from his body with a blow he would have been proud of if he had not been the recipient. I will not give many more details because, though I am a sadist, I am not a braggart.

I made one more cut that day as he squirmed on the floor. Without going into detail, I mention that he will never visit a whore again. I might also mention that he would not even successfully jerk off because he had neither a hand nor a prick.

When my mother died two months later without ever regaining consciousness, I visited him again. No disguise this time. I told him why I was there and then promptly killed him. I didn't hesitate. I smiled.

3 0

SCENES FROM AN
ITALIAN RESTAURANT

"I'll meet you any time you want,
In our Italian restaurant."
- Billy Joel

Actor's Script – Scene 2

I now realized that at sixteen, I was on my own. I guess I could have worried about child protective services trying to put me in a foster home because I was underage. I didn't. As long as I could present myself to the world as an adult, no one cared. No one came for me. I proceeded on my way, picking pockets and shoplifting. It never occurred to me to use the talents that I had displayed *with* the butcher (or *as a* butcher). That is, until I got caught.

I was playing the part of a very, very old Italian man in Little Italy. I was doing pretty well for quite a few days just by standing on the corner with a tin cup, occasionally singing some off-key version of "Volare" in an old, raspy voice. The marks were mostly tourists, and I got a little sloppy with my presentation. It was too easy. Then...

A mixed group of older and younger men was heading into one of the nicer restaurants. They stared at me, and I mistook this for interest and perhaps a big payday. One of the younger ones came right up to me and stared me in the face.

"Don Provenzano, your table is ready and waiting," the maître de respectfully announced as he leaned out the door to the crowd waiting to go in. Everyone listened except for the young man who came toward me.

"Guy, c'mon, leave the old man alone," rasped the impatient father to his son.

"Wait, I want to speak to this guy," the annoyed son replied.

"Goombah, I think that your accent sounds like it is from Messina."

I just smiled and indicated that we must be, as he said...goombahs. I knew enough to know that it was a term of endearment...a companion...an accomplice.

"How wonderful to have the eternal city of Rome so close by," smiled Guy Provenzano, putting his hand on my shoulder as if we were old friends.

"Certo," I replied, being glad I had learned the word for yes.

"We often went from seeing the Pope at the Vatican early Sunday morning and then returning by lunchtime for my mother's pasta in Messina." This time, he displayed a smile to me that I could not understand.

"Si, Messina," I mumbled just before Guy's fist caught me in the solar plexus.

"Son, what are you doing to that old man?" His father was livid with Guy until the son pulled off my gray wig. This was followed by a very powerful right cross to my jaw, and I lost consciousness.

"Messina is in Sicily, you asshole. It's where my father came from... but you didn't." In fact, I am pretty sure you are not even Italian."

We were in a room with no windows, just Mad Guy Provenzano and me. His friends and family were nowhere to be seen. He made me remove my makeup, thus revealing the real me to him.

"But what gave me away?"

"You mean before you screwed up Italy's geography?"

"Yeah."

"A real Italian man would work 24 hours a day for any money...or he would starve...but he would never, ever beg. Too much pride... perhaps...false pride. And if there ever was such desperation for his family that he had to beg, he would never do it in Little Italy. You know why?"

"Pride?" I mumbled.

"You know, I might just make an Italian out of you yet."

I noticed his mood lightened slightly, and he sat in a chair across from me. He then took out a stiletto knife and flung it into the seat of the wooden chair I sat in. It stuck in the chair...right in between my balls.

"So, do you want to tell me what's going on? What's your real story...ah...goombah?"

Faced perhaps with terminal castration, I spilled my guts to Mad Guy Provenzano. I did this as I had never done before — or since. As he abruptly got up from his seat across from me, he smiled.

"Keep the knife. I might just have a use for a boy...er, man of your talents."

Three months later, he gave me my first of many "missions." When he wanted me for something, he always called and asked me to meet in "our special place"—that same Italian restaurant where he had discovered me...and almost castrated me. It was always a little game to see if he could recognize me in my ever-changing disguises.

Sometimes, I would be a particular ethnic group, which was always the easiest guess for him because most of those personas seemed out of sync with the high-end Italian restaurant. The one that fooled him the most was when I showed up as a sexy broad. He had no idea until I opened my mouth. (I still had not perfected my female voice). However, regardless of my costume, he gave me my assignment in a business-like manner, never showing any reaction to my current theme. To my best recollection, I have "performed" for him on seventeen occasions. I even got to the point where, after an even dozen, I did one "on the house." He liked the fact that even his relatives and friends didn't know he was behind a hit when I worked for him. Deniability. However, I'll never forget my first hit—my tryout.

Disguised as a nerdy musical college student, I attended a party for incoming freshmen at the Berklee College of Music in Boston. It was a test of my abilities as "The Actor." In the real world, I had not even graduated from junior high. However, I was a fast learner as far as faking it for the few days necessary.

I was invited to a party thrown by upperclassmen. It was the end of the first week of school, and they wanted to welcome fellow New Yorkers to their geeky little world. I blended right in...I always do.

I found my mark, a certain Joseph Tinley. I eventually got him to come and listen to some really rare jazz albums I had in my room. I don't know if he was naïve...or maybe even gay...or just such a music dork, but he followed me to a deserted room that I pretended to be my dorm room. Before he was able to realize that there were no jazz albums or anything else in the room, I had rendered him unconscious with a pressure point maneuver I had studied by watching military films.

When he came to, I had him bound and gagged. Mad Guy had insisted that this guy's death had to look like an accident. Therefore, I did my research and found that each year, a certain number of college kids die of alcohol poisoning. That was going to be the method of nerdy Joseph's demise. Of course, he initially refused to cooperate. However, when I drew black lines on each of the knuckles of his fingers, he looked at me with questioning eyes.

"You see, my little friend, for every minute you do not drink this quart of 100-proof vodka, I am going to cut off one of your fingers... right on the dotted line." I pulled out the stiletto Mad Guy had given me and placed it delicately on his right index finger. The look of horror on his face was priceless. He played the piano, and his fingers were his future. His fingers were his life. He drank.

Alcohol poisoning happens when a person takes in too much booze, too fast. The body doesn't have enough time to become unconscious as a self-defense mechanism. Systems shut down, and that's all she wrote.

I brought home a local Boston paper that vividly described the tragic story of a life cut short by the stupidity of college drinking. Mad Guy was extremely pleased. I had accomplished what none of his regular gang had been able to—a perfectly executed hit with no sloppiness or mistakes.

"This is the beginning of a beautiful relationship," Mad Guy said to me as he handed me an envelope with more money than I had ever seen in my life. That was in 1967. Here we are in 1990, and it is still a beautiful relationship.

Since that time so long ago, I have only met Guy while in disguise, but I cannot forget that he is the only person who knows what the real Jerry Marchant, The Actor, looks like. Yet our loyalty works both ways, so I just returned from playing one of my most significant roles ever. I am intrigued by this job. Yet if you ask my mark, she'll never know or recognize my real name ...or my face. You see, my target is now my audience. I am performing for her in my role as her patient.

Mad Guy wants to know if Dr. Maggie Evers is talking to anyone whom she shouldn't be talking to. Especially someone connected to him who could do him legal harm. Once I infiltrate her defenses and see her files, I will know, and I will report. What my employer will do with that information is up to him. Sometimes, he just wants me to investigate. However, sometimes, he asks me to *take care of* matters. I like that. Remember...The Actor is a sadist.

I believe my role as a Holocaust survivor, Josef Stern, is developing nicely. I am getting to know Dr. Maggie Evers. I can tell she feels deep empathy for me. Today she left me alone in her waiting room. It was not hard to pick the lock to her office, where I found her files very interesting.

Oh, Nicky Glue, you've been a very bad boy.

PART III

YESTERDAY'S GONE

*"But that was yesterday.
And yesterday's gone."*

1966 -1975

31

SEEMS LIKE SUCH
A LONG TIME AGO

"Seems like such a long time ago,
I was walking on a lonely road.
Getting tired of dreaming alone,
Like all the lonely people I have known."
- Jim Croce

Maggie's Memos and Memories

I was driving out to finally see my sister, Aylin, one of only two people I know who are still alive from the summer and fall of 1967. The other is her husband, DJ.

I now know the story of all the evil that occurred. Yet, I need something else—I need Aylin and DJ to fill me in about the beauty of those times. I need to hear more about Johnny, Gio, Tinman, and Bracko. I need to relive the closeness of the band. I need to reminisce about my family—Mom, Dad, Siobhan, and Jimmy. I needed to remember Michael, my friend and my second dance partner.

I need to hear the "good people's" side of the story.

When Aylin opened the door, I was numb. It had been seventeen years…a lifetime ago…half of my actual life ago. Yet I was immediately transported back to all that was my childhood.

"Maggie," mumbled Aylin in a subdued voice, trying desperately to hold back tears. She failed. She ran to me and embraced me in a bear hug that squeezed the living shit out of me. It felt good. I had not hugged, kissed, held hands, or shown or felt any human emotion since 1975. It's a long story, and I will get to it eventually. For those years, I was building the much-mentioned brick house to surround my feelings. This embrace was about music, dancing, egg creams, loving parents, and sisterhood. It was also all about what we had lost in 1967.

We eventually found our way to the den and talked like we had never been torn apart. DJ left us alone but occasionally popped in and asked if we needed anything. The last time he did this, I told him to stay.

"DJ, we've got him. We've got Provenzano. Nicky confided in me the story behind each of the murders that he engineered. His recollections were horrendous, and I listened to every minute detail. Mad Guy was a scheming, conniving dirtbag who covered his tracks well. Except he slipped up once and only once…and Nicky Toto told me of the one murder he personally committed on his cousin Guy's direct orders…and more importantly, he will swear to it in court as soon as witness protection is arranged."

"Holy shit. We got him…er, you got Mad Guy," screeched DJ. Let me call Goody, Leo, and the DA. Let me get the ball rolling." He left the room in an excited frenzy.

Aylin and I were again alone, but there was no joy on our faces.

"Who?" softly whispered Aylin almost inaudibly.

"Who? What do you mean?"

"Maggie, who did Nicky admit to killing?"

"Bracko."

She nodded in acceptance.

"Aylin, how come you didn't ask who killed our brother?"

She didn't reply immediately, as if she were weighing some great decision.

"Aylin, what aren't you telling me?"

She stared at me blankly.

"Aylin, what the hell is going on? You're shutting me out...just like in 1967. It's one of the reasons I left home."

I began to feel angry, recalling all the feelings of being abandoned by her. I considered leaving. And still, she stared at me.

DJ walked into the room. He spoke somberly...void of all the joy he had displayed a few minutes before.

"She didn't ask you who killed Jimmy because she already knew who did it...she witnessed your brother's murder first-hand."

"What the fuck? What are you saying? How come I never knew this?"

"Aylin was meeting Jimmy at the store that night and was just outside at closing time. From there, she witnessed everything ...the assault...and the deaths of her father and brother. She saw everything."

"And the hitmen didn't know about her?"

"They never saw her as she silently left the scene. The shock of what had happened put her into a mental haze. She blocked the whole affair out of her conscious mind for years. As a therapist, you can understand this repression...this blackout of memory, better than I do. Her internal struggle with knowing what she had seen and not remembering it led to years of drug and alcohol abuse. She has lived with the guilt of that night ever since. She sorely regrets her actions in the years that followed, especially because of what it did to your mother, Siobhan, and you."

"Aylin...I just thought that you were a selfish...a selfish..."

"Bitch? Is that the word you are looking for, Maggie? Because I was. I caused so much pain to Mom and everyone."

DJ said no more but merely nodded at Aylin as if he were encouraging her to tell me the rest of the story.

"Three years after the tragedies...the deaths, I was listening to old tapes of the band. Jimmy always forgot to turn off the tape recorder when they finished recording a tune. I liked those parts of the tapes best. I would listen to the byplay between the guys, and it brought me back to the good times. Only on one particular tape, they were making fun of one of the local hoods. The physical description forced the memory back into my mind. I knew that it was Sammy Crespo and Sal Timpani who killed our father and brother."

She stopped as if contemplating whether to go on, whether to give me the final piece to the puzzle.

"Holy shit! Where was I when all this was happening?"

"By that time, you were a fourteen-year-old who was dealing with her loss and the craziness of her oldest sister."

"Nicky told me that some 'crazy broad' killed Crespo."

Aylin said nothing. She bowed her head and pointed to herself.

Thinking she was feeling guilty for killing the dirtbag, I reacted by forcefully insisting that he deserved it. It was then that she started to cry, and DJ rushed to her side,

"Her attempt to…to do away with Crespo didn't go as expected. He saw through the phony seduction she had used to get him alone. In the ensuing struggle, she did…uh…kill him."

I was confused. DJ continued.

"But there was a price for her revenge. Unknown to her or me, she was pregnant with our baby. The damage that Crespo inflicted on her caused her to lose that baby, our son. She almost died. She almost bled to death, but the doctors were able to save her. However, there was a cost. She was unable to have children after that."

"Oh my God, my poor Aylin," I moved toward her and held her tightly like I had held no one in fifteen years. DJ continued.

"Finding out that her revenge had caused her to lose the baby affected her mentally. She had a complete and total meltdown. Your mother called her priest, Father Hanratty, who was a take-charge, but loving kind of guy. He understood the neighborhood and knew if Mad Guy found out that a young girl had taken out one of his closest minions, he would be enraged," explained DJ, "Only one person knew who had lured Crespo to his death?" A faint smile could barely be seen on DJ's face.

"Who?"

"Mad Guy asked the bartender who had witnessed the faux seduction. He lied and gave a phony description of the young woman who had left with Crespo—wrong height, wrong hair color, wrong facial features."

"Why would he do that?"

"Because the bartender was Charlie Catalano. Charlie suspected that three years prior, Guy had killed his son, Vinnie "The Cat" Catalano. He stayed on as a bartender because he needed the job, but more importantly, he was hoping to screw Mad Guy in any way possible. Lying about Aylin was his first cut. And now, more than two decades later, he is giving info to the DA that will support Nicky's testimony."

DJ and I looked at Aylin, and to our surprise, she smiled a little.

"I'm okay now, Maggie," she said, taking DJ's hand.

"But she wasn't then. Father Hanratty created a complicated cover story to hide Aylin's act while she recovered physically and mentally for years."

"He announced from the pulpit that Aylin was in a novitiate and that she was training to become a nun. He even backdated her vocation to before Crespo's death."

"Sonofabitch," I muttered. I never believed my sister's religious devotion for a second and thought it was just another trick by Aylin. It was the final straw for me. I ran away before I ever saw her again.

"I am truly sorry for that," whimpered Aylin, speaking for the first time since the story began. "I was in no state to think of the consequences to anyone—myself included."

"Blame me. I was complicit in the deception. Your mother and I knew, but we decided the truth might get out if you and Siobhan were to find out. I never thought of what it would do to you. I'm sorry," confessed DJ in a muted tone.

For a long time, we said nothing. We were emotionally spent.

32

SOMETIMES A FANTASY

"Sometimes a fantasy,
Is all you need."
- Billy Joel

Maggie's Memos and Memories

"$\mathcal{I}$ always suspected Mad Guy was behind Bracko's death, but I couldn't prove it."

"Well, now you can," I gloated.

"Bracko," whispered Aylin. "I had a crush on him."

"We all did," I responded. "But Aylin, you had a real boyfriend... DJ."

"Not then. I thought DJ was a jerk."

"Thanks a lot. But, you know, I wanted you even then. Who knew it would take over five years to win you over?" DJ smiled at Aylin.

"All I ever thought of was Bracko," I confided in them. "I just wish I knew more about him. I was so young, and my memories are fading. I remember being at practices and dancing with him and Michael.

Yeah, Michael, who Bracko brought to the practices. We played, we danced, and we…"

"Finger Danced? Do you think we didn't notice the game that the three of you played? We thought it was cute." DJ finished my thought.

"DJ, please tell me more. I need to hear about the good times— from good people."

"Maggie, I'll do better than that." He nodded at Aylin and left the room quickly. He returned holding a thick manuscript.

I was confused.

"Is that the book you are writing about Mad Guy's takedown that I just read?"

"No, *Empire of the Mad* was started only six months ago when Leo and Goody brought me in to record the story of Guy's case. This is the book I have been writing for more than twenty years. It is the story of the band—Those Born Free. When I started it, I never thought it would be a post-mortem." DJ. pensively held the typed sheets— emotion seemingly stopping him dead in his tracks.

"I started researching while Those Born Free were still practicing in 1967. I was going to give a first-hand account of the band's rise to stardom. Then it became something else altogether after their demise at the Driftwood Club. I even spoke to some of the guys after the debacle. I have had to assume certain parts of the story to fill in the blanks. Because of that, this book is written as a novel, just like the book about Mad Guy."

"Why haven't you published it?" I asked.

"Because the story won't end…it won't ever be complete until I find Johnny, my best friend and the only band member who might not be dead. It may take me years, even decades. However, this story has to have a conclusion before I do anything with it."

"So why are you showing it to me now?"

"You wanted to know about Bracko, so I pulled out that chapter. You heard about his gruesome death. But you need to hear the untold parts of his wonderful life. In the weeks after the band's demise, but before his death, he needed to talk. Yes, I know you're skeptical because Bracko never spoke to anyone. But Bracko was human, and with his life in disarray, he needed someone to lean on. The lawyers had advised the band members not to have contact with each other. So, he called me. We spoke a lot. I learned Bracko's story like no one else."

"What do you call it? What is the title of the book?"

"I have been working on it so long that I simply call it *The Book*. Still, I have played around with some names that might work. I just don't know if any of the ideas fully catch the essence of the group...or their story."

"Try them on me."

"Well, my latest is *Brothers of Forever*—because of their strong bond as friends and bandmates."

"Nice."

"Another idea was *A Band Lost in the Wind*—because they are all only remembered by a few of us."

That title hit me hard because of the reality of all our losses. I thought that would be a good title. And then DJ hit me with his third title, which also brought back beautiful memories of the band...but also confusion that I couldn't explain.

"You probably don't remember any of their original songs—those that would have been on their first album. However, I do. I had a hand in writing many of them, along with the guys. Yet their best song, by far, was "The Thief of My Forever," and I had nothing to do with that one. It was Bracko's original idea, but the entire band contributed to making it spectacular."

I said nothing, but I remembered that song. I remembered it very well. I also thought that I had heard it long after the band was gone. I knew that was impossible. Yet...

"There were so many lines in the song that were prophetic to the events that would soon happen."

DJ started to sing...

We were living lives of passion,
Never wanting to go slow.
Never thinking about tomorrow,

Never choosing to say no.

He suddenly was choked up; Aylin continued along with the faltering DJ ...

We had the promise of a dream,
To keep our fates at bay.
Then came the Thief,
And took it all away.
Away...

"Yeah, right now, if I don't call it *A Band Lost in the Wind,* I will call it *The Thief of My Forevers.*"

With that, he handed me the pages he had written.

33

HELL IS FOR CHILDREN

"Hell, Hell is for children,
And you shouldn't have to pay for your love,
With your bones and your flesh."
- Pat Benatar

An Excerpt from *The Thief of My Forever, A Band Lost in the Wind,*
Brothers of Forever, or just *The Book.*

*R*occo Brackowski had been the product of a mixed marriage. No, he was not biracial or anything of that nature. In the Queens neighborhood where he was born and raised, his father, Stanley Brackowski, a third-generation Polish boy, had married a young girl of Italian descent named Josephine Ferrigno. At first, Josie's family had been reluctant to accept such a mismatch, but the young girl had convinced her parents by citing the fact that it could have been worse—the Poles were at least Catholic.

The Ferrigno family had accepted the marriage even more readily when Josie announced she was pregnant and due to give birth around the couple's first anniversary. Unfortunately, Josie suffered through a difficult childbirth and only lived long enough to hold her child once. At that moment, she named him Rocco after her father. Having an Italian first name and a Polish last name seemed incongruous. Yet, that had been Josie's dying wish, so it became a reality.

After a very short period, Rocco's mere existence reminded Stanley of how he had lost the love of his life. Alcohol was consumed much more frequently, and with it, the illogical obsession of blaming the young boy for his mother's death grew stronger. By the time young Rocco could walk, Stanley pushed him down at the slightest perceived annoyance the boy might offer. However, no matter how inebriated Stanley became, he never allowed Josie's family to see any of his abusive behavior. He also went to great lengths to limit their interaction with their grandson.

Frustrated, the Ferrigno family withdrew their attempts to see the boy. Unconsciously, he was also a reminder to them of their deceased daughter. Eventually, in the solitude of their home, Rocco became a victim of his often irrational and frequently drunk father.

Yet, in the nature versus nurture discussion, Rocco became the poster boy for nature. Because of his treatment, he should have grown into a mean and violent bully. Rocco was just the opposite. When he emerged from his shy and silent cocoon, he was a loving and feeling person who would do anything to help anyone. Over six feet and powerfully built in his teens, Rocco could have been a bully with no equal. Indeed, he could have probably taken on his father when he commenced his unprovoked beatings. Instead, he was submissive to his father in the home, perhaps unconsciously believing that his father was correct in blaming him for the death of his mother.

Until recently, Rocco had been alone. In that solitude, he had secretly taught himself the guitar. He released all the pent-up emotions of his young mind and body, focusing them on the fingers that fluidly ran across the strings of his instrument. It showed. There was no more skilled guitarist in his area, perhaps in the entire city of

DANCING WITH THE LOST

New York. Yet all his abilities stayed hidden from the world, including his abusive father, who might irrationally destroy his instrument in a fit of rage. Yet in the last year, Rocco's world had changed. Though his father still consistently attacked him, he had found an outlet filled with friendship, loyalty…and maybe even love.

Often, while his father was in a drunken stupor and Rocco wished to play, he would take his electric guitar (sans amplifier) to the Garden of Eden. As fanciful as the name sounded, it was merely an overgrown garden in the back corner of the public schoolyard. Years of neglect had resulted in a perimeter with a wall of bushes that withheld any view of events occurring in its equally overgrown interior. Mainly, this place was used by local druggies to hide their transactions and usage of their choice of poison. Getting high was the main event; thus, it took on the ironic name of the "Garden of Eden." Yet there was enough seclusion that the lone guitarist could practice his craft without contact with those using the garden for other purposes. Until the day Rocco met Tony and Johnny.

Rocco had heard a gasping sound near him in the brush and came upon Tony Provenzano, who was near death from huffing an extreme amount of glue. Beside him, there were two strangers, Johnny Cipp and Gio DeAngelis, whom he would eventually come to know. The three combined to save Tony's life…but not his brain.

As a result of his near-death experience, Tony was left with severe mental deficiencies and had the thoughts and actions of a young child. Months later, when his family allowed Tony to revisit the world, he somehow found his way back to the Garden of Eden. There, a chance encounter brought Johnny, Rocco, and Tony together. An improbable friendship developed among the three, and Rocco and Johnny often played guitar for Tony's amusement. His inability to remember or pronounce "Rocco Brackowski" led to Tony's mangled version of the guitarist's name. What came out was "Bracko." In his usual mode of kindness, the newly christened "Bracko" accepted the name as his own.

This new person, this "Bracko," had friends. He had Tony and Johnny. When Johnny asked him to join his band, Those Born Free, he met Gio, Joey Tinman, and Jimmy Mac. With all the practices at Jimmy's house, he also met the drummer's sisters, Aylin, Siobhan, and Maggie. His world was now filled with many people who cared for him.

Yet each night, he went home to the beatings. Each night, he poured out his feelings into his guitar. Each night, to quote George Harrison of the Beatles, his guitar gently wept.

34

THE THIEF OF MY FOREVER

"In time, time takes everything,
No memories to treasure.
How long will he steal from me?
This Thief of my forever."
- Those Born Free

An Excerpt from A *Band Lost in the Wind* (or *The Thief of My Forever*, *Brothers of Forever*, or just *The Book.*)

*I*t had probably been one of the happiest moments of his short and sad life, but he was exhausted. He had brought an idea for a song to his group, Those Born Free, and they had liked it. They had worked on it for endless hours, adding to and then perfecting the words and music he had written in the pain and solitude of his basement.

During this joint effort, each group member shared their burdens and fears, and those feelings were incorporated into the lyrics. However, it all started with one of Bracko's beatings. Early that morning, Bracko had committed some minor mistake that had riled his father to the point where his right fist pummeled Bracko's left eye. After his father left for work, he iced his injury as always and then went on with life.

The band had always had to tread lightly around Bracko's injuries. He, in turn, always avoided discussion with flimsy excuses. The band was now confronted with devastating evidence of what was going on. Still, Bracko would not talk about it. However, during a break in practice, he began playing a tune he had composed. With it were lyrics that obtusely told of his plight. The band picked up on it and, without a spoken word, played along with him. During the course of the very long day, each member added verses to Bracko's song, each revealing a part of their soul. When it was all over, they talked...even longer than they had practiced.

The band was no longer a band, but a group of five loyal friends bonded for life. The song would become their anthem...and, perhaps someday, their first hit record. Yet, in the end, Bracko had to go home.

After he had snuck down the basement and hidden his guitar, his father followed shortly after. This intrusion was never good news. By Bracko's calculation, Stan Brackowski had already consumed his nightly six-pack of beer and followed it with either two or three shooters of Seagram's 7 whiskey. Whenever his father came into Bracko's living space post-blotto, suffering was the order of the day. Yet the younger Brackowski never escalated the situation with any verbal or physical response.

"What the hell are you thinking? You come in and go down to this shithole basement you call a room without talking to me?" As he screamed these words with spittle frothing on his lips, his two hands grabbed the collar of Bracko's shirt and pushed him against the wall.

I'm thinking that it is more important to hide my guitar than to see you.

I'm thinking that this shithole of a basement is my only escape from you, and I couldn't wait to get down here. I'm thinking that I hate you. Bracko's thoughts were never verbalized.

"You got nothing to say to your hard-working dad who puts a roof over your head and food on the table?" Stan now started to slap Bracko's face...a face already black and blue from a previous beating.

I have nothing to say...for now. When the band hits big, and I have my own money, I'm out of here. And even if we don't hit it big, I'm gone as soon as I turn eighteen.

The slaps became more vicious. Stan had decided that using his open hand was more humiliating to his son than his usual punches. Bracko, for his part, stared straight into his father's eyes, displaying no emotion at all.

In our battle of wills, I will show no weakness. That will be my only victory.

Eventually, Stan Brackowski, fatigued, found his way up the stairs to the living room couch. There, he would fall into an alcohol-induced coma. When Bracko was sure of his father's nightly state, he slipped up the stairs and outside onto the stoop of their home. There, he would breathe fresh air and dream about his future.

"Mister, you look kinda messed up," announced a squeaky voice from a neighbor's door to the slouching, beaten Bracko. "I mean, you need some help or something?"

A young boy emerged from the door of the house next to Bracko's. On this block of Cambria Heights, houses were only separated by a pseudo-driveway that led to a garage in the backyard. Those garages became storage sheds, as it would be impossible to navigate any vehicle through the narrow "driveway" without hitting one of the houses enclosing it. Therefore, one house's door was never far from the others.

"Hi, kid...yeah...I'm okay," responded Bracko, shocked that the boy, whom he estimated to be about eight, was soon standing next to him.

"You don't look okay," said the boy in a concerned voice.

"Looks can be deceiving."

"What does 'deceiving' mean?"

All Bracko could do was laugh…for the first time in a long time.

"No, really. I'm okay. What's your name, kid?"

"Michael. I used to be called 'Mickey' because my dad liked Mickey Mantle. But…"

"But, what?"

"When he left me and my mom, she told me she always liked Michael better."

"Well, hello, Michael. My friends call me Bracko."

"Bracko…that's a funny name. Your friends call you…wait…does that mean we are friends?"

"Sure does," chuckled Bracko, extending his hand to shake.

"Wow, my first friend. Well, my first friend outside of school." Michael's hand gripped Bracko's.

"C'mon, you must have many friends in this neighborhood…on this block. You're a cool kid."

"No, I need to stay in the house all day. My mom is sick. She won't say it, but…I think…maybe…that is why my dad left."

Bracko could think of nothing to say. It seemed this boy understood his world. Perhaps he understood it better than Bracko understood his own.

"I gotta go check on my mom. I guess I'll see you around."

"You definitely will," whispered Bracko, a rare smile adorning his face.

Bracko and Michael often met on the stoops in front of their homes— but only on nights when Michael's mom and Bracko's dad were asleep. Though almost ten years apart in age, they felt at ease talking to each other. Bracko felt like a big brother to the boy, who desperately needed someone to help him cope with his problems. Yet Michael talked little about his mother, and Bracko, not at all, about his father. Their brief nightly conversations were primarily to forget these complications.

"I've heard you play the guitar. You're really, really good."

"Wait, you could hear me down in my basement? Oh sh...shoot, I thought that no one could hear."

"Doesn't your dad like to listen to you?"

"No! I only play when he is not home." However, Bracko would not elaborate, and Michael didn't want to seem nosy. Finally, He realized that the younger boy was asking a legitimate question that a real friend would answer. Bracko used no words, instead pointing to his most recent black and blue location. He then nodded his head toward his house.

"He..."

"Yup."

As if to take Bracko's mind off his problems, Michael looked at him with a hopeful look.

"I wish I could play guitar like you."

"Why?"

"Because it looks and sounds like fun. Besides...I want to be just like you."

"No, you don't."

Michael looked seriously into Bracko's eyes and, without flinching, spoke firmly, "Yes, I do."

Often, Michael would knock on the basement window to let Bracko know that his mother was sleeping and that he was hanging out on his stoop. However, the designation as a "window" was perhaps a gross exaggeration for the four-by-six-inch slit that barely allowed light into the room. Why a long-forgotten builder had bothered to include this in his floor plan was lost in the winds of time. This tiny portal was often the only means of communication between Bracko and Michael. On one occasion, it changed the lives of both of them.

"Bracko, help…please…my mom," screeched Michael into the glass partition that had not been opened in decades.

Without hearing another word, Bracko leaped from his bed and bolted up the stairs and through his house. Luckily, Stan Brackowski's stupor was particularly deep that evening as Bracko ran out the door to his waiting friend.

"She…she…was walking from the kitchen and…then she was on the floor."

"Okay, show me."

Bracko entered his friend's home for the first time. Although there had been attempts to clean it as much as possible, none of them had been made recently. However, Bracko's quick inspection of the house was cut short by the sight of a frail woman barely moving on the floor. He turned her over, and a dazed expression met his gaze. *Good, she was conscious.* He lifted her and brought her to her bedroom and laid her down. A smile finally came to her face when she saw her son, Michael, and standing behind him was the tall, strong boy who had carried her to her bed.

"You must be Bracko," gasped a barely audible voice.

"Yeah," mumbled Bracko. He could not understand what he was seeing. Michael's mom couldn't be over eighty pounds. Her head was wrapped in a dull gray scarf that was partially displaced, revealing her hairless head.

"Go get me some ice from the freezer," Bracko commanded Michael. He sensed the sick woman wished to say something she did not want her son to hear. As Michael left the room, her raspy voice spoke.

"Cancer, but Michael doesn't know or understand."

Before she could utter another word, Michael interrupted by yelling from the kitchen that he couldn't get the ice cubes from the tray.

"I'll be back in a second. I don't want Michael to be upset." Bracko tried to smile, but confusion and anxiety overwhelmed him as he passed into the kitchen. There, he found Michael frustrated by his inability to dislodge the ice. However, more distressing was the fact that the young boy stood in front of an empty refrigerator.

Bracko said nothing. He released the ice cubes from the tray, put them in a dishcloth, brought them in, and placed them on an elbow that seemed to have taken the brunt of Michael's mother's fall.

"Susan...er...Susie...that's my name."

"Well, Susie, I'm going to call for an ambulance."

"No, I don't have any money to pay...and there is no one to care for Michael."

"Let me worry about it," replied Bracko quickly. In reality, Bracko was just a 17-year-old kid. He didn't know what to do.

As they heard ambulance sirens in the distance, Michael walked up to his mother's bedside, and Bracko, for the first time, observed something unusual. Susie placed her right hand on the bed beside her. She then positioned her right index and middle finger as if they were legs standing...waiting...but for what? Michael soon moved closer to the bed and placed his two fingers facing his mother's fingers. Slowly, they moved in a syncopated motion together. They both smiled while Bracko stood dumbfounded.

"We do this...our finger-dancing...we do it to remind each other that someday she will teach me to dance so that she can dance with me at my wedding."

Bracko took one look at the woman in bed and knew that would never happen.

35

TIME IN A BOTTLE

"But there never seems to be enough time
To do the things you want to do
Once you find them."
- Jim Croce

An Excerpt from *The Thief of My Forever, A Band Lost in the Wind,*
Brothers of Forever, or just *The Book.*

*B*racko had never really had a childhood. There were only the beatings and the guitar playing in the solitude of his room. Though it was true that this had led to his incredible development as a guitarist, but at what price? At age 17, he had very few social skills. Those that he did have were the direct result of the support and friendship of his bandmates.

However, nothing prepared him for dealing with a 31-year-old terminal cancer patient and her 8-year-old son. But that was Bracko.

He gave everything he could to anyone who asked. Therefore, no one who knew him would be surprised to find him at the hospital bedside of a woman he had known for less than two hours.

"Are you related, young man?" asked a doctor, looking at a clipboard with only passing interest in either Bracko or Michael. Bracko had made enough visits to emergency rooms courtesy of his father to know he needed to be related to the patient to get any information.

"Yeah, I'm her brother...Rocco." After that statement, Michael looked strangely at Bracko and quickly received a quick but loving kick to keep him quiet.

"Okay, then you must know that her breast cancer has metastasized and..."

"Are you an idiot?" screamed Bracko in a rare show of emotion to the doctor. He then rolled his eyes toward Michael, trying to mute the conversation. The doctor seemed unaware of his insensitivity to the young boy standing just a few feet away.

"Michael, are you as hungry as I am? I saw a snack machine down the hall. Go get us something." Bracko pulled out some coins, and Michael soon left the room.

"Oh...sorry about that," cooed the doctor.

"You should be. That's her 8-year-old son. I don't think he needs to hear anything from you. Let his mother tell him when she is ready."

"She is terminal. There is no help for her. However, she does have some time left, and that's not the reason for her fall today. She's here because she hasn't eaten in days, and the lack of food...well, that's her immediate problem."

"I...I didn't know," mumbled Bracko almost to himself.

"I spoke to her. It's been financially tough since her husband left. What food she can afford, she gives to her son."

"Shit!" was all Bracko responded, but now he thought back to all the times that he had shared something on the stoop with Michael. The boy had devoured whatever was given to him, yet many times, Bracko noticed him putting some in his pocket. He had always thought it would be for some time later, when actually it was for someone else.

The band had been playing dances frequently, so Bracko had saved some money. This stash would be his "getaway fund" if the band did not succeed. He didn't know where he would get to, but it would be away from his father—anywhere away from his father.

Now, quite often, he hit up the fund to buy food and other necessities for his next-door neighbors. He reasoned that Those Born Free was doing so well that it would not be long before money would no longer be an issue. Yet, in his heart, he knew that even if the band did not bring fame and fortune, he still would have been there for Michael and his mother.

Bracko understood that he was not the long-term solution to their problems, but he didn't know what was. He realized this the same night he had taken her to the hospital. With no health insurance coverage, Susie had been strengthened by infusions of all sorts of healthy substances...and then sent home. Bracko could not even drive yet, so they depended upon the kindness of a nurse whose shift had ended to get them back to Cambria Heights. For now, Bracko would do what he could do.

36

JOIN TOGETHER WITH THE BAND

"We don't know where we're going,
But the season's right for knowing
Oh, won't you join together with the band?"
- The Who

An Excerpt from *The Thief of My Forever, A Band Lost in the Wind,*
Brothers of Forever, or just *The Book.*

The years 1966 and 1967 were defining moments for the band Those Born Free. The five young musicians had found each other and almost immediately developed into a tight-knit quality band. They had practiced seriously for an exorbitant amount of time to reach their goal as professional musicians.

They had also formed a strong bond as friends. They could finish each other's thoughts as well as they could predict the next note each member would play in a song. They were truly headed for stardom... until they weren't.

As the five musicians toiled to make their music professional enough to pursue a career, those attending their practices not only enjoyed the music but also shared in the laughs and good times.

The three McAvoy sisters danced and sang along with the band, all the while dreaming of romantic involvement with the three eligible bachelors in the group. All three girls were stunning beauties with matching auburn hair and green eyes. Their smiles lit up the otherwise dark, dank basement of the McAvoy home.

Yet, they were not the only ones at the practices. Johnny Cipp's girlfriend, Maria Romano, could also be found there, often just staring at her boyfriend. Maria, who was 17 years old, could have been an older sister to the McAvoy girls, who fit the age pattern nicely with Aylin (15), Siobhan (13), and Maggie (11). Maria very often danced, sang, and laughed with the girls. At times, she thought of them as if they were indeed her siblings.

Sometimes, Johnny would take a break while the band played a simpler song that didn't require his bass playing. His friend Gio switched from his rhythm guitar duties to bass, and Johnny took Maria in his arms and danced. The McAvoy girls would sigh with envy and often would ask Maria what it was like to be held by someone who loved her.

Often, the band also had another visitor named DJ Spinelli. A classmate of Johnny's at Bishop McCarthy High School, the group frequently used his beautiful poetry to create lyrics to their original songs. DJ and the band worked hard to create tunes that would have been on the first album if the band had lived.

DJ also had his eye on Aylin McAvoy. She was less than two years younger, and he foresaw some point in the future when she would be old enough to date. Her youth aside, there was a band rule that none of the musicians would ever consider any of the young girls as anything other than a "sister." This law was amended to include DJ when he started attending practices. Though DJ never spoke of his wish to be with Aylin, it seemed evident from how he looked at her.

There was a clash of wills at those times when Jimmy noticed this attention. DJ's interest and opportunity ended with the murder of Jimmy McAvoy in the summer of 1967.

One of the most unusual visitors to the band's practices was Tony Provenzano. One of the former "princes" of the crime family, he had suffered irreversible brain damage during one stupid night of huffing glue. Indeed, Tony would have died had not three members of the band saved his life in the sarcastically named Garden of Eden.

In that same garden, the diminished Tony had formed an unusual friendship with band members Bracko and Johnny. Ironically, this friendship was one of the determining factors in the destruction of the band and the death of four of its members.

And then there was Michael. To her sisters' amusement, Maggie had become close friends with the young boy when Bracko had started bringing him to practices. Neither Aylin nor Siobhan could understand the strange "finger-dancing ritual" that Maggie, Michael, and Bracko shared. It was cute but crazy. While their fingers danced to the music, the two young children took their cues from Bracko, intermittently laughing throughout the practice as they performed their strange finger magic.

Yes, it was a happy little group that attended the band practices. The good times came to an abrupt stop in June of 1967.

37

LITTLE CHILDREN

"I wonder what can I do around
Little children like you?"
- Billy J. Kramer

Maggie's Memos and Memories

I finished reading the story as it had existed so far, and then DJ walked back into the room.

"So, what do you think?" DJ questioned.

"I like it. I think it captures the gist of Bracko's personality. But, DJ, I can add to this story…about Bracko…and Michael…and the band as I knew them. You can incorporate my thoughts into your book or disregard them. I just think that I have to get it out there. Give me a pen and paper and a few minutes to write."

I recall the first time I met Michael Powers vividly. I think it was the Fall of 1966. But I'm not sure. He was a scrawny little kid about three years younger than me. But he did have cute going for him. He had jet-black hair and piercing blue eyes, set against a face with very delicate features and an extremely pale skin tone. However, he had a contagious smile that lit up the room. I liked him from the very first time Bracko brought him to a Those Born Free practice.

"I'm teaching him guitar and wanted him to see a band in action," I remember Bracko saying. That was only partially true, and Gio saw through the façade and called him on it.

"Who are you trying to fool? You're babysitting—call it what it is," crowed Gio.

"I'm not a baby," reacted Michael in one of the only times a smile left his face.

As Gio was about to continue his harangue, Bracko gave him a stern look that said...*Don't.*

As practice continued, I watched Michael soaking up every bit of the joy that the music created by the band brought. It was about an hour later when I noticed Michael's fingers. As we sat on our basement steps, his index finger and middle finger rested on his worn jeans. Without him even thinking about it, they started to move rhythmically to the music. Immediately, my surprised look turned into a tiny giggle as I looked from Michael's fingers to Bracko's eyes. With a hint of a smile, Bracko nodded, affirming my suspicion of where the guitarist had first seen the "dancing fingers" he had taught me.

I looked Michael in the eye and then let my gaze drift down to my fingers, which were "dancing" with his. We both laughed...and then laughed harder when we noticed Bracko also joining in the reverie. No one else in the room...not my sisters nor the rest of the band... caught on to our little secret ritual.

Michael did not attend all practices because he had so much going on at home. I imagine that anyone else telling this tale would not even remember him enough to mention his name. However, to me, he was special. We listened to the music, finger-danced, and on one memorable occasion, we actually danced.

The band was playing "Slow Dancin' (Swaying to the Music)" by Johnny Rivers. It was the craziest thing—something rock bands never did—For that one song, they sang a cappella—no instruments. Johnny Cipp was the one person in the five-man band who didn't sing. Therefore, he became an onlooker for that tune. He placed his bass guitar on its stand and stood awkwardly, emanating uselessness. He then realized he could dance with his girlfriend Maria while the band harmonized. Not counting my middle-aged parents, it was the only time I saw real love first-hand. When Johnny and Maria gazed into each other's eyes, their look became the very definition of love in my mind.

While this same song was being performed at another practice, I noticed Bracko looking over at Michael and waving his finger. I didn't understand until Michael approached me and asked me to dance. I realize that he was eight and I was eleven...and that his head only came up to my shoulder, but it was more than fun. It was exciting. I fantasized that someday, my husband and I would dance to this song at our wedding and feel the love I witnessed with Johnny and Maria. Yeah, *slow dancin' swayin' to the music*.

38

NEVER GO HOME ANYMORE

"You can never go home anymore (Mama!)
No, I can never go home anymore."
- The Shangri-Las

Maggie's Memos and Memories

With Michael's visits infrequent, I made a point of going up to see him at his house. He could not leave too often because he cared for his mother. We would sit on his stoop, and conversations would flow easily. Sometimes, it centered on comic books, school, and the world in general. However, mostly we talked about the band and music.

Bracko was teaching Michael the guitar, and he often played what he had learned from his master. With not much else good going on in his life, he poured all his emotions into the guitar. My sister Aylin told me later that this had also been the case with Bracko. The guitar was the outlet for all of his feelings. At the time, I had no idea what she was talking about. I just know that Michael became a close and dear friend to me.

One night at dusk, Bracko emerged from his house to see us talking.

"So, is a party going on out here without me?" he joked. However, that was so unlike Bracko. He had no sense of humor."

"Nope," I answered, "just killing time."

"Is it okay for you guys to come with me and see something special?"

"I'll go check that my mom is okay," offered Michael.

"What my family doesn't know won't hurt them," I added glibly.

We had only traveled a few blocks when we began to hear the beautiful sounds of four girls singing in harmony. As they came into view, I could not believe my eyes.

"They're good...very good," blurted Michael.

"They should be, they're the..." Bracko began, but I interrupted him.

"The Shangri-Las," I screamed.

"Who?" questioned Michael.

The girls' voices flowed through the humid air, and for a moment, we stood hypnotized by their talent. Bracko leaned against the lamppost, arms folded, his expression unreadable. Michael nudged me, eyes wide with wonder, but confused.

"Michael, these are real stars. I have seen them on American Bandstand, and my sisters and I have a few of their records. 'Walking in the Sand' and 'Leader of the Pack' are my favorites."

"But what are they doing here?" stammered Michael.

"Well, the Ganser twins live right over there," Bracko said, pointing to a well-kept one-family home. "Mary and Betty Weiss live down the street."

"You mean they live here...in Cambria Heights?" babbled Michael.

"Well, when they are not on tour," answered Bracko.

As the Shangri-Las finished up their version of "You Cheated, You Lied," they noticed us staring.

"Hey, Bracko, how are you doing?" shouted Mary, the youngest of the group, "Why don't you get your guitar and give us some backup?"

"No, I gotta get these two guys home soon." Bracko announced, "This is Maggie, and this is Michael," he said as he tapped each of us on the shoulder.

"Okay, Maggie and Michael, we're going to do our new song for you. It's called "Never Go Home Anymore." This time it was Betty, the oldest of the group, speaking.

"You know them?" Michael was in awe.

"Yeah, they heard me playing the Garden of Eden once and asked me to sit in on one of their rehearsals."

I hardly heard Bracko and Michael as the performance of the Shangri-Las enthralled me. Years later, their song (which became a hit) meant even more to me on a personal level. Their words could have been the story of my life after I left home, abandoning my mother and sisters.

Do you ever get that feeling
You wanna kiss and hug her?
Do it now
Tell her you love her

Don't do to your mom
What I did to mine
She grew so lonely in the end
Angels picked her for their friend

And I can never go home

anymore
And that's called sad.

39

THE WAY

"But where were they going without ever knowing the way."
- Fastball

Maggie's Memos and Memories

When Bracko died, Michael was crushed. He now had no protector, no savior, no friend to help him with his mother. Somehow, he always found the inner strength to go on.

I'll never forget one of the last times I saw him. I was grieving my brother and father, and he was grieving Bracko. Yet he had also known my father and brother from hanging out at the band practices, and the grief was mounting for both of us.

One day, he looked at me and said, "Let's go."

"Where?" I responded.

"To the cemetery and see them,"

"What?"

"Yeah, we can be with them one last time."

"Do you know how to get there?"

"Yeah, my mother took me there once to visit her parents. I remember it's just down Springfield Boulevard… maybe in Springfield Gardens. *Monty*-something. That's what the cemetery is called.

"I'm game. When?"

"How about now?"

He went into the house and came out with a small paper bag.

"What's that?"

"We might get hungry on the way, so…"

"I'm hungry right now."

"Okay, so we eat and then go." He handed me a sandwich.

"What is it?"

"Peanut butter and sugar. It's all I eat. Before he…um…ah…left, Bracko left me a pound of sugar for my mother's tea, three jars of Skippy Peanut Butter, and a few loaves of bread that I keep in the fridge. I got creative."

We ate, and it wasn't bad, though I doubt the lunch was going to win any nutrition awards. In the long term, this could cause problems with a person's teeth. I remember thinking about the candy store… and the dentist above.

"Ready," he announced, and I saw a rare smile on his face. He had lost so much of his joyful exterior after Bracko's death.

He may have visited that cemetery before, but only in a car. The walk was excruciatingly long…the miles took their toll on our young, short legs. However, we eventually arrived at the "Monty-something" (Montefiore Cemetery). We easily found my father's and Jimmy's grave sites. I was numb. I thought that I would cry hysterically, but I didn't. I stood in quiet solitude, thinking about how much I loved and missed them. Michael saw how I felt and came over and held my hand, a very mature thing to do for an eight-year-old. He asked me if I wanted to move closer to where they lay, but I couldn't. I told him I wanted to leave. I guess maybe that was the moment when I began pouring the foundation for my brick house.

Finding Bracko's grave proved to be much harder. He and his father had been laid in a Potter's Field. With no money available, a

DANCING WITH THE LOST

very small stone lay in the mud, marking his final resting place. We only found it because a kindly caretaker looked up the location in the record book and took us to it. Left alone, I watched as Michael approached the stone and knelt in the mud. He beckoned me to join him. To my surprise, I joined him at the gravesite this time.

"My Momma says dancing brings people heart to heart and soul to soul," Michael murmured almost inaudibly. He then placed his index finger and middle finger on the stone. He took my hand, put it across from his, and nodded. I placed my two fingers facing his.

"The end should never be the end. We should always dance with the lost."

We danced.

I only saw him a few times after that day. There was no one watching over *me* anymore because they were all grieving. I took as much food as I could carry from our pantry and brought it to Michael.

In November of 1967, his mother died. I only knew this because his house was dark and locked up when I went there with food. A neighbor told me that no one lived there anymore. Looking at Michael's darkened home and the burned-out shell of Bracko's house standing next to it, I thought...where do I go to dance with the lost now?

40

WASTED ON THE WAY

"So much time to make up everywhere you turn,
Time, we have wasted on the way.
So much water moving underneath the bridge
Let the water come and carry us away"
- Crosby, Stills, Nash, and Young

Maggie's Memos and Memories

*A*ylin and DJ read my pages later that day and looked at me, dumbstruck.

"I had no idea how badly you were hurting. I was selfish and only thought of *my* pain. But your life must have been horrible for you to run away at seventeen years old," sobbed Aylin. She stared at me, waiting for a comment, but I could think of nothing to say that wouldn't hurt her, so I remained silent.

"Maybe she doesn't want to talk about it anymore?" interjected DJ.

"No, goddammit, we have been silent for too long. We've wasted too much of our lives already. Let's get through this. Let's get the past out so we can deal with it and move on."

I thought *I did need to move on, but I can't.* To use a biblical term, the times of the band...the times of Those Born Free—were the alpha and omega. It was the beginning of everything and the end of everything. The years of the band were, without a doubt, the happiest time of my life. I often try to recreate that feeling and have come close occasionally. I started to relate this to DJ and Aylin.

"The dynamics of the people involved were amazing and could be the basis of one or more books. DJ, I have confidence that the entire book will capture that feeling. I was the youngest person in the room, except for Michael. I, therefore, missed many of the nuances of what was happening. I will do my best to probe my memories and recreate that world — a beautiful, passionate world that surrounded a band called Those Born Free."

"Maggie, what do you remember?"

I think it was 1965 when our brother Jimmy (they called him Jimmy Mac) met up with Johnny Cipp and Gio DeAngelis. I get confused because I know another guy was there, but he was soon gone. In his place were Bracko and a cute guy named Joey, who played the keyboards. For some reason, they called him "Tinman" all the time."

"It was because his last name was 'Tinley.'"

"I never knew that. I remember Gio was a loudmouth, and we covered our ears when he spoke because he tended to use bad words. Aylin, I remember you told me that Gio could use the 'F-bomb' as all seven parts of speech and claimed you had heard him do just that in one sentence. A skill that was certainly worthy of the Guinness Book of Records."

We all laughed at that, and Aylin continued my thought.

"Yes, Gio was the frontman that the audience would never forget. He was sometimes obnoxious, but those of us who got to know him understood that he had a heart of gold and was loyal to a fault... especially to his best friend, Johnny. They had grown up together, played sports together, learned the guitar together, and now were in a band together. That is why when tragedy hit the band in 1967 and both went missing, it was assumed that they ran away together. Nothing in the two decades since has dissuaded anyone from that scenario until Nicky told you that Mad Guy had killed Gio. But there was another scenario that we believed for many years."

"What was that?" I interjected.

"Johnny was madly in love with Maria, who was always at band practice. My sisters and I questioned how Johnny could have run away without her. The answer came to us four months later when Maria left home and was never seen again. I believe Maria left to join Johnny, but I'll never know."

I continued the narrative, "Tinman was unusual. Tall and handsome, with strong facial features, he was often quiet and reserved. His screwed-up home life left him reclusive except when he was with the band. He was a classically trained keyboardist but had a passion for rock and roll. He only came to life when the band was practicing or playing…"

"Bullshit, bullshit, and more bullshit," screamed Aylin. "We know all this shit. We lived it and have talked about it for over two decades, even while you were away. We will never get over it. But, Maggie, you need to move on."

I ignored her.

"And then there is Bracko. With his playing…with our conversations…with his honorable actions…with his loyalty and devotion to people…he stole my heart…"

"Stop!" She now spoke a bit more calmly, but her piercing eyes shook me from storytelling.

I did. I remained silent.

Aylin stood up, approached me, and grabbed me by my arms. She gently shook me.

"What about you? You've had a whole lifetime since I last saw you, seventeen years ago. As much as we all remember and care about that brief time, we have moved on. What have you done in that time?"

I spoke no words. My expression betrayed no feeling.

"Maggie, nothing can be so bad that we can't discuss it."

"Maybe, not so bad…but it might be too sad for me to relive. Did you ever think of that?

Now, she was the one who was speechless.

"Maybe there is a reason I don't discuss my past—that I keep it locked away." I could see she was frustrated, and still, seventeen years of my pent-up emotions exploded in that moment.

"But maybe it is time to unload it all…on you," I screamed at her, letting go of years of rage. Just as suddenly, I stopped and stared into her eyes. I expected her to back down. She didn't.

"I'm ready."

I heard only the crumbling of my house. The bricks had started to fall.

I told them my story.

41

LONELY PEOPLE

"This is for all the lonely people,
Thinking that love has passed them by.
Don't give up,
Until you drink from the silver cup."
- America

Maggie's Memos and Memories

"To be perfectly honest, ages twelve to seventeen are a blur. After the devastation of 1967, a depressing gloom overcame what was left of our family. I was too young to understand what was going on with the rest of you.

"Our mother took care of us. She protected us from the outside world and tried to shield us from the bad memories. However, it destroyed her. She was in a perpetual state of sadness. She became obsessed with certain audio tapes that she found of the band's practices.

"On some of them, the tape had been left running after the band stopped playing, and you could hear Jimmy talking with all the exuberance of his youth. You could hear our father interacting with Jimmy on more than one tape. Mom became obsessed with those tapes and often sat in the basement playing them repeatedly.

"Besides our mom's malaise, I had lost you, Aylin—not physically, but emotionally. You seemed more lost than the rest of us and soon fell into destructive choices in your life. That's my therapist mode slipping into this tale. Meanwhile, I spent those years… the ones when I needed you most, alone. I was in a continuous cycle of reliving the joys of the past and mourning the loss of those joys."

"Maggie, I, too, listened to the tapes. That is where I discovered who had killed Jimmy and our father. As I told you…I did something about it. It changed my life. What a damn waste. I wish they had never recorded them."

"No, Aylin…Mom, Siobhan, and I needed them." Occasionally, I would also sneak down and listen to the tapes. However, I listened to the music and the conversations. It brought me back to a time of happiness. I was transported back to songs, the dancing, the jokes, and the byplay of the guys interacting with each other. The tapes, and later music in general, became my companion, my solace in a world gone mad. For those five years, all I remember is the music. It helped me tune out a world I didn't want to be in. I became obsessed with listening to 1960s music, and even today, as a 34-year-old, I infuriate my peers with my fixation on British Invasion and Garage Band songs. I had nothing else."

"But, Maggie, you survived, and you thrived. You hold three degrees and are a well-established therapist. You must have gotten your act together."

"Oh no, not at first. Yes, I received that formal education, and I learned some techniques along the way. However, I thought the whole system was about research and not dealing with people. Don't get me wrong, I did it, and I did it well, but I developed an inner philosophy about the hoops and rings they made me go through to get the degrees."

"But you have a B.S., an M.S., and a PhD, right?"

"Yeah, I do, but I always laugh when people say that because I'm thinking…"

*B.S. stands for **Bull Shit***
*M.S. stands for **More Shit***
*PhD. - **Piled higher and Deeper***

"So then, how did you get so good at your job?"

"Before I ever started school, I had an excellent role model. Aylin, I guess this is where I finally tell you the story of my life. It's a story I never thought I'd tell…I never thought I could tell."

"Maggie, you don't have to if it will cause you pain."

"Aylin, I'm way past that. I think it is time to let someone in."

"Thank you for letting it be me."

"Well, who the hell else could it be?" I laughed. "You and DJ are the only people I know well enough to tell my story. You are the only people who were around when it all began. So…"

Aylin sat closer and held my hand. DJ stared at me from the chair across from us.

"I needed an escape and therefore left home at 17 years old. I joined the Navy."

"You what?"

I held up my hand to stop her protest.

"Let me get through this."

PART IV

THE WIND

"I listen to the wind
To the wind of my soul
Where I'll end up,
Well, I think only God knows."
- Cat Stevens

Key West – 1973

42

A PLACE IN THE SUN

"There's a place in the sun,
Where there's hope for everyone,
Where my poor restless heart's gotta run."
- Stevie Wonder

Maggie's Memos and Memories

I don't remember much about bootcamp. There was discipline and organization—two things that helped me cope with the emotional fatigue I had felt since 1967. I went about my business with a clear purpose. It helped that I was doing something useful by training to be a nurse...well, at least a nurse's assistant. I felt a sense of fulfillment in helping people, and I thought this might be a direction I would take with my life.

I also enjoyed the camaraderie of the friends I made after being stationed in perhaps the most desirable Naval air base in the United States—Key West, Florida. The base is actually in several locations around the southernmost key. The planes fly out of an airstrip on the island of Boca Chica. However, the Trumbo Point Annex is actually on the island of Key West, only a mile from the center of one of the biggest party towns in the entire universe. The housing was within walking distance of Duval Street, a thoroughfare that had more bars than I could count.

Now, I don't want you to think that I was a big drinker because I wasn't. I saw what losing control could do to a person as I watched someone I loved self-destruct. However, no one asked for proof of age if you wore a uniform. For the most part, I kept my head down and learned how to be a good, helpful person. Despite the allure of Key West's vibrant nightlife, I often found myself retreating into quiet evenings, content with the rhythm of my thoughts and the steady routine of my days.

Eva, however, was the opposite—a whirlwind of energy and persuasion. She seemed to have made it her mission to introduce me to every corner and character this crazy town had to offer. Our friendship had blossomed in the warm, tropical air, and though I resisted many of her adventures, Eva's spirited persistence was impossible to ignore.

It was on one particularly balmy evening that she succeeded in pulling me out of my shell. Armed with her irresistible enthusiasm and a mischievous grin, she declared that a proper initiation into Key West life was long overdue. Reluctantly, I agreed, curious despite myself about what the night might hold.

I was considering making the Navy my career. If I had done that, my story and my life would have been a great deal simpler. I didn't make that choice, and my life evolved in a much different way. And it all started one night in a bar. It was a chaotic set of events that could never have been planned — or even foreseen. On one random night in Key West, Florida, in 1973, I *thought* I saw my past... and I *know* I saw my future.

It was a hot August evening when my world changed. I had been stationed in Key West for six months and had turned eighteen during that time. Eva first asked and then bullied me into going into town. Mostly, I had been keeping to myself for my entire time in the area.

There was fun to be had in every nook and cranny around the main drag of Duval Street, but I had shied away from participating in any of it. It was not a morose solitude, but my extreme enjoyment of calm in my life. I was doing nothing. However, I was doing it with a smile on my face and enjoying every moment.

I can't remember what Eva said to change my mind, but I soon found myself at the sunset ceremony at Mallory Square. For those unfamiliar with the concept, it is a nightly celebration signifying nothing more important than the sun setting on the horizon of the Gulf of Mexico. Depending on the weather, the number of participants varies from a couple of hundred to thousands. Because all those attending have a drink in hand, it usually does not even matter if the setting sun can be seen through the clouds. Yet, it's a boisterous, fun time.

"Okay, my sweet innocent Maggie, we've only just begun. Now it's time to begin the Duval Crawl," prattled Eva.

"The What?" I questioned.

"The Duval Crawl, my dear friend. You see, this avenue in front of us is exactly one mile long...and has more than a dozen bars. The idea is to hit each one of them, even if it means crawling to the last few, because you're so plastered you can't walk. Thus, the term Duval..."

"...Crawl. Yeah, I get it, but it doesn't sound like my kind of thing," I murmured, almost sounding like I was apologizing.

"Well, Maggie, it should be. I need to get you out more often and make you have more fun."

The conversation became mute when we were joined by two other fun-loving buddies from our Naval station. Dee was a natural platinum blonde with blue eyes, facial features, and a body to die for. There was no doubt that whatever bar we went in, she would garner all the attention of the male inhabitants...and that was not a bad thing. I liked being out there, but under the radar.

Eva and Dee took over every bar we visited. Inevitably, Dee would yell, "I need another Margarita," and some guy or group of guys would make that happen. However, the "Duval Crawl *Rules*" required that we keep moving…much to the disappointment of many of the opposite sex.

Our other compadre, Sandy, was laid back—like me. She had stylishly short hair and a cute face. She was short, maybe a little over five feet. She was dressed in a pantsuit that did not attract many of the men. That was okay with her. She didn't want to attract *men*.

"I'll be leaving you guys when we get to my side of town," spouted Sandy. I understood. Key West had a very enthusiastic gay population that centered around the southernmost section of Duval. We understood that Sandy was more at home there, and it didn't bother us in the least. She was a good friend. I would like to think we were enlightened for the early 1970s, but it was more like the rest of the country was in the dark ages when it came to sexuality.

I didn't qualify for my Duval Crawl Award certificate because I only had a margarita in every third or fourth bar that we walked into. Still, I was a few notches above buzzed when we entered Reilly's Irish Pub. Because of this, I cannot swear to the validity of the next part of my story.

We were surrounded by a bunch of fun-loving (equally inebriated) guys who were busy making passes at Dee, and to a lesser extent, Eva and me, when I heard a song. It was a tune from long ago, and I thought I recognized it. Yet, I thought that impossible.

The singer, sitting alone with only his guitar for accompaniment, was just finishing up his last few minutes of his set. I thought I heard a lyric that sounded like, "…of my forever." I truly believed that I had heard "Thief of My Forever"—a song created by my departed brother Jimmy's band. I had last heard it in our dark and dank basement, and no one here in Key West, fifteen hundred miles and six years removed from that basement, could know the song. I looked to see who was singing.

My gaze was fixed on the elevated stage at the rear of the club, where I observed the singer. I'll never know if it was the abundance of margaritas or an overactive imagination that deluded me into thinking that this scraggly-looking performer could be one of the two "survivors" of Those Born Free. It would be an astronomical coincidence if either Gio or Johnny had arrived here in Key West, and I had just happened to run into them. I sought further proof but was dissuaded when the show's emcee spoke.

"Let's hear it one more time for Captain Jack Paradise," he bantered with the crowd before introducing the next act. I looked over at the performer, but I still had no closure. His hair was the same color as Johnny Cipp's—jet black, but this guy's hair flowed below his shoulders, and he had a full beard that covered much of his face. The Johnny I knew always had relatively short hair and was clean-shaven. And there were other inconsistencies. Johnny was the only member of the band who *didn't* sing, so being a solo artist down here made no sense at all. However, here in Key West, the abundance of bars meant that the standard for singing talent required to get a job was low. In addition, Johnny loved Maria Romano, and she was nowhere to be seen.

Maria had run away from home four months after Johnny went missing. We always assumed that she had gone to join Johnny wherever he was hiding. These final thoughts led me to want to investigate this person named "Captain Jack Paradise." As he packed up his guitar and made to leave the club, I followed. If Maria were around, surely, he would meet her.

"You can't go," slurred Eva.

"Stay, Maggie," bubbled Dee, who I thought hadn't noticed I was even there all night.

"Sorry, something came up...I gotta go."

Dee was soon engrossed with the three guys vying for her attention. Eva gave me an exaggerated look of disappointment, followed by a halfhearted wave. I tried to keep my eye on Paradise as he exited onto Duval. I followed him through the Truman Annex and found myself approaching Fort Zachary Taylor Beach. I knew this area well because a substation of the Naval base was located at Sigsbee Point, separated from the public beach by a ten-foot-high hedge and a chain-link fence. I had completed some required training with some of the Marines stationed there.

Leaning on that fence, I kept my distance and tried to determine a way to confirm my suspicions. If this guy met Maria on the beach, that would be a dead giveaway. However, short of yelling "Johnny" and seeing if he reacted, I was at a loss about what to do next. Being timid, all that came out of my attempt to call was a whisper of his name that no one more than three feet away from me would hear. And yet, someone heard it.

"If you are trying to get his attention, you are going to have to do better than that," announced a voice from the other side of the hedges —an unseen interloper.

"Who's there?" I snapped.

"Does it matter?" a male voice answered.

"Yes, it does."

"Ma'am, excuse my language, but you are chickenshit."

I detected a slight accent that was not readily recognizable to me.

"Do you want me to yell his name?" interjected the interloper, "I can offer that service to you."

"No, thank you. I am not even sure if it is his name."

"Now, in my opinion, you are as crazy as you are chickenshit."

"I didn't ask your opinion. I mean, what kind of pervert sits by a fence and listens to other people's conversations?"

"Ma'am, first of all, I don't hear any conversation besides the one between us. Second, I am doing my job. This is my post, and I am guarding against suspicious persons who might want to degrade the security of this base."

"Yeah, like who?"

"Well, like crazy people who talk to themselves on the other side of the fence, that's who?" He boomed this with all the force of a drill sergeant giving orders to a recruit. Yet, in his voice was a certain tone that allowed me to know he was teasing. The unidentified person, possibly Johnny Cipp or Jack Paradise, on the beach, thirty yards away, felt his privacy invaded and left. Whatever emotional inspiration he was getting from the moon-soaked beach was gone. I thought of running after him but was too confused by my conversation with the unknown person on the other side of the fence and hedges.

"Now, see what you did. You scared the mystery man away."

"I'm sorry," murmured the mysterious Marine, definitely apologetic.

"It's not that important. I just thought that guy was someone from my past. But I realize I need to move on from that past...meet new people...do new things...have adventures."

"How about starting right now?"

"What does that mean?"

"Hi, I am Lance Corporal Danny Evers... and Danny is my full, legal name—not Daniel or Dan. How would you like to meet me tomorrow night for a..."

"A date?" I finished his sentence. "But you have no idea what I look like."

"And you, Ma'am, have no idea what I look like. But then again, I don't think I proposed marriage yet, so we both have an out." I decided then and there that I was going to start taking chances and making life worth being there.

"Meet me at Sloppy Joe's at 8 p.m. tomorrow. I'll have a red flower behind my ear."

"Me too," he answered. Then I heard a superior officer speak to him, and they both started walking away.

"Maggie's my name," I yelled through the bush, hoping he heard me. I don't know what the officer would have thought if he had also heard me.

I never saw or sought out the mysterious musician again. I was too busy building a relationship with Danny to ever do the Duval Crawl or visit Reilly's Irish Pub. If he had been Johnny, it was just a case of Those Born Free helping me again.

43

REMEMBER WALKING
IN THE SAND

"Remember...walking in the sand,
Remember...walking hand in hand,
Remember... the night was so exciting,
Remember...his smile was so inviting."
- The Shangri-Las

Maggie's Memos and Memories

$\mathcal{N}$o one would ever mistake Sloppy Joe's for a quiet, intimate place to meet. It had a lively, party atmosphere that drew hundreds of people who frequented the place while the music was playing, which was usually all day and all night. The menu consisted of Sloppy Joe sandwiches, Sloppy Joe fries, Sloppy Joe hot dogs, Sloppy Joe baked potatoes, Sloppy Joe...well, you get the idea. The concept of melted cheese mixed with seasoned ground beef was a recipe that permeated every inch of the bar that had invented this American delicacy. Long gone were the days when Ernest Hemingway would spend most of his nights drinking at this bar. In fact, in modern America, probably more people have heard of the Sloppy Joe sandwiches invented there than one of America's most talented writers.

The fact remained that I was using this massive venue to hide from this Danny character until I got to look at him first. I must admit that I was a coward...I didn't even put the flower in my hair. I wanted to see him before he saw me. If I didn't like what I saw, well...

I scanned the tables and entrances looking for a guy with a flower behind his ear. I realized that maybe he didn't even have to be an Adonis at all. Any guy who had the self-confidence to walk into a bar filled with hundreds of people (many of them his fellow Marines) with a flower stuck behind his ear was some kind of special.

Then I saw that he actually *was* something special, and he was also an Adonis. He stood about six feet with the kind of body you would expect on a Marine. His face was chiseled with features that would not be out of place on the cover of Gentlemen's Quarterly magazine. I could not ascertain the color of his hair because it was cut very, very short in the manner of all Marines. It didn't matter because hair would have only covered his beautiful features. I was blown away.

Could this really be the voice on the other side of the hedge? I quickly attempted to put my flower in its designated location. However, I was flustered, so I first stuck it in my ear, then placed it backward before finding the correct location. It didn't matter; he was already on his way towards me.

"Weren't sure, were you?" he chuckled.

"What do you mean?"

"I saw you put your flower in at the last minute. But I don't begrudge you. A beautiful woman like you can't be too careful."

I blushed. Flattery will get you everywhere! Okay, modesty aside, I could look in the mirror and recognize my credentials. God had blessed all three of the McAvoy sisters with nice features, luxurious auburn hair, and bright green eyes. The body was all me, the product of hours of hard work. Still, I looked at the man standing in front of me and thought to myself, *Am I good enough for him?*

As if to answer my unspoken question, he took the flower from behind his ear, added it to a small bouquet he had hidden behind his back, and then presented them to me, saying nothing but smiling broadly.

"I'm…I'm Maggie," was all I could think to say.

"I know."

"Oh, so you heard me last night."

"Yeah…and so did Captain Ryerson."

"Oops."

"He reamed me out and then said, 'Is she worth it?'"

"Well?"

"You certainly are…and more."

Right there and then, I wanted to hug him…so I did.

"I'm Danny. Not Dan or Daniel to people I care about. So, you can call me Danny."

Boy, was this moving fast, and I loved it. It only took us five minutes to realize we had to leave Sloppy Joe's if we were ever going to have a real conversation without the blasting noise.

"We gotta get out of this place," I shouted to be heard above the din. Without thinking, I reverted to my love of music and finished the line from the 1965 song.

We gotta get out of this place
If it's the last thing we ever do.
We gotta get out of this place,
There's a better place for me and you.

I didn't know then, but suspected, that Danny was about 22 years old. That would mean that he was close to my deceased brother's age. He should have caught on to my song banter because he was of an era when the song was popular. At worst, he should have thought I was corny and dismissed my attempt at humor with a simple 'no comment' and a smile. He didn't. He just stared at me and said nothing.

"You know...the Animals song," I prodded and received only a blank stare. We spoke no more, and we found our way out into the street where relative quiet prevailed.

I think we're alone now,
There doesn't seem to be anyone around.

I thought the Tommy James and the Shondells' hit would elicit recognition. Again, I was wrong.

"You talk funny," he quipped, but then started to chuckle openly. "I know you were singing another song. But to be honest, I didn't know that one either."

I put my arm in his to show my affection and to soften the effect of my next comment.

"What? Did you grow up on Mars?"

"Sort of," he answered me, very seriously looking into my eyes. He didn't elaborate on the response, at least not yet.

We walked and talked for hours. Mostly, the conversation was superficial, focusing on the basics and life as a Marine. It seemed like we were two boxers who were feeling each other out before committing to anything serious. Yet we laughed a lot...and held hands. I was thinking this could become something special.

Eventually, we found ourselves on the same beach that only the night before we had communicated through the bushes and chain link fence. He looked at me and pointed further down the shore to a place with more privacy.

"Why? Is there someone right behind that fence and bush?" I asked.

"There is *always* someone stationed there—day and night—24/7. Tonight, it is one of my friends—a guy named Joe Hebert."

"I don't believe you," I teased.

"Hey, Joe...," he began. I know that I should have learned my lesson, but I couldn't resist the musical implications.

"Hey, Joe, where are you going with that gun in your hand?" I *sang* to the fence, and Danny looked at me like I was crazy (again). He then spoke in all seriousness.

"Of course, he's got a gun in his hand. He's on duty. I don't...Oh, I see, another song reference that I don't get."

Before I could even respond, the unseen voice on the other side of the bushes sang the next line of the lyrics of the Jimi Hendrix hit.

I'm goin' down to shoot my old lady.
You know I caught her messin' 'round with another man.

"That's what I'm talking about. Joe gets it!" I teased my bewildered date. "One of Jimi Hendrix's best."

"Huh?" was Danny's confused response.

"Though I prefer the version by the virtually unknown group The Leaves," quickly responded the unseen Joe from his hidden location on the other side of the hedge.

"He gets me!" I shrieked, "Hey, Joe, how do you feel about wearing a flower behind your ear...at Sloppy Joe's bar?"

"Huh," was now Joe's response, but he quickly changed his tone, and we could now hear the very flustered voice of Joe Hebert barking, "No, Captain Ryerson, just talking to myself."

Danny and I almost burst our guts holding in our laughter as we quickly and quietly moved away from the fence and down the beach. When a safe distance from Joe and the omnipresent Captain Ryerson, we sat. He put his arm around me. I put my head on his shoulder.

"You aren't kidding. You don't know who Jimi Hendrix is...do you?"

"Nope."

"Okay, until further notice, I am still assuming your planet of origin is Mars...or maybe something farther away like Neptune or Pluto."

"No...Ocracoke," was his only response.

44

I'M LIVING ON AN ISLAND

"I'm living on an island,
Every day,
When my friends come over,
We go out and play."
- Howard Livingston and the Mile Marker 24 Band

Maggie's Memos and Memories

"What the hell is an ocracoke?" I asked, baffled at his statement.

"It's where I grew up," Danny answered without giving the slightest clue as to what that had to do with musical knowledge.

"Yeah, so?"

"Well, it's an island."

"Big whoop," I said, remaining confused and telling him so. "I grew up on an island too...Long Island."

"How many people?"

"Well, counting all four counties...eight million...give or take a couple hundred thousand."

"My island has five hundred...give or take one or two."

"Okay, that is small. But what...nobody had a radio?"

"Wouldn't do any good. We don't have reception from the mainland."

"Where the hell is this island?"

"I told you...Ocracoke."

"Okay, forget that I first assumed you were talking about a plant popular in Southern cooking and a soft drink created in Atlanta and sold worldwide. You know, okra and Coke."

It was now Danny's turn to smile...and show some patience with me.

"Let me start at the beginning. You've heard of the Outer Banks... right?"

"Isn't that like a long beach in North Carolina? One of my friends from training camp was from Nags Head."

"The Outer Banks are two hundred miles long, and Nags Head is at the northernmost point. I was about 202 miles away from there."

"Okay, now you've lost me. How can you be further away than the Outer Banks are long?"

"Ocracoke," replied Danny, and a broad smile took over his face. "My home—born and bred."

"Explain, please."

"The island was once joined to the Outer Banks, and we were the southernmost point of the road."

"And?'

"In 1846, a hurricane overwhelmed the narrow strip of land that kept us joined to the mainland, and we became an isolated island with no access to the rest of the United States except by boat. We are still that way; our only access to civilization is by ferry. So, you can imagine no TV or radio signals were traveling the airwaves to us."

"How horrible," I gasped.

"No, not really. We may not have had *your* world, but the people of Ocracoke did have *our* world. We had wonderful beaches and a sense of community. We had wild horses roaming freely on the island. Being separated from everyone else, we even developed our own dialect of speech. We call it Ocracoke Brogue."

"So that's the strange accent I hear when you speak."

"Oh, it's not just an accent. We have about four hundred words that are unique to us…and the famous pirate, Blackbeard, was killed on Ocracoke."

"Okay, if it is so wonderful, why'd you ever leave?"

"That's very personal."

"C'mon, more personal than me knowing that you speak an exotic language…or that you know nothing about American music and culture. Or that horses run wild on your little island."

He said nothing…only staring at me blankly.

"Okay, I'll go first if that is what it takes for us to get to know each other." My tone sounded angry, but actually, I was merely feeling frustrated. However, he was still not responding, so I broke the ice.

"Six years ago, my father and brother were murdered. And all my friends, who just happen to be in my brother's band, also died or disappeared. And my best friend, Michael, an eight-year-old boy, also vanished from my life."

"Oh, I'm so sorry," he started, but I cut him off.

"I'm not done. My mother went into a shell of depression, and my older sister, Aylin, now alternates between being a drug addict and going to rehab. I forged my mother's signature to join the Navy to get out of that hellhole of a life while I was still underage. Can you match that, Danny Boy, because not many people can."

"No, my life was nothing like that. It's just a thing that sort of meant a great deal to me."

"Let's hear it, Danny Boy."

"It's nothing compared to your story."

"Spit it out, Danny Boy," I challenged him.

"What's with this Danny Boy?"

"Just another song you wouldn't know. Quit stalling," I countered.

45

SEA OF HEARTBREAK

*"I'm like a lost ship
Adrift on the sea"*
- Everly Brothers Version

Danny Boy's Story

"There's a certain place on my island that I passed by every day of my life while I was walking to school. It was a cemetery."

"Okay, you're freaking me out now." He didn't respond to my comment but continued his tale.

"Very few people realize that when World War II broke out, America did not immediately join the fight against Hitler. However, when we did join the hostilities, the armed forces were severely unprepared...especially the American Navy. From January to May in 1942, almost four hundred commercial ships were sunk in American waters by German U-boats. Such a high percentage of them were destroyed off the Outer Banks that the area became known as "Torpedo Alley" by captains piloting ships through our waters. The United States lacked the resources to halt the carnage. Old timers on Ocracoke would tell the next generation that they could read newspapers by the light of the flaming debris off the coast each night."

"Holy shit," was my emotional response to my lack of knowledge of these events.

"Britain came to our rescue and patrolled our shores until we could build enough ships to do so ourselves. However, they suffered heavy casualties saving American lives."

He paused, and I could see raw emotion on his face. Yet I still didn't know where this was going.

"In May of 1942, the HMS Bedfordshire exploded right outside our kitchen window, and all 37 aboard died. My father and grandfather rushed to the shore, hoping to find a way to help. They stayed all night looking for survivors. In the early hours of the morning, the bodies of four deceased British sailors washed ashore."

He stopped speaking. He looked morose for a few minutes, and I said nothing. Finally, he began again.

"My father and grandfather saw to it that they had an honorable burial on Ocracoke. There, those four sailors' remains rested under the protection of the United States. Eventually, our country, out of gratitude, leased the land on which they were buried to the United Kingdom. That small cemetery is now considered actual British territory. The British Union Jack flag now flies over their final resting place, which lies on "British" soil, and each year a memorial ceremony is held by the Royal British Navy and the United States Coast Guard."

He stopped speaking, but I sensed that there was more. I hugged him and comforted him—this guy I had barely just met.

"My father and grandfather enlisted a few weeks later. My father was only eighteen, so he would not have been drafted yet. My grandfather was forty-four years old and would never have been able to enlist if he had not lied about being a bit younger to the local recruiter. He was an excellent cook, and as a result, he was given a cushy job on a destroyer in the Pacific. Unfortunately, as the Japanese grew desperate, they resorted to Kamikaze flights, suicide missions where they flew their bomb-laden planes into American ships. My grandfather died in July of 1945, less than a month before the end of the war."

"And your father?"

"He came back alive...obviously, or I wouldn't be here."

"I suspect a 'but' in that statement, Danny."

"Wow, I graduated from Danny Boy."

"I sense this is too serious for joking around...and you're stalling again."

"My father was on the USS Indianapolis," Danny whispered reverently. He expected a reaction out of me and got none.

"I said *the* Indianapolis." He was incredulous that the name meant nothing to me. In reality, very few in America were knowledgeable of the fate of the Indianapolis. This was because when the ship sank, a veil of silence was placed on all matters concerning the disaster. Almost four decades after its sinking, the story was told as a cautionary tale by a main character in the movie *Jaws*. Many thought it was fiction, made up to enhance the movie's plot. If I didn't know better, I would have thought Danny was angry, rather than frustrated with my ignorance. He calmed himself down and told me the story.

"The USS Indianapolis had completed its mission of delivering the uranium to be used for the atomic bomb that would be dropped on Hiroshima, Japan. This bomb would end the war, and in the aftermath of that spectacular story, the fate of the Indianapolis was overshadowed."

"You're right. I never heard of it."

"And you call yourself Navy?" This last statement was mixed with what I thought was a glimpse of a smile. When I heard the rest of the story, I quickly realized I must be wrong.

"Because of its top-secret mission, the ship was under strict radio silence. Therefore, when it was torpedoed on July 30 and sank in twelve minutes, no one knew. Three hundred men died in the actual sinking of the ship. Almost 900 went into the water with no lifeboats and very few life jackets. They stayed there for three and a half days, many dying of dehydration and starvation…and then the sharks came. First, they ate the dead bodies that were floating but eventually started to pick off the floating live sailors who had survived. Only 316 of the 900 who went into the sea survived when the sinking was finally discovered. Those who survived watched at least 160 of their fellow sailors eaten alive by sharks."

"Oh my God," was all I could express.

"My father was one of the survivors, but only because a friend saved him. He was knocked unconscious when the torpedo hit, and he was floating in the water when his best friend followed him in and held his head up until he awakened. Days later, my father watched Danny Cranston being attacked while he clung to my father's hands. My father beat on the shark's head furiously. But it was too late to save Danny, who was eaten alive while clinging to my father.

"Yeah, my father came home, but he was never quite right. He would fade away at times in thought, and we knew where his mind had gone—back to those horrible memories…back to the sea of death, the sea of heartbreak…back to his friend."

"And he named you Danny…not Dan or Daniel."

He nodded in recognition of my insight.

"They never found my grandfather's body, but we gave him a headstone anyway and placed it across from the British cemetery that had inspired his enlistment. As a child, I knew I would enlist in the military. I knew it every time I passed by the British cemetery and the grave of my grandfather. The dedication…the sacrifice. I admired it … I aspired to it."

I stared at him…speechless. What could I say? He continued.

"I was in the Marines for three years when I got word that my father had taken his own life…another victim of the Indianapolis tragedy. He's buried next to the headstone memorializing my grandfather and across from the four British sailors…right there on Ocracoke Island."

I had only known Danny Evers for less than two days, but his compassion, loyalty, and everything else about his personality had stolen my heart. I knew from our first date that I was going to marry this man.

HERE IN THE CONCH REPUBLIC

"The rest of the world
A million miles away
But in the Conch Republic
We're doin' okay."
- Howard Livingston and the Mile Marker 24 Band

Maggie's Memos and Memories

The Conch Republic was founded in 1982, but if I had not left seven years prior, I would have been right in the midst of that "rebellion." It would have been fun. It all started with the United States government blocking US 1, the only road connecting Key West to the rest of the world. At the time, that road was also the main thoroughfare for illegal drugs coming into the country.

To those who were not in the drug trade, the blockade was a major inconvenience. Therefore, Key West declared itself an independent country—The Conch Republic. The first act of the new "country" was to seek foreign aid from the United States. It was all done tongue-in-cheek to highlight the problem, but also to have a little fun. This story of the Conch Republic just about captured the two sides of Key West —both the bad and the good: the persistent drug problem and the unbelievable fun (with or without those drugs).

Again, I wasn't there for that secession, but it does portray both the heaven and hell of Key West, both in the 1970s and in the present time. Hedonism reigned supreme on the farthest outpost of contiguous America. Many came down for vacation and never left after being seduced into a lifestyle that revolved around the sun... some fishing...and a whole lot of drinking and drugs. For those who followed that path, life expectancy was not exceptionally long. To those of us sane and sober, we referred to these unfortunates as the "Key-wasted" who suffered from "Keys Disease."

However, Danny and I were in the service, and therefore, we towed the straight and narrow. Yet what would come to be called the Conch Republic could still be a paradise. When we weren't busy fulfilling our obligations, there were long walks on the beach, scuba-diving and snorkeling, swimming, fishing, boating, music in the clubs...and so much more.

And then there were the nights. In the interest of propriety, I will not go into much detail. Let me just say that there was a great deal of passion accented by heavy doses of tenderness. Use your imagination. Life could not have been more perfect, and on a moonlit night on the same beach where we had first talked through a fence, Danny proposed to me. Of course, when I broke into a chorus of...

Going to the Chapel
And we're going to get married.

... he didn't get the reference to the Dixie Cups' hit song, "Chapel of Love." We were married on August 29, 1974, on that same beach.

47

NIGHTS IN WHITE SATIN

"Nights in White Satin.
Never reaching the end."
- Moody Blues

Maggie's Memos and Memories

*D*espite my previous statement about nights of passion, I was a virgin when Danny Boy and I married. This was a rare occurrence in the "free love" attitude of the late 1960s and early 1970s. As much as I would like to say that this was a moral decision, it had a lot to do with my being a social recluse from the age of 12 to 18. After meeting Danny Boy, it was much more about making our marriage commitment something special. It's hard to explain, but Danny was a bit old-fashioned in his thinking, and we jointly came to the decision…and it was worth it.

Our wedding night was everything I could have hoped for and more, and my obsession with 1960s music led me to liken that night to the Moody Blues' song "Nights in White Satin." Okay, that probably wasn't a subconscious thought, as I made a point of actually wearing white satin for the occasion. However, as the passion grew and grew, it did seem like the prophetic lyrics of "never reaching the end" were also true...and neither one of us wanted that night to end...and it didn't until the sun shone through our bedroom window after a night of lovemaking.

But it wasn't just the wonderful nights. The days following our wedding were a whirl of laughter, music, and sunsets we could never have dreamed of. The beach became the backdrop where we sketched plans for the future, imagining a life after our service to our country was completed.

Danny and I laughed at the ongoing byplay that found me speaking in song lyrics and his total lack of any knowledge of them. One day, he turned the tables on me as we walked in the sand.

"You don't know what it's like. Baby, you don't know what it's like...to love somebody...to love somebody," he spoke (not sang) in a deadpan monotone.

"You're shittin' me, right? Did you think I wouldn't notice you quoting the Bee Gees? What did you do, look at the album notes with the lyrics when I wasn't looking?"

"Maggie, you got me what can I say, "I'm a Loser, and I'm not what I appear to be."

"Oh, Danny Boy, it appears as if you found my Beatles album, too."

He suddenly stopped and looked at me with that mischievous glint in his eye, the one that always signaled he was about to surprise me. I braced myself.

"You know, Maggie, I may not have ever heard the tunes you remember and enjoy, but I can tell when you've got a song in your heart."

His attempts to mimic my love of songs were awkward and endearing, and together we'd often burst into laughter, drawing curious glances from strangers passing by. Those were golden days—the sun, the salty air...and the love. We built a life together and somehow the weirdness of my musical obsession was symbolic of that partnership.

I'd hum, he'd whistle off-key, and somehow, in that blending of our voices and the sincerity behind it, we found our harmony. I began to realize that what made our love unique wasn't just our shared moments, but the way our differences fit together like the perfectly sung duet.

But time, as it always does, brought change. The outside world started to press in through newspaper headlines and late-night conversations—and all the beauty of our love could not prevent reality from intruding on our dream.

And there is one final song that came out eight years after our wedding day that still haunts me.

48

GOODNIGHT, SAIGON

"And we said we would all go down together."
- Billy Joel

Maggie's Memos and Memories

On December 27, 1974, Danny received notice that he was being deployed to Vietnam. However, this was not as terrifying as it would seem. This was not the same Vietnam that had taken the lives of over 50,000 American troops. In all of 1974, only one American died there. The draft had virtually disappeared, and America seemed to be settling into relative quiet after the conflict, both abroad and internally, between people with different views on the war.

For Danny Boy and me, it was more of a question of the end of our idyllic life in Key West. I was still stationed there and had started college with the idea of continuing in the field of therapy. I hadn't decided whether it would be ministering to people's bodies or their minds. Eventually, I became a mental health professional, but that's later on in my story.

I thought about how much I would miss my husband, Danny, like I had never missed anyone before. Upon introspection, I realized that was not true. My life had been an ongoing story of loss. I still miss my father and brother. I miss my other "brother," Bracko, and my best friend, Michael. Those losses were like fresh wounds that were reopened with Danny's departure.

It was some consolation that this was not the same Vietnam War as in 1967-1968, when half of all American casualties occurred. Over 28,000 Americans died in those two years of losses. Yes, 28,000 families were feeling what I was feeling about my family and friends at the same time in 1967.

Of course, back in 1967, I was unaware of the war. I was turning twelve and oblivious to the world around me. Now that my Danny was going over there, I tried to focus on how less dangerous a situation he was heading toward. The one consolation was that when he returned, we would both be near the end of our enlistments, and we had decided it was time for a change. The paradise of our Key West playland would give way to a beautiful future in an as-yet-undecided location.

49

BROKEN DREAMS

"One more illusion shattered,
One more broken dream,
Oh, that the morning brings the light."
- Justin Hayward

Maggie's Memos and Memories

"Maggie, I'll be fine. It'll be a cushy job standing at the guard post at the embassy."

"Danny Boy, no talking to strange women through the fence. You know what that leads to."

"I don't speak any Vietnamese," he teased and then quickly followed with a second statement that touched my heart. "Besides, I can't do any better than I did that night at Zach Taylor Beach."

He always knew the right thing to say.

"I love you," I whispered in his ear.

"I love you. In fact, when I'm away, I'll write home every day...and send all my lovin' to you," he answered.

"Holy shit, I created a rock and roll monster. Are you actually quoting the Beatles to me as your last words?"

"No, not my very last words."

"Maggie, I've been thinking maybe we'll start that family we talked about. You know…when I return."

"I'd like that."

"So, I thought of quoting Paul Anka and his song, 'You're Having My Baby.'"

"I like the concept but cut the corny song medley. Paul Anka… really? Seriously, though, when you come home, I think I'd like to start our family."

In reality, we had decided on this in several discussions in the weeks leading up to his departure, but it was reassuring to hear him say it again. We kissed, and he turned, starting to walk toward the transport that would take him halfway around the world to a conflict that was winding down. I will never forget that beautiful smile on his face as he waved goodbye.

It is now 1990. I still do not have any children. Danny Boy never came home.

I awoke on the morning of April 30, 1975, to the news that the Viet Cong had surrounded the city of Saigon. Pictures on TV screens showed the last Americans escaping from the roof of the embassy building in a helicopter.

The American plan to honorably exit the war by turning over the fighting to the South Vietnamese had failed miserably, and now the only mission for the United States was to get the hell out. To facilitate this scenario, the Marine Security Guard battalion at the US Embassy in Saigon was quickly moved to a compound adjacent to the airport. As a prelude to the capture of the city, a rocket attack was launched by the Viet Cong on the airport. That strike resulted in the last two

American casualties of the entire Vietnam War. One of the victims was Lance Corporal Danny Evers.

I always thought that the ride down the length of the Outer Banks to Ocracoke would be a joyous occasion. I would be meeting Danny's family for the first time, and a large group of family and friends would welcome me. Instead, I was now making that journey with what seemed like half the United States Marine Corps. I knew that there would never be any doubt that the Marines would do him right. However, it almost seemed as if this was extra special because Danny was the last casualty of the very long war.

In the end, the Vietnam War had torn America asunder with differing opinions about what should be done. During that time, some returning servicemen were unfortunately treated with disdain. That was all gone now, and perhaps in this backwater section of North Carolina, it never existed. I had no way of knowing. All I saw were hundreds of people lining the streets of every populated area of the Outer Banks, waving flags with serious faces of sadness. And it was all for my Danny Boy, the last death of the war.

We had started the National Scenic Byway at the northern end of the Outer Banks at Whalebone Junction, where US 264 meets NC 12 in Nags Head. Soon, we were flanked by only sand and the Atlantic Ocean to the east and the sand and the Pamlico Sound to the west. I could only think how beautiful this would have been with Danny. Perhaps we would have enjoyed the Shipwreck Museum or climbing to the top of the Cape Hatteras Lighthouse. After our seemingly endless journey, we would have taken the ferry over to the island of Ocracoke and have been lovingly welcomed by Danny's family and friends.

As it was, Danny Boy was laid to rest next to his father and grandfather and across from the four valiant British sailors who had so long ago inspired him. I sobbed all through the eulogy given by his commanding officer and did indeed totally lose all restraint when they gave him a twenty-one-gun salute and played taps. His mother (whom I have come to know and love) held me upright even though she was also weeping uncontrollably. After the official ceremony was completed, there would only be one final act to draw the curtain on a beautiful man's life. How could I know that when I lovingly teased him with the "Danny Boy" moniker, it would prove prophetic?

I was Irish to my very core, and Danny Boy knew that somewhere centuries ago, his ancestors had emigrated from there. So, a friend from the corps sang the final tribute to the man I had loved briefly but intensely. I heard and sang along with every word, but specific phrases evoked such emotion that I was choked with tears and unable to continue.

> *Oh, Danny boy, the pipes, the pipes are calling.*
> *From glen to glen, and down the mountainside.*
> *The summer's gone, and all the roses falling,*
> **It's you, it's you must go, and I must abide.**
>
> *But come ye back when summer's in the meadow,*
> *Or when the valley's hushed and white with snow,*
> *I'll be here in sunshine or in shadow,*
> **Oh, Danny boy, oh Danny boy, I love you so!**
>
> *But when ye come, and all the flowers are dying,*
> *If I am dead, as dead I well may be,*
> *You'll come and find the place where I am lying,*
> *And kneel and say an Ave there for me.*
>
> *And I shall hear, though soft you tread above me,*
> *And all my grave will warmer, sweeter be,*
> **For you will bend and tell me that you love me,**
> **And I shall sleep in peace until you come to me!**

50

IF THE SUN COMES UP

"If the sun comes up
Without me tomorrow,
You'll be fine
You'll be fine."
- Trace Adkins

Maggie's Memos and Memories

J was not yet 21. I was a widow. Those days were a time that I never want to relive. But I will because they are part of my story...the story of the third pig in the brick house who survived.

For most of the weeks after he died, I roamed around the base in a fog. People knew the story—*There goes the wife of the last casualty of the Vietnam War.* My friends all tried to console me, but I couldn't help but think that strangers all pointed at me behind my back as if to say, *Yeah, that's her...what a tragedy.*

Eva, of course, was there for me, but what could she do? Often, she would convince me to go to the bars on Duval Street to try and take my mind off everything. However, I was not a big drinker and did not want to become one. As I looked at all the people who lay around wasting their lives in Captain Tony's, Sloppy Joe's, and Reilly's, I was sure that was not the path I wanted to take. Yet, I did not know what I could do.

The Armed Forces honor their dead. The Navy was willing to let me take as much time as I needed to mourn. And so it was that I found myself roaming the streets of Key West in a never-ending pattern from Mallory Square to the East End beaches. Somedays, when I was particularly lazy or morose, I just walked off the Truman Annex base and onto the adjoining Zach Taylor Beach. That could be tough. That was where we met. That was where we had our last night before he shipped off. The night before we said our loving farewells at the airport, we had walked hand in hand along "our" beach. I vividly remember that conversation, though for some reason I had tried to forget it. But it all came back to me one day while I sat alone at the beach. It was sunrise, and in the beauty of the moment, I remembered our final time there.

"If I don't...," he started, and I cut him off rather quickly.

"Don't you frigging even think like that," I screamed, the tears starting to flow.

"Maggie, I'm a Marine, and I am not going there to play checkers. We have to allow for the possibility that..."

"Shut up, you damn well better shut up," I vehemently answered.

He held me tight, and we talked no more about it. Yet I knew what he was saying, and I let it guide me through my turbulent future. If he didn't come back, he wanted me to live my life to the fullest without him. And that's just what I did, all the while knowing that he would be looking down on me and pushing me to succeed.

Months later, I still roamed the streets—thinking about my future. One day, my rambling walk led me to a place I had been once or twice during my tour of duty in Key West—Saint Mary, Star of the Sea

Church. Saint Mary might be the star of the sea, but the land folk hardly populated the place. The "Live-for-today" lifestyles of Key West in 1975 left the pews of this church incredibly devoid of human life, even on a Sunday morning. Therefore, I was utterly alone on the Monday morning that I entered the doors and sat down to pray. But that was okay. Just me and God—I could handle that. I sat for what seemed like hours, and perhaps a certain kind of peace came over me. I cried. I mean, I cried like there was no tomorrow, and it felt good. I was now ready to deal with my grief. I would move on. He would want that.

"Are you okay?" a soft voice whispered from behind.

I didn't immediately answer, thinking that perhaps I had imagined it.

"I'll leave you to your solitude if you wish. God knows you will find that here in this church...especially on a Monday. The only time there are fewer people here is on a Saturday night. But then again, this is Key West."

Now I needed to know who was mocking this church for its sparse attendance. I turned and almost laughed out loud (for the first time since...) to find it was a priest who was speaking. Because he had made me smile, I invited him to sit and talk with me.

"I'm Maggie McAvoy Evers, and my husband just died in Vietnam."

He said nothing at first and let me tell him my story — my whole story, all the while patiently holding my hand and looking me in the eyes.

"How old are you? Because I believe you have suffered quite a bit in a very short time."

"Aren't you going to give a God pep talk? You know, all this suffering will be penance and get me into heaven sooner."

He laughed extremely boisterously at that one.

"You don't seem like the type to buy into that sort of reasoning?"

"You're right, Father, I am a Catholic-school-raised-go-to-church-every-Sunday-Irish girl from Queens, New York. Well, not so much lately. Maybe that's it. God punished me for not going to church anymore."

"If that were the case, there would not be anyone alive in Key West! No, God doesn't work that way. He lets us find our own path."

"Are you sure you're really a priest?"

"Naw, got the costume from a thrift shop."

"And to pull off the act, you hang around in a church."

"'A man's gotta do what a man's gotta do,' as my father used to say,"

We talked for what seemed like hours about everything and about nothing. Sports—I was a Yankee fan, and he was (Yuck!) a Red Sox fan. Politics - He thought that it was a good thing that Nixon resigned due to Watergate; I couldn't care less. Key West – He liked to swim at Higgs Beach, and I preferred Zach Taylor (no surprise there).

And then I hit him with what I thought was an innocuous question.

"Okay, pseudo-priest, what is your story? I've told you everything about me. Fess up, what's going on with you?"

"Other than to tell you, I am a priest. I don't think my story would interest you."

"Try me."

"It's not a great story. Not a happy story."

"All the better. I could use the lift from hearing somebody else's woes."

He got really serious very quickly. I got up and started to walk out, all the while screaming incoherently.

"Don't go," he begged.

"I don't buy this one-way giving. How do I know you're for real?"

He stood as if I had torn out his heart.

"I've never told anyone my story, but if it helps you to move on… and maybe it helps me to move on…I will."

HEROES AND VILLAINS
IN THE NIGHT

"There were heroes and villains in the night,
Not apparent at first sight
Who's good? Who's bad?
And who's just entirely insane?"
- Chris Delaney and the Brotherhood Blues Band

Father Rizzo's Confession

"*I* had always wanted to be a priest. It sounds crazy. But, yeah, when they talked about vocations and all the other guys were laughing it up in the back of Sister Mary the Fairy's eighth-grade classroom, I was different. All of my friends assumed that if anyone took a vow of celibacy to become a religious person, whether a nun or a priest, they were gay. Because the nun who taught us pushed the religious life, they tagged her with the name "Mary the Fairy."

"Sister Mary helped me find someone to talk to about pursuing a religious life. I then attended a high school exclusively for young men who aspired to be priests. Needless to say, 50% of them dropped out when the hormones kicked in and they couldn't resist the urge to be with the opposite sex. It's a good thing they figured it out early.

"For my part, I had quite a few dates to ensure I was in the right state of mind. I liked girls—I mean, really, really liked girls. However, in the end, I just felt that I had a more profound commitment to God. No one outside of those of us who made that choice could understand how I felt.

"However, there was a third group of those in my classes, both at the seminary prep high school and the seminary itself, who were using their vocation as an escape. They *were* gay. I grew up in a rough part of Boston, and fighting was inbred in us as much as rooting for the Red Sox. Who you fought was not always particularly defined, but often it might be Italians versus Irish. This proved particularly interesting for a young Patrick Rizzo, a half-Italian, half-Irish boy who wanted to be a priest. While the Italians didn't trust me because I was half Irish, the Irish didn't trust me because I was half Italian. Yet, I was a step above the gay kids who were despised by all. In a world where you could get pummeled for making the wrong comment, it paid to hide your sexuality. Many did this by becoming priests. No one questioned you then. The tough guys might think you are crazy to give up girls...but at least you were not gay."

"Wait a minute, your name is Patrick Rizzo? That is a weird combination. Where I come from, they called that a mixed marriage," I interrupted.

"That's better than being called a 'McWop." He smiled. However, from his tone, I knew this story was going to take a serious turn very soon. "Some of those guys were lucky enough to understand how they felt and left the seminary, and in most cases, left town for more welcoming locations. In our area, the closest one was Provincetown, on Cape Cod. At the same time, others headed to further destinations, including here in Key West. Many of them truly were religious and stayed. What was the difference between heterosexual and homosexual celibacy? In both cases, you weren't getting any action—to put it bluntly. However, in certain situations, the religious life was merely a façade —a means of hiding reality. I encountered one such person in my first year as a full-fledged priest.

"Huh? I'm not following. You were a priest, and another priest was gay. How did you know…and why did you care?"

"Because I walked in on him while he was…"

"You're kidding?"

"With an altar boy—a twelve-year-old altar boy."

"Oh, shit."

"I knew the boy and knew he was embarrassed by the situation. Beyond that, I knew nothing about how and why Father Fitzgerald, the bastard, had misused this innocent boy."

"It isn't what it seems," Fitzgerald tried to excuse himself.

"I think it is exactly as it seems, you fucking asshole," I answered.

"Hey, watch your language, we are still in church," he countered.

"Hey shithead, you think that God is going to be upset with my mouth, after what you were doing with yours?"

"I ushered the boy out of the room and walked him home. He was my priority. As we approached his house, he spoke for the first time."

"Father, I want you to hear my confession."

"You did nothing wrong," I tried to console him.

"I don't want to go to hell."

"I thought about counseling him, not to feel guilty, and telling him so much more. At that moment, he knew what he wanted. As he went into vivid detail about all this predator had done to him, I grew angrier. I didn't show it. I stayed calm for the boy's sake and listened. When he was done, he showed me a small smile. I suppose he felt relief that it was over, both with Fitzgerald's actions and the confession.

"At that time, the church's philosophy was to conceal such behavior by reassigning priests. I was going to approach every authority that I knew and tell them what I had seen. However, I feared there would be no repercussions for the bastard. I made one final comment that I will regret for the rest of my life. It was not that I made the comment, but rather that the result was death. I told the boy to tell his parents what had happened.

"Weeks went by, and the boy occasionally came by to talk. He was moving forward and doing reasonably well considering all that he had been through. As expected, Fitzgerald was transferred to a parish a mere ten miles away. I fought with the church authorities. My position was that he should be in jail, or at the very least, the church should strip him of his position while waiting for a more public action. I did not have to worry for long."

"Wait a minute. Are you allowed to tell me any of this?" I interrupted.

"I haven't told you names. I haven't even shared the details with you...and eventually the story did become public knowledge on its own. I am speaking in generalities, but I am still pushing the boundaries of confidential confessions. But you needed to hear my story. You forced me to tell you."

"That's your defense?" I smiled, laughing amid the story would have been inappropriate.

"It is, and I'm sticking to it."

He became very serious.

About a week after Fitzgerald was transferred, a man came into the confessional.

"Are you Father Rizzo?"

"Yes."

"I want to know if it's true that Father Fitzgerald was transferred because he was abusing the altar boys?"

"I'm sorry, but that is between him and God."

I didn't flat-out say yes or no. The church had sworn me to secrecy, which meant shit to me besides losing my job. However, the boy's confession had locked me into knowing the entire story under the seal of confession. Therefore, I adhered to the excuse provided by the church leadership.

"Bullshit! You know. You caught them. My son told me so today," said the man angrily to me.

I said nothing.

"Okay. We'll do it your way. I want to make my confession."

"Go ahead," I said with trepidation.

"Fitzgerald molested my son. My son told me so this morning."

"This is not your confession," I interrupted, thinking he was merely trying to still get information from me.

"Oh yes, it is. Give me three Hail Marys to say. I blew the bastard Fitzgerald's brains out this morning."

52

END OF THE LINE

"Well, it's all right, even if the sun don't shine.
Well, it's all right we're going to the end of the line."
- The Traveling Wilburys

Father Rizzo's Confession

*C*haos reigned in my life from that moment on. With the police on the case, I was asked several questions about both the boy and his father. I answered none. I not only respected the boy's privacy but was bound by the seal of confession with the father. I was also asked questions by my superiors, who already knew more of the story than the police and wanted to keep it that way. They didn't want the story of a pedophile being murdered after the church did nothing to punish him for his violations of both religious and civil law. It was a scandal waiting to happen, and I was in the middle of it. Although the police were not entirely sure of my role, my name appeared in relation to the story in all the Boston papers.

Was I a pedophile like my superior, Father Fitzgerald? Had I been covering for him? What did I know? Many in the city assumed that it was Fitzgerald who had confessed to me, and I had done nothing. Eventually, the storm died down, and people came to understand that the whole matter had been settled with "street justice." There was almost a party when the boy's father made a plea deal that involved only probation as a punishment. In confessing to the civil authorities, he told the entire story as I have relayed it to you, and so I did not reveal anything that I was not permitted to. However, I was toast as far as being a functioning priest in Boston.

"But you did nothing wrong," I tried to console him

"Didn't I?" Father Rizzo answered with a very pained look on his face.

"No, not from my point of view."

"From my point of view, I did plenty wrong." He now grew increasingly agitated.

"I didn't find out about the pervert sooner. It was happening right under my eyes."

"Not your fault, your job description doesn't include being a private investigator...does it?"

"I should have pushed the church leaders to do more to Fitzgerald besides simply hiding him in another parish."

"The Catholic Church's hierarchy has moved slowly for over two thousand years, and you think you could have somehow changed that. I think there's more that's bothering you, Father. What is really bugging you?" He thought for a long while, and I could see the sadness in his eyes.

"The boy..."

"What about the boy?"

"I should have walked him all the way home, and I should have spoken to his parents that very day."

"But the boy confessed to you, and so you couldn't tell them."

"Not true, I could tell what I saw."

"I wouldn't beat yourself up about it."

"I wanted to move on...start over. The cardinal couldn't get me far enough away. He had a friend in the diocese down here and pawned me off on them."

"I would say we are the lucky ones to have you."

"What have you known me...less than an hour, and you think you can tell that I'm good?"

"Didn't I tell you. That's my superpower." With that, we both smiled.

"I'm trying to start over here in Key West."

"How's that going?"

"It isn't. No one ever comes in here. This is literally the end of the line. A few blocks down is a sign that is Mile Marker 0 of US Route 1. There is no more road in America, and you can't go any farther without getting wet. You're the first person to come in here on a weekday in ages."

"So maybe you should go to them," I blurted out, not thinking about what that meant. "Go to where those who need you are. Don't sit in this church expecting them to come to you."

"Yes, yes, that's it. People who need help are not in here—they're out there. That's where I need to be."

———

I volunteered at the church during my final months in the Navy. I set up a food bank for those who drank more of their meals than they should. I organized and scheduled AA meetings while Father Rizzo combed the back alleys and beaches looking to help those who needed it. Most importantly, I attended most of his counseling sessions— listening and learning. I knew I wanted to help people the way Father did, but without the religious commitment. Though looking back at all these years, my social life wasn't much different than a religious person who took a vow of celibacy. I have been helping people for almost two decades, and it is only recently that I have tried to help myself. I really am going to work on that.

He and I became very good friends, and I still visit him from time to time. He helped me through a difficult period and started me on my life's work of counseling. I like to think that I had a small part in the beginnings of his mission, which has helped so many. Eventually, he did receive some notoriety.

People magazine did a whole spread on him in 1986. By then, he had let his hair and beard grow out and looked like the Baltimore Catechism version of Jesus. He was single-handedly ministering to the addicted and destitute. The magazine called him the "Saint of the Key-Wasted." A funny thing was that Father Rizzo did not want his real name used and insisted that the article refer to him only by the name everyone in the Keys knew him by. Ever the humble individual, he wanted the emphasis to be on the mission rather than the man.

He served in anonymity, not wishing any credit for all his good works. Therefore, the title of the People piece read. "Saint of the Key-Wasted...a Man Named Padre."

53

I'VE BEEN LONELY TOO LONG

"I can see me lost and searching
Now I find that I can choose, I'm free.
I've been lonely too long."
- The Young Rascals

Maggie's Memos and Memories

"And so, Aylin, now you know everything. You know why I haven't loved or been loved since 1975. You know why I have built a wall around my heart to protect it from being broken. Why I haven't had any relationships, serious or otherwise, since the day I buried Danny Boy. Padre might be my only real friend in this world."

"You have us," interjected Aylin.

"Yeah, that's gonna take some getting used to."

"We're going to get you out of that shell. Get you to meet people. Get you a damn life."

"I think I might be ready."

Aylin and DJ smiled at me. It had been a long day, and they had fixed up a room for me to crash in. However, specific vivid memories resurfaced in my consciousness while I was telling the story. First, there was the recurring memory of having heard "Thief of My Forever" sung in Reilly's Pub all those years ago. Had I imagined that?

I had been so enamored with Danny Boy that I never pursued the issue. Should I have? That will forever remain a mystery. It's not like I am going barhopping years later trying to find the elusive Captain Jack Paradise. If I cared, I could ask Padre the next time I call him if he knows of this guy.

I had a sudden brainstorm. I knew that DJ had taken up the guitar. Indeed, for many years, my newly discovered brother-in-law had been a member of the famous Chris Delaney and the Brotherhood Blues Band. He had written most of their hit songs and had a Grammy sitting on the mantle of the fireplace that blazed not five feet from me. He had only quit the band to take care of Aylin after her near-death incident.

"DJ, can you sing 'Thief of My Forever' for me again?" I asked.

"Er...I will, but I don't like to. I swore I would never play it for anyone except Aylin. It's not right. Johnny, Bracko, and the others should be the only ones who ever perform it. I sang it for you the other day to help you to understand."

"DJ, Maggie was there when they wrote it. She is family."

"I know that."

Reluctantly, DJ picked up his guitar and looked at me with resignation and sadness. He tuned the instrument and then looked me straight in the eyes, as if saying, "Do I have to?" I nodded as if he had spoken those very words. He began to play and sing the song somberly. I could tell this was hard for him. When he was finished, I looked him in the face with a logical question, at least, to me.

"DJ, weren't you even tempted to record that song with Chris Delaney's band when you were with them?"

His response came in a tone as close to rage as I have ever seen in my soft-spoken, mild-mannered brother-in-law.

"Never, never will the songs of Those Born Free be played or sung in public until I can play and sing them with Johnny. They had a whole album worth of hits that we could have done with Chris Delaney. However, we all agreed it was a sacrilege to do them now... or ever."

"I'm sorry I brought it up," I reacted defensively.

"No, I'm sorry I jumped all over you. It's just that the whole Nicky Toto-Mad Guy Provenzano thing is bringing it all back to me — and not in a good way.

I attempted to distract him from that.

"Do you know the other songs that they practiced in our basement?"

"I should, I wrote all or part of most of them...and I wrote and still write most of the songs that Chris Delaney and the Brotherhood Blues Band perform."

"Wow, I am impressed that I am related by marriage to rock royalty. Did you write their biggest hit, "Dancing on the Other Side of the Wind?"

DJ hung his head, not replying at first. Without any elaboration, he mumbled, "Yeah."

'Hey, Dumbshit, tell her about that song...or I will," interjected Aylin.

"Go ahead," DJ conceded with the air of surrender.

"Really?"

"Yes, really."

"Maggie, the band...DJ's band wanted to perform the Those Born Free catalogue of songs, but DJ steadfastly refused. They had a record contract and no obvious hit song to headline it."

"Well, we did have one prospective hit... 'I Could Love You, If You Live' and I was even reluctant about that one."

"Why? I remember it from the early 1970s. It wasn't your biggest hit, but it made the top ten. Why didn't you lead with that?" I was confused.

Now it was Aylin's turn to hang her head, yet she nodded to DJ, telling him it was okay to tell me that story.

"The song is about…it's about your sister."

Aylin nodded her head.

"She had almost died from a drug overdose at Woodstock, and while I sat at her bedside, not knowing if she would make it, I started to sing to her."

DJ looked down at the guitar that he still held and started to play and sing.

I could love you,
If you live.
But that doesn't seem to be.

Lines down your arm
Are doing you harm.
And it's breakin' my heart to see.

He stopped and looked at Aylin, trying to decide if this was too painful for her. She made a hand sign for him to continue.

I could love you
If you live.
But that doesn't seem to be.

That monkey got a hold.
Of your damn soul.
Won't you listen to my plea?

He stopped, and Aylin reached down and pulled up the sleeves of her blouse to reveal arms that had been untouched for almost two decades. She then took her husband's hand.

"But still, we didn't think we had that one big hit. The band members were all easy-going guys, but there was a bit of tension. Should we do Those Born Free songs...or not?" It was then that I devised a solution, a compromise. Instead of a song *by* that band, I wrote a song *about* Those Born Free... 'Dancing on the Other Side of the Wind.'"

"I never knew what that song was about, but I loved it. Its meaning was lost on me, but then again, in those years, I was preoccupied with Danny Boy and the good times and bad."

"Well, Miss Maggie, as Bracko used to call you, you of all people should have, or could have gotten some of the symbolism. Where do you think I got the idea for 'Dancing?' It was that whole thing about you and Michael and that whole 'dancing fingers' routine."

"You're kidding me?"

"Just before Bracko died, he told me about Michael and his mother...and how dancing was a symbol of living and loving...and all things good. And so, when the band died, I couldn't help thinking that they were still 'dancing' ... living and loving...on the other side. The metaphor fit perfectly. I was already writing the book about them, and, as I told you, I was considering the title *A Band Lost in the Wind*. It seemed the logical next step to write the song that they were dancing on the other side of that wind. So, Maggie, you were a part of that hit."

I didn't feel like I had done anything special, but I thanked DJ for making me feel valued. I was moved by the fact that two people cared about me. I said goodnight to them and went to the guest bedroom, hoping for a good night's sleep.

In the middle of the night, I awoke. The discussion about Michael and me finger-dancing brought back a memory that had long been locked in my unconscious brain. In the vast depression following the death of my husband, Danny Boy, I had thrown myself into charity and volunteer work with Padre. Yet still music, as always, was my constant companion. I listened to the radio in the car while running errands for the mission. I had a small transistor radio in my room, which played music that would calm me enough to sleep.

That same radio sat on a shelf while I meticulously organized the foodstuffs for Padre. I was a bit OCD when it came to organizing the donated food. I was lost in the menial tasks that could take my mind off the loss of my husband, and listening to "Oldies" on the radio helped.

This was 1975, and I found it amusing that the music of the 1960s was now considered old. But it was. The Disco craze was in full bloom, and that music made me want to vomit. Oh, my poor Bee Gees, who had created such great songs in the '60s like "To Love Somebody" and "Massachusetts," had morphed into the falsetto singers of "Stayin' Alive." Yet, as I tossed and turned sleeplessly in the bed, my mind recollected something that had been lodged in some secluded region of my unconscious memories.

My small radio had fallen, and as I tried to retune to my favorite oldies channel, I came upon a radio station playing new music that wasn't disco. The loud, manic musing of the disc jockeys belied the fact that he was playing new, mellow tunes reminiscent of a bygone era. It was a style of music reminiscent of the 1960s. I listened because I found the whole concept amusing—a revival of music that was only five to ten years old. Then, a song came on that shook me to my very core. At another time or place in my existence, I would have sought out more information about the tune. I would have needed to know who wrote and sang it. I would have either verified or rejected my conclusions about this person.

How old would Michael be, 17 or 18, in 1975? How could he have recorded a hit tune? Yet as I listened to the clear-voiced lyrics of the song, I knew that it had to be Michael, as the singer softly proclaimed in a very melodic voice...

The end should never be the end,
That's why I always dance with the lost.
Dance with the lost.

However, I decided to focus on my current endeavors. Maybe someday I would...

54

DANCING WITH THE LOST

"The end should never be the end.
That's why I always dance with the lost."
- Powerhouse

Excerpt from The Queens Undies

*I*n 1968, a Queens College sophomore named DJ Spinelli was excluded from participating in his college newspaper due to favoritism and politics. Wishing to write anyway, he created an independent alternative paper, which he named the "Queens Undies." It circulated the college campus and was well received. Eventually, it focused its articles on the burgeoning music scene of the late 1960s. Its creator, however, eventually dropped out of college and abandoned the paper. In its place, he pursued a very successful career as a songwriter and guitarist with an extremely popular band known as Chris Delaney and the Brotherhood Blues Band.

In 1975, an English major looking for a creative outlet for his writing found some old copies of the "Queens Undies" while poking

DANCING WITH THE LOST

around some neglected closets in an underutilized classroom. Jason Karzakian decided to recreate the popular music paper of the previous author. He sought permission from the original creator, D.J. Spinelli, who wrote back, "Thrilled...go for it!"

Karzakian decided that his inaugural issue would feature an interview with the very young lead singer of a group named Powerhouse, whose first single was topping the charts. Not coincidentally, they were due to perform at the college that very night. Considering that the interviewer and the interviewee were of the same age, it seemed that the conversation would go smoothly.

Though the singer was pleasant and cooperative, many of his answers were enigmatic. When Karzakian tried to probe deeper, he was left wondering what this guy's real story was. It would be the only known interview of the singer who went by the stage name of "Mickey Bracko," but whose real name was Michael Powers.

"Queens' Tragedy Creates Beautiful Music"
May 13, 1975
By Jason Karzakian

Unlike many of the overly made-up groups of today (think KISS), Powerhouse is a relatively clean-cut, low-key band. Their number one hit "Dancing with the Lost" has risen quickly on the charts and portends a great future for the Los Angeles-based group. They offer an alternative to the heavy metal and disco genres that dominate the current music scene.

I spoke with lead singer and guitarist Mickey Bracko while Powerhouse took a break from doing a sound check at our own Colden Auditorium. While he freely admits that Mickey Bracko is not his real name, the singer was evasive in discussing many topics from his past life. However, he is an incredibly endearing individual whose ever-present smile and positive attitude seem to be too good to be true.

Karzakian: *So, Mickey, how are you enjoying your tour of New York?*
Mickey Bracko: *I'm loving it. It brings back old memories—both good and bad.*
Karzakian: *Explain, please.*
Mickey Bracko: *I was born and raised in Queens...at least until the age of nine.*
Karzakian: *And then?*
Mickey Bracko: *Well, I was lucky enough to be adopted after my mom passed away in late 1967. My new family moved out of state, and I left behind my whole world.*
Karzakian: *First of all, I'd like to offer my condolences on your loss. It must have been tough to lose someone at such a young age.*
Mickey Bracko*: I didn't just lose my mom. I lost everything else in my life. I lost all my friends too. When my mom was in her final stages of cancer, I had the support of a large group of friends. There was a girl named Maggie, who was a little older than me, and she would often come to visit and comfort me when I was feeling down. I never got to say goodbye to her or all the others.*
Karzakian*: Others?*
Mickey Bracko: *In the final days of my mother's life, my next-door neighbor, a kid younger than I am now, took both my mother and me under his wing. He would bring us food, help me clean the house, and give my mother her meds. He even helped me with my homework. But most importantly, he taught me the guitar.*
Karzakian: *Wow, this guy must be very proud of you.*
Mickey Bracko: *No, he's dead.*
Karzakian: *How?*
Mickey Bracko: (No answer)
Karzakian: *How did you cope with all that loss?*
Mickey Bracko: *My mother had a little game she played with me toward the end. She always told me that she would dance with me at my wedding. She always said to me that slow dancing always brought the hearts of two people as close as they could be...and that it was the ultimate symbol of love. As she grew weaker and weaker and couldn't get out of bed, she would have*

me sit beside her, and we would mimic dancing with each other by making our middle and index fingers into dancing couples. It was all she could do. We called it finger-dancing. We were doing it when she...

Karzakian: *It seems symbolic of a beautiful relationship between you and your mother.*

Mickey Bracko: *Funny thing about it is that Mom told me to share it with anyone and everyone I cared about. And so, I shared it with Maggie, and I shared it with...*

Karzakian: *The guitarist?*

Mickey Bracko*: Yeah, him.*

Karzakian: *Why so mysterious about him?*

Mickey Bracko: *I don't know. However, I must tell you that I have never discussed the topics I am sharing with you in this interview.*

Karzakian*: I am honored that you chose me instead of the writers from Rolling Stone or Jamz.*

Mickey Bracko: *(chuckles) You're a young guy like me...just looking for a break. I feel comfortable speaking with you.*

Karzakian: *Thanks*

Mickey Bracko: *His name was Rocco Brackowski, but everyone called him Bracko.*

Karzakian: *Your...your...name.*

Mickey Bracko: *Yeah, Bracko. I use it as a stage name as a tribute to him. I will never be half as good as he was.*

Karzakian: *Now you're being too humble.*

Mickey Bracko: *You never heard Bracko play.*

Karzakian: *True.*

Mickey Bracko: *Above and beyond the guitar, Bracko and Maggie were everything to me in my mother's final days. But there were others. Maggie and her two sisters, Aylin and Siobhan, took me under their wing at practices.*

Karzakian: *Practices?*

Mickey Bracko: *Bracko was part of a band named Those Born Free. Every moment that I could leave my mother safely, I would go and watch their practices. It was my salvation. Music saved my sanity. But it was not just the joy of hearing great music, but also the feeling of being part of something* *special. There was camaraderie among all those at the practices. The other four band members also treated me like a younger brother, and so did Maggie's sisters and other people who attended the practices.*

Karzakian: *That seems special.*

Mickey Bracko: *It was. Whenever Maggie saw me getting depressed, she would smile at me and then point down at her hands, with her two fingers in a position to dance. I would feel better. Sometimes Bracko would be playing the guitar, and somehow his fingers would move in little dance-like motions.*

Karzakian: *And so that all ended when your mother passed away?*

Mickey Bracko: *No, it ended way before. In July of 1967, when I was still eight years old, Bracko died in a house fire. There would be no more band practices, no more lessons, and no more visits. Maggie would come by my house and try to cheer me up for the first few months.*

Karzakian: *And then?*

Mickey Bracko: *One of the last times I saw Maggie we walked two miles to the cemetery to say goodbye to Bracko. Without even thinking, we both went up to his headstone and danced with him...dancing with our fingers.*

Karzakian: *I...I'm at a loss for words.*

Mickey Bracko: *Maggie's father and brother Jimmy had died in a robbery of their family store. My eight-year-old mind could not comprehend two tragedies so close together. Then, in late November, my mom passed away, and I had no one. There was no one to dance with. They were all gone...lost.*

Karzakian: *Now I understand. Now I get it. You...*

Mickey Bracko: *I was left to dance with the lost.*

For those readers who have not heard or have not truly understood the words, I've asked Mickey Bracko's permission to reprint them here.

Dancing with the Lost
By Powerhouse (written by Michael Powers)

Life shouldn't be so hard.
It shouldn't be so real.
It shouldn't cause you pain
It shouldn't make us feel

Yet Dancing brings us heart to heart
It bonds our souls together
It brings us love
A love that lasts forever

Chorus
I've felt that kind of love
Yet it always has a cost
The end should never be the end
And so, I dance with the lost
Yes, I dance with the lost

Very few have come
and touched me inside
I gave to them
What from the world I hide

Those with whom I've danced
Whose feelings shared so deep
I gave them all of me
Even as they now sleep

Chorus
I've felt that kind of love
Yet it always has a cost
The end should never be the end
And so, I dance with the lost
Yes, I dance with the lost.

Only twelve people read the interview, and the paper soon folded after its second issue. It certainly was not seen by Maggie McAvoy Evers, who was stationed on a naval base in Key West, Florida. She was busy making funeral arrangements for her recently deceased husband.

55

IT'S MY LIFE

"It's my life, it's now or never,
But I ain't gonna live forever.
I just wanna live while I'm alive."
- Bon Jovi

Michael's Story

*M*ichael Powers (alias Mickey Bracko) never told the whole story in his interview—the entire story of his past...and the probable story of his future.

Michael was alone for the last days of his mother's life until...out of the blue, a married couple decided to take him in. He only knew them as people who had taken pity on him after the fire next door took Bracko's life and left him with no support. They had seen and heard about the fire and made Michael their son.

The adoption story had a dark side. Though the couple took Michael in, it was out of pity, not love. When they moved out of state, he lost touch with his past, including Maggie, who had been more like a sister than a friend. His new home was full of arguments between the husband and wife. Confused, he kept to himself and focused on his guitar, following the pattern that his idol, Bracko, had used to escape reality.

In 1971, when Michael was fourteen, his adoptive parents separated, and his "mother" moved back with relatives in New York. Away from the influence of his "father," his mother became a much calmer and loving person, and for three years, Michael had a relatively normal existence on Long Island. A genuine bond of love developed between them. Yet, when his mother considered reconciliation with his "father," Michael left home. He felt bad for leaving his "mother" and hoped that his act of defiance would help her reconsider her choices. It didn't work.

Michael took what little money he had and hopped a bus for points west, eventually making it to Los Angeles. As a broke and homeless high school dropout, his prospects were bleak. The one thing he did have going for him was his guitar playing, and he was quickly involved in the area's music scene. He assembled a group of musicians who would mesh perfectly with the sound he envisioned.

They got their big break when a talent agent saw them performing at a local club and soon signed them to a record contract. From there, it was a roller coaster ride to stardom. He poured his heart out into their hit song "Dancing with the Lost," and soon, they were on a whirlwind tour to promote their album, named Powerhouse I.

But soon the wheels came off. While the rest of the musicians in his group were gifted in playing their instruments, they were not as gifted in their personalities. There were constant fights brought on by a case of attaining fame way too fast. Two of the members of the group were seriously developing drug dependencies.

By the time Michael Powers gave his interview to Jason Karzakian, he could see the writing on the wall. There would be no future with Powerhouse, and surprisingly, it did not bother him at all. He had said what he had to say musically with the songs he had written. In truth, he did not like the life of a rock star and longed for the stability that he had never had.

Powerhouse would join the never-ending list of "one-hit-wonder" groups. Yet, with complete rights to all the songs on the album that they had produced, Michael Powers was now financially secure. His path was clear when his "mother" announced she was leaving his "father" for good.

He returned home to Long Island, New York, and this time, he was financially independent. He purchased a small house for the two of them, located far from the city, and chose a path for the rest of his life. He went back to school, obtained his GED, and earned a college degree from Stony Brook University. By 1982, he secured a position as a music teacher in a Suffolk County school district. At last, he achieved a level of stability that allowed him to relax and enjoy life.

PART V

ON THE DARK SIDE

"The dark side's coming,
And nothing is real."
- John Cafferty and the Beaver Brown Band (from the movie Eddie
and the Cruisers)

June 8, 1990

WITH A LITTLE HELP
FROM MY FRIENDS

"I'm gonna try with a little help from my friends."
- Joe Cocker (by way of the Beatles)

Maggie's Memos and Memories

*D*ue to legal issues, I have been unable to speak to Nicky Toto. After he agreed to testify and enter the Witness Protection Program, the DA's office cut off my contact with him to avoid any potential disruptions. They did not consider that they had only gotten this far because of me.

During this period of inactivity, I have readjusted my life and my priorities. I rented a house near my sister Aylin and her family. The house is located on Lake Panamoka, where I often spend my weekends, reflecting on my life. This reflection is to prepare me for the future. Meanwhile, I met my nephew, Robbie Mac, whom I adore and look forward to getting to know better once this whole Provenzano/Toto game is done.

Yet, I couldn't help but feel a pang of frustration at being sidelined.

The nights spent piecing together fragments of information and the hours spent convincing Nicky to take the leap feel so far away, overshadowed by the bureaucracy of the law. But I must remind myself that the goal is bigger than me. Justice, after all, is a team effort. Yet revenge will be mine alone.

Still, there were glimpses of light among the darkness. Memories of how far we had come lift my spirits. I could remember Nicky's hesitant nod when he finally agreed to testify, his face pale but resolute. Those moments were my victories.

Nicky has continued his normal routine while arrangements are being made for Mad Guy's arrest in June. He informed his cousin that he was visiting friends in Atlantic City. In reality, he is currently in a safe house in Queens.

As for myself, I am moving forward. I will never forget my father, my brother, and the friends I lost in 1967. I will also remember Danny Boy, despite the brevity of our time together. My "third little pig" persona has helped me thus far, but I feel ready to leave that "brick house" and experience the real world. Although I still feel apprehensive about the future, I sought support. I contacted my friend Padre yesterday. He provided encouragement and boosted my confidence.

"Maggie, you are a significant presence in this world. Do not forget it," said Padre.

"No, Padre, YOU are the significant presence in this world. You have saved many lives down there. I have done nothing to compare to your mission in Key West."

"A mission, I will remind you, Maggie, that was your idea. Did you forget that? I was in a quiet state of malaise, content to wait for people to walk into my church. You, my dear, kicked me in the ass and got me moving."

"So, how's the body and soul saving business been going down there? I'm sorry I haven't been able to visit in a few years."

"I can't do enough, but even one human saved is a small miracle that I thank God for each night."

"How are you handling everything all by yourself?"

"I'm not. I have always had a series of recovering alcoholics who offer to help with the day-to-day chores, so I am free to work with the people."

"That's good to hear."

"Yeah, right now I have this wonderful man, Jack...he helps me with everything. He mows the lawns, paints, and does maintenance on the church...I mean everything."

For a split second, I thought of asking Padre if Jack's last name just happened to be Paradise, but then I remembered his credo. As close as I was to Padre, he was never going to break his rule of keeping all his charges anonymous. Hell, he even kept himself anonymous—using Padre instead of Father Rizzo.

"I wish I could come and help you out down there, but I am tied up."

"Maggie, you've done more for me than anyone else on this planet. Besides, it sounds like you're on the right path with your relationship with your sister. Grab all the good times you can get. You've suffered more than many people twice your age. You lived through the tragedy of your family...and the loss of Danny Boy. And yet you have accomplished so much. You served your country, you got me started on my mission, and now you are helping innumerable patients work through their problems with therapy."

"I couldn't have done it without you. I never would be the therapist I am without learning from you how to be empathetic."

"Maggie, you were always the one quoting songs from the sixties."

"So?"

"Remember the one by the group America? I think the song was called "Tin Man?" There's a line that fits our relationship. 'Oz never did give nothing to the Tin Man...that he didn't already have.' I couldn't have helped you find your calling if it wasn't already inside you to help people and understand them. Don't you ever forget that."

"Well, maybe."

"There is no maybe about it. Don't ever think that you haven't done your share of good in this world...Maggie...hold on a second."

"Padre...you there?"

"Sorry, Maggie, I gotta go, we just got a big donation of food for the pantry...Jack, please put it in the basement. Okay, bye, sweetheart...be strong. I know you'll always do the right thing."

Padre got me to thinking about all the people I had helped in life. I knew I could do this. I could get Nicky to tell the truth on the stand... and in the process, perhaps, give him some peace.

Besides Nicky, I still had an important job to do. My current roster of clients (we don't call them patients anymore) includes Josef, the Holocaust survivor, a burn victim suffering through the mental and physical trauma of having his face disfigured, various women, and one man whose partners physically abused them.

One of my specialties is grief counseling for people who have suffered the loss of a loved one. Gee, how did I end up working on that? With Padre's pep talk, I was ready to return to the city and help with Nicky Toto's finale.

DEATH IS NOT THE END

"Not the end, not the end
Just remember that death is not the end."
- Bob Dylan

Maggie's Memos and Memories
June 15, 1990

*I*t's over. Just like that, all the efforts of all of us to bring Mad Guy Provenzano to his day of reckoning were for naught. The FBI, as well as local NYC police, were set to execute a raid to arrest Provenzano for the death of Bracko last week. Except it didn't happen. Guy went missing the night before his D-Day, and it was suspected that he had gotten advanced warning and fled.

That fallacy was debunked when his body washed up on a Connecticut shore. He had drowned in the Long Island Sound. If anyone briefly suspected that this had been a boating accident, they were dissuaded by the fact that his brother Tony's body washed up a day later with numerous bullet holes in his torso.

The current narrative has a rival gang boarding the boat. When they attempted to take Guy, Tony bravely stepped in front and was taken down. I find that hard to believe because for the last decade or so, Tony had deteriorated to the point where he barely functioned as a human being. Yet Tony was a loyal person; however, probably not to his brother, who treated him like absolute shit.

Blood was found on the lower deck of the boat, but so far, it is not a match to Tony or anyone in any recorded database. I suppose that in the next few months, the authorities will sort everything out. At least, I hope they will.

June 16

I have returned to my home office in Astoria. I am waiting for Nicky to make contact, as there has been no communication from him since the discovery of Guy and Tony's bodies. The safe house was left empty, and the federal marshals responsible for Nicky's protection are undergoing disciplinary action due to procedural failures. The official explanation stated that, following Mad Guy's death, their presence was deemed unnecessary. There is uncertainty regarding whether they were involved in the incident.

Some suspect Nicky of the crime, but after knowing him for over six months, I doubt he is capable of killing. He deeply regretted giving in to Guy on one or two occasions, but that hardly seems enough motive to kill. I need to speak with him.

Other theories include a wide variety of suspects, ranging from members of Desiderio Gomez's gang to internal members of Provenzano's gang, and even his own family. Guy was feared but not loved. Yet, did anyone have enough balls to do something about it?

The Gomez theory appears to be the most sensible. After all, the police records showed that Guy had (allegedly) sent Joey Pasco and Nicky Toto to kill the rival gang chief. However, there was no proof that anyone in that gang had tried anything. They had a motive, but did they have the opportunity? Perhaps whoever took over leadership

DEATH IS NOT THE END

in either the Gomez or Provenzano gang was happy with the developments as they occurred.

The long-standing rumor has it that it was his cousin and consigliere, Richie Shea. After hearing Nicky talk about Richie, it seemed like he was a man who enjoyed power, but not violence. Nicky often told me that Richie was pleased with where he was. Still, motivation is also strong here because the members of the Five Families of New York recently conferred on Richie the power that had belonged to Guy. Is Richie a wolf in sheep's clothing?

And then there are his sons, or rather his son Dominick. He is often referred to as D-Mon by many who know him. Though only in his early twenties, he has shown a propensity for violence found only in someone as evil as his father. Nicky spoke openly of his fear of his nephew. Perhaps, D-Mon would take out Richie next and claim the throne.

Guy has a second son who was the bane of his father's existence. Carmine Provenzano had left home at 18 to follow a gay lifestyle. He is now a drag queen who performs under the stage name "Carmen Lola Brigitta." According to Nicky, this made both Guy and D-Mon want to order a hit on Carmine/Carmen. However, there is no indication that the prodigal son felt the same way and would have taken his father out first.

So, for now, everything is a mystery. It may stay that way forever. I need to talk to Nicky before I jump to any conclusions. I don't think the murder of Guy will be solved. Too many people are simply saying, "Good riddance."

I can only dream that somehow one of the band members came back from the grave (or in the case of Johnny Cipp, wherever he is) to do the deed. I usually do not encourage violence, but in this case, I would. I really would.

5 8

LOOKING FOR THE
NEXT BEST THING

"That's why I'm looking for the next best thing
Looking for the next best thing."
- Warren Zevon

Provenzano Gang Headquarters

"*M*arone, are you so *stunad* that you don't show any respect to an elder?" he announced as he stood inside the door to the Dew Drop Inn, which housed the reorganizing remnants of the Provenzano crime family and its associates.

"Who the fuck are you?" responded Joey Pasco, who just happened to be the closest one to the door when the outsider walked in. Pasco gave him the once-over. The stranger's jet-black hair was combed straight back on his head. Because Joey estimated the man to be in his sixties, the color was obviously out of a bottle. The matching pencil-thin moustache was something he only saw on the much older generation who did not know or care that it had gone out of style. His clothes were impressive and could have been tailored in the old

258

country, specifically Milan. However, the finishing touch that pinned him as old school was the De Nobili cigar held in his right hand. No one in the entire universe smoked these smelly, crooked little stogies...except maybe the kind of person who would spend their lives playing bocce in the park.

"Hey, *Jamoke*, I got *oogatz* to say to you. I want to see my nephew."

"And who might that be?"

"You *jabroni*, you might find yourself with a stiletto up your ass if you don't talk to me with some *rispetto*. Then again, you probably don't even understand what I'm saying to you because you don't speak Italian. *Stugats*, I doubt if you are even Italian at all."

"You better have some great credentials to speak to me like that, or old man or not, I'm going to beat the shit out of you. And the name is Pasco, and my family is from Calabria."

"And my name is Provenzano, Antonio Provenzano, and my family is from Sicily, and we eat Calabrese punks like you for breakfast. Dominick Provenzano was my brother, and I just lost my nephews, Guy and Tony." With that, the older man took his De Nobili cigar and crushed it into the chest of Joey Pasco. He pushed past him and proceeded to the office located at the rear of the bar. The furious Pasco made an ill-advised attempt to grab the older man but was held back by some of his friends.

"What part of 'Provenzano' didn't you understand?" screamed Donnie "Donuts" Nuzzio as he held Pasco in an arm lock to prevent him from making a terrible mistake. Antonio Provenzano turned his back on the commotion and walked into the office, where he faced a confused Richie Shea, the newly confirmed leader of the family.

"Hello, Nephew."

"I heard every word of your exchange out there. Pasco is an idiot, tough and violent, but more importantly, who the fuck are you? And how come I have no recollection of seeing you?"

"The United States government offered me an all-expenses-paid trip back to Sicily in 1954. I left the empire I had built to be run by my older brother Dominick."

"You were deported."

"That is one way of putting it."

"And now?"

"I am back to claim what is mine."

"Again. Respectfully…over my dead body."

"That could be arranged if that was what I wanted to happen. Death is my specialty."

Shea moved to the door to ensure that reinforcements would be available if he needed them.

His erstwhile uncle held up his hand, smiled, and closed the door.

"That won't be necessary. You see, I'm just having a bit of fun with you. There is no Antonio Provenzano…at least that I know of."

The older man immediately stood up straighter, gaining height. His eyes took on a new, younger, more cunning look. He smiled.

"Let me properly introduce myself…I am The Actor."

59

DEVIL IN DISGUISE

"You're the devil in disguise,
Oh, yes, you are."
- Elvis Presley

Provenzano Headquarters

*A*s Shea's door closed, Joey's anger could not be held in check by his friends. Indeed, attempts to calm him by filling him full of Johnny Walker Black only seemed to fuel his resolve to have it out with the intruder. He had no concept of who he was dealing with.

"Ah, The Actor...I bet you could tell some stories about Guy's vendettas and...well, let's call it what it was...Guy's madness."

"I thought your cousin was a very reasonable and well-paying employer."

"You would. From what Guy told me about you; you were just as crazy as he was—maybe more so."

"Beauty is in the eye of the beholder."

"Okay, let's get down to it. Why are you here? And what do I call you? What did Guy call you in your years of association?"

"Simply, The Actor. That's what Guy called me, though he was the only one who knew my real name…the result of an unfortunate incident more than twenty years ago when I underestimated him. Now, that knowledge has died with him."

"Mr. Actor," began Richie Shea, seemingly to mock the killer facing him, "I will have no use for your services, I do things differently than my cousin."

"We'll see about that, *Lieutenant*," returning the disrespect by using Shea's last police rank. This slight was meant to serve the purpose of showing Shea that he knew every detail of his life. It was also to show that he did not think him ruthless enough to lead the Provenzano gang.

"You've said your piece. There's the door. And I would watch your back. Joey Pasco is a real hot head."

"That amateur, please don't make me laugh."

Richie shrugged. He had warned "The Actor." There was little more he could do.

"You misunderstand. I'm here because I've completed part of a task for Mad Guy. I wanted to know if you wanted me to continue. Guy paid me 5K to snoop on a suspected turncoat in the organization. If and when I got proof of his guilt, he would generously reward me for taking care of the problem."

"We all know what the euphemism 'taking care of the problem' means, and I don't want any part of it."

"Even if it means your entire organization is at risk?"

"Quit beating around the bush. If I understand you correctly, you have already been paid for…er…your research. So, let's have it."

"My, my, aren't you rude. You could have at least offered me a drink."

"Listen, *Mister* Actor, I don't like you...or need you. So, say what you have to say, and please leave. Was that polite enough for you?"

"Okay, but I would like the first shot at the kill after you hear what I have to say."

"Shit or get off the pot. You have already been paid for that part of the job, so spill it."

"Nicky Toto has been talking to the cops and DA for months. He gave them enough that Guy would have been indicted within the week if..." The Actor didn't know how sensitive Richie was about his cousin's demise and therefore didn't finish his sentence.

"I hope that you are intelligent enough to get this pun, but *that ship has sailed*," smirked Shea about Guy's death by drowning while on his boat.

The Actor could handle most insults, but attacking his intelligence infuriated him. However, as always, he controlled himself, thinking maybe he would do something at a later date. Then, he returned to his professional attitude and decided that the investigation into Guy and his organization was no longer his problem. Though he had been looking forward to slitting the throats of Nicky Toto and Dr. Evers—and not just for the paycheck. Without a word, he turned and left Richie Shea's office.

As he left, he returned to his Antonio Provenzano persona, stopping mid-room and lighting his smelly DeNobili cigar and blowing smoke in Joey Pasco's direction before exiting the bar.

60

BAD THINGS

"I don't know who you think you are,
But before the night is through,
I'm goin' to do bad things to you."
- Jace Evers

The Streets of Queens

*J*oey Pasco waited a few minutes before acting. He then rushed to the back door of the bar and exited onto a street that ran parallel to the thoroughfare that ran in front of the bar. He knew that a quarter of a mile away, a dark alley intersected the main street, and there he would trap this asshole, Antonio Provenzano. He would teach him to respect the person the gang always called the "Backdoor Man."

Joey chuckled. He had received this nickname years before, when the Doors' song of the same name was popular. *The men don't know, but the little girls understand* went the lyrics and his tendency to use and abuse other gang members' lady friends had not gone unnoticed. Yet, few had had the nerve to confront Pasco. He was violent, and maybe just a little bit nuts.

However, today he truly was a *Backdoor Man*—quite literally. At the exact location that he had chosen, he sprang from the shadows with his sharpened stiletto in hand. He held it to the throat of his disguised target, never knowing that he was dealing with a much younger and agile opponent.

The Actor, for his part, stayed in character and did so with his usual calmness.

"A-ha, the Backdoor Man strikes."

"How do you know my nickname, you old piece of shit?" countered Pasco, losing some of his calmness to anger.

"Little foolish Joey, I know many, many things about just about everything. Oh, and I am not an old piece of shit, as you called me, but rather…"

With that, the elder Provenzano character disappeared, and his entire demeanor and voice changed as he spoke, "I think it is just the right time for you to meet The Actor."

Without missing a beat while speaking, The Actor's Cuban heeled boot rose and then rapidly descended to crush Pasco's right foot. This action caused his assailant to flinch ever so slightly, but enough for The Actor's right hand to grab the wrist that held the stiletto, forcing its owner to drop the weapon. A quick blow to the Solar Plexus caused Pasco to lose his breath and fall to the dirty pavement inside the darkened alleyway.

"I like mine better," mocked The Actor as he now pulled out *his* stiletto, which was significantly larger. He placed the blade so that it was just beneath Pasco's left eye.

"Can we talk about this? I didn't know who you were. I…I idolize you and what you have done for Guy through the years."

"Why, thank you. But…flattery will get you nowhere, and I am going to give you a little reminder of your run-in with me. Well, then again, it will only be a reminder if I decide to let you live."

With that, the Actor slid the blade down Pasco's cheek, creating a four inch gash from his upper cheek to his jaw. He expected Joey to scream like a banshee at the incision, but instead the victim just stared at him, showing a toughness that The Actor had never expected.

"Backdoor Man is a weak nickname. From now on, your friends can call you 'Scarface.' You know, like 'Scarface' Al Capone." Pasco said nothing but merely stared right into the eyes of The Actor.

"So, if my friends are going to call me that, it would mean that I will see them again." The blood from his cheek ran into his mouth. He spat it out defiantly, but not in the direction of The Actor.

"You know, I think you are right. You are a lot tougher than I thought. A bit stupid, but you've got guts, and I like that. More guts than your new boss, that's for sure."

The Actor helped Pasco off the floor and handed him a handkerchief to staunch the bleeding on his cheek.

"What does that mean? You don't respect the Provenzano family?"

"I did, but not with Shea in charge." The Actor thought long and hard before he continued. He had never shared any thoughts, feelings, or information about anything to anyone else in this world. However, Shea had disrespected him, and therefore, he owed him no professional courtesy. Indeed, he could exact a bit of revenge.

"The coward wouldn't act on the information that I gave him. Information that could change *your* life."

"Okay, now you have my attention," Pasco anxiously responded, patting the handkerchief on his still bleeding wound.

"Nicky Toto was goin' state's evidence against Guy. He was giving them a murder conviction on a silver platter in return for his own chickenshit life."

"That motherfucking rat...yeah, but none of that matters with Guy being dead and all," Pasco remarked disappointedly.

The Actor let out a bellowing laugh.

"What's so funny?"

"Maybe you are as stupid as I originally thought. With Guy gone, who is Nicky going to trade for his freedom? Think the Gomez murder...think the Rothstein murder two decades ago."

"Dammit, sonofabitch, how do you know all this shit?"

"My methods remain my secret. However, I will mention that Nicky spilled his guts to his therapist, Dr. Evers."

The Actor could see the fury building in Joey Pasco. He would truly miss out on "taking care of" Evers and Toto. The sadist in him, unfortunately, would not receive his pound of flesh. However, he took some vicarious joy in knowing that they would be "taken care of." He might even help the effort along—just for fun.

61

COME ALIVE

"We wake up in the morning,
Some of us in Heaven
Most of us in Hell."
- Capt. Kirk Douglas and Hundred Watt Heart

The Streets of Queens

*T*he Actor knew that Joey Pasco was going to do something. He also knew that The Back Door Man had no idea where to find either Dr. Evers or Nicky Toto. Indeed, no one knew where Toto was since he had slipped out of protective custody.

Interestingly, the only person with whom The Actor had shared any human feelings had been Mad Guy Provenzano. Perhaps it was their shared love of sadism, or maybe the longevity of their association, that made The Actor miss the mob boss.

"Okay, Joey *Scarface,* I am going to help you get the ball rolling. In memory of our dear departed comrade, Guy, I am going to help you out this one time—no charge. Meet me at 24—15 23rd Street in

Astoria in two hours. Be smart enough not to be seen by the inhabitant."

"And who the fuck is the inhabitant?"

"The eminent Dr. Maggie *McAvoy*-Evers."

"Wait…wait the doctor is…."

"Yes indeed. She is one of the McAvoy clan who so annoyed Guy. And none of you *jamokes* figured it out. It is no wonder the gang never progressed as it should."

Pasco was going to complain or maybe defend his gang. But in the end, he realized he didn't care. It was all about survival—his survival. If this mysterious Actor could help, who was he to argue?

Exactly two hours later, Pasco stood at the rendezvous location alone. Had The Actor played him? Eventually, he noticed an extremely old man shuffling down the street. His yarmulke was askew on his head, and Joey had the impression that the very senior citizen's next step could be his last. His glasses were so thick that it was hard to ascertain the color of the eyes that lay behind them.

"Nice work on the cheek," commented the octogenarian. Joey had taken the opportunity during the layover to have his face stitched by a local mob medicine man, an unlicensed doctor who was paid well to do his job and tell no tales.

"Actor?"

"No shit, Sherlock."

"I never would have known."

"Umm, that's the general idea. I am beginning to think I overestimated you. Never mind, here's the plan. I go in, and when the doctor is subdued, I will signal you to enter. Then I leave, and you are on your own. Mad Guy can thank me from hell."

"But how?"

"I play the long game. I have been Dr. Evers' patient for four months, just waiting for a moment like this when I might need to get close to her…very close."

With that, he walked off and right up to Dr. Evers' office door.

Holocaust survivor, Josef Stern, held a special spot in Maggie McAvoy-Evers' heart, and The Actor knew it. She would never refuse to see him while he played this role. Today was no different.

"Josef, how are you?" Maggie greeted him almost automatically with that phrase every time she saw him. This time, she could see the answer on his face. He was not well.

"*Chavver, devenen*...please," moaned the erstwhile "Josef."

"I don't understand, Josef. You know I have picked up some of your Yiddish, but..."

"Friend, pray for *mir*, um me."

"Come in, Josef. Come in and talk to me."

The Actor shuffled in, seeming so bereft with grief that he could barely walk. Maggie led him to the couch, helped him into his seat, and then sat beside him.

"My Rifka...she is gone."

"Oh, no," responded Maggie in a very unprofessional tone.

The Actor, in his role as Josef, began to wail uncontrollably, and Maggie pulled him into her embrace, letting him cry on her shoulder. She couldn't see the broad smile spreading across The Actor's face. She remained unaware of the hypodermic needle hidden in his right hand. She would remain unaware of anything at all for quite a while. After laying the unconscious Dr. Evers on the couch, The Actor signaled Joey Pasco to join him in her office.

"She will be unconscious for about fifteen minutes. The paralytic drug will make it impossible for her to move even the slightest muscle for at least an hour. After that, you can torture her until she tells you where Nicky is."

"What if she won't tell me?"

"Oh, *Scarface*, as much as I'd love a little torture in my day, you just have to learn to do these things yourself. That is especially true in case

I decide to take on an apprentice at some point. Let's see what you got?"

Joey took out his stiletto and moved toward the incapacitated Dr. Evers.

"Okay, Scarface *Stunad,* she has to be awake for you to get anything out of her. And when she is awake, you have to control her, so use your stiletto to cut some of the phone cords and tie her to the chair. However, leave one outgoing line alone. We will need it. Take the scarf from her neck and put it in her mouth."

Joey did as instructed and then looked to The Actor for approval.

"Now, did you bring the five-gallon can of gasoline that I told you to get?"

"Yeah, it's just outside the door."

"Well, bring it in. It's not doing any good out there."

Joey went and retrieved the can and placed it on the floor between them.

"Okay, now what is the first thing you are going to do to get her to talk?"

Joey put the stiletto to her face.

"No, no, no, no. First, the victim must believe that you are going to mame her but leave her alive. She won't talk if she thinks she is going to die."

"Yeah, but what if I cut her face?"

"Nope. That only works if the subject is vain. I don't believe Dr. Evers is. Also, the victim can't see the results of your efforts. Therefore, it is not as terrifying."

"Just spit it out. What the fuck do you think I should do?"

"I use a method I call the 'digit demoralizer.'"

"Huh?"

"I cut off a finger every time the person resists. It is excruciating and very visual. I started that method more than twenty years ago with my first kill for Guy. A kid who played the piano. I got him to kill himself before he would let me take a single finger."

"I am in awe."

"Yes, maybe I will see if one of the local colleges is interested in me teaching a course titled, *Methods of Torture for Fun and Fortune.*"

Joey started to laugh so hard that he lost his balance and fell onto Dr. Evers' desk. The papers she had been working on fell haphazardly on the floor. The Actor immediately reacted and gathered the papers to place them neatly back where they had been.

"Severe OCD. It's a professional hazard. You start to worry about every little detail, and then it becomes compulsive. But I am working on..."

The Actor stopped midsentence and stared at one of the papers he was organizing."

"Dr. Evers, you are a genius," chortled The Actor. He took the paper and ran his fingers down to a location halfway down the page and laughed.

"What? What is it?"

"She's got Nicky's location and phone number."

"How?"

"She must have realized that Nicky needed his supply of oxygen. So, she gathered a list of companies in the city that fit the bill." The Actor held up a list that had the names of six companies. Five names were crossed out.

She must have called the six companies, using her credentials as a doctor, to figure out which one was servicing Nicky. She probably then told them that she had to verify the company's address for her patient. It's all right here—phone and address."

"So, we kill her and then we go kill Nicky."

The Actor shook his head in frustration.

"I am rethinking this whole apprenticeship idea. You really don't get the whole picture. If you can draw Nicky here and then do away with both of them, it can look like Nicky came here to kill her and things went wrong. The cops will think that he got angry because Guy's death screwed up the whole deal. And then there is the interesting method that Nicky used to do away with her."

"What the fuck are you talking about?"

"You're going to burn the place down."

"How will that help?"

"Nicky already confessed to doing that to Harry Rothstein and that Bracko character twenty years ago. The cops will think it is exactly his *modus operandi*."

"His what?"

"His method of doing things. I'm going to call Nicky."

"Why will he listen to you?"

"Because I am The Actor. After four months of being her patient, I can imitate Dr. Evers' voice perfectly."

"Wow! You can do that?"

The Actor just shook his head.

"After I make the call, I am out of here. This is your kill...actually, that will be kills. I want to see if you can pull it off."

"I got this covered. You'll see."

"Okay, then, The Actor will make his exit."

62

SHOWDOWN

"You better get ready,
For a showdown tonight."
- Doobie Brothers

Dr. Evers Office

Twenty minutes later, Nicky could be seen exiting a taxi. He had been inhabiting a local hooker hotel in neighboring Long Island City. He was not using the services available but instead chose the facility because it was familiar and not affiliated with the Provenzanos.

Inside Dr. Evers' office, Joey's fingers drummed nervously on his thigh, every tap echoing the tension winding through his chest. Joey paced the cramped room, rehearsing what he'd say, picturing Nicky's face when the moment arrived—a mixture of confusion and regret, perhaps even a flicker of realization about all that had led them to this point.

He glanced again at the battered clock, its slow, deliberate tick serving as a countdown. Joey remembered their past together with mixed feelings—laughter from handball courts intertwined with Nicky's cowardice at the Men-at-Arms, now nothing but echoes, drowned by the present.

Whatever bonds had survived the years were gone. For Joey, tonight would be a reckoning—the solution to every slight and injustice of their shared past. Joey waited for the inevitable sound of Nicky's halting step outside the door.

At a younger age, Nicky might have strolled the entire distance from his makeshift hideout to Dr. Evers' office. Now, his disability made it even difficult to make the short walk from the cab to the front door. Indeed, he struggled to remove the eighteen-inch-long cylinder that contained his life-saving supply of oxygen from the back seat.

As Nicky shuffled up the steps, Joey stared at him through the half-drawn blinds and wondered when his former friend had become such an invalid. They had been close as kids. When did Nicky become such a fool, such a clown? Joey tried to remember when his hatred of Nicky began. Was it the incident that permanently branded him with the "Nicky Glue" handle that made him lose respect for his friend? Joey liked to think that he would not have put up with the glue incident at any age or from any person. In this matter, Joey was only fooling himself. He would have done anything to please Mad Guy Provenzano—absolutely anything.

Perhaps his resentment began with that first hit. Nicky could screw up almost every job given to him, and he was still Provenzano blood. Everyone knew that Nicky had chickened out of actually setting the flames on the Rothstein store, but did anyone say anything about it? No, Nicky moved on to bigger and better assignments despite his ineptitude. His research on Those Born Free had been pathetic. He had failed to make anyone—Vinnie the Cat or Guy—aware of the band's underage status. The Provenzano gang and Mad Guy himself had spiraled downward from that very moment. That one failure should have been the final nail in Nicky's coffin, but instead, he was given even more responsibility. He was to commit the first phase of Guy's vicious vendetta—the murder of that guitarist with the weird name of Bracko.

Nicky screwed that up. He allowed a witness to survive his botched arson of Bracko's home. If Joey "Back Door Man" Pasco had made all these mistakes, he would be "taken care of" as the gang liked to say. Yet, privileged "Little Nicky" was "punished" by being exiled to a cushy job with the Las Vegas branch of the mob. Poor Nicky!

There, Nicky was given the dream job of supervising a ranch — a ranch full of extremely young girls who were used for the pleasure of mob bosses and other paying customers. Rumor had it that Nicky never made use of the opportunity to sample the merchandise because he was loyal to his family and wouldn't cheat on his wife. What a jerk. She left him anyway when the story of the ranch was made public. Can you imagine that Nicky was subdued by a young Midwestern girl named Becky Simmons, who tricked him and escaped with all the little girls?

Surely that should have been his end. Nope. Richie Shea again intervened and stopped Mad Guy's wrath against their cousin. Now that same Richie Shea didn't care that Nicky had ratted to the cops. Well, Joey Pasco was going to be the man that the gang needed. Joey was going to do what others didn't have the guts to do. He would put an end to this clown, and no one would be the wiser that he was involved.

When Nicky rang the doorbell, Joey pressed the buzzer that unlocked the front door, allowing entry into the house-turned-office. In a weak falsetto voice that would not fool anyone but the dullard Nicky Toto, Joey beckoned the visitor into the back office.

"Surprise," gleefully yelled Pasco, as if welcoming Nicky to a birthday party instead of his own homicide. Toto stared at the immobile Dr. Evers rather than the Glock aimed at his head.

"What the Hell?"

"Remember when we were teenagers, we used to wonder about how and where we would die? Well, Nicky, I have an answer for you."

"But why this? Why me? Why her?"

Pasco threw a file at Nicky's feet.

"I was going to tell you to read it, but I just remember how really stupid you are."

Nicky made no move to pick up the folder. He could guess what was in it.

"So, you've been eating the cheese…you know ratting on us…on me especially—just to save your own goddamn ass."

Nicky was silent. He knew Joey Pasco was right. He had expected this retribution from the very beginning. His only mistake was that he had expected it from Guy. With his cousin's death, he had let down his guard. When nothing happened in the past few days, he figured he was in the clear. Still, Nicky needed to know where he stood with the cops and what was happening with his deal. When Dr. Evers reached out, he responded immediately. Now he realized it had not been Dr. Evers on the phone. She would never lure him into a trap. She would never betray him.

"Joey, do whatever you want to me, but leave Dr. Evers out of this."

"Stupid Nicky Glue, you know that's what they called you behind your back when you were young and strong. Now that you are feeble and dragging around the air you breathe, we say whatever we want. Why, in God's name, would I let her live? So, she can finger me instead of you? Stupid, stupid, stupid."

"So, you think you can get away with knocking us both off and no one will notice?"

"Nope. You underestimate my genius. You always have."

"What the hell are you talking about?"

"Those records that you didn't read, but I did, tell your story…and a fine story it is. They tell how you torched that old man Rothstein."

"Yeah, but you were there, and you lit the match and…"

"But…aha, I wasn't there for that weirdo named Bracko. That was all you. You come across as a serial arsonist to me. That's probably what the cops will think when you do it a third time."

It was then that Nicky first noticed the odor of gasoline in the air. It all became clear.

"Yes, poor Nicky Glue, disgusted that he had been tricked into ratting by his therapist, decided to end her the way he knew best—with fire. However, the stupid schlep didn't realize that his oxygen tank was an accelerant and was trapped in his own scheme. Poor Dr. Evers and Nicky were engulfed in flames and died as they had lived together...as rats."

Nicky started towards Joey, but the Glock faced him only three feet away. He would never get close enough to reach the gun. Disheartened, it was then that Nicky noticed Maggie's eyes were open. Pasco picked up on it.

"She's awake now, but the paralytic drug in her body will probably last another fifteen or twenty minutes. That's why I want you to untie her right now so we can get this show on the road. Oh, if you think of trying anything, I'll just put a bullet in both your heads and let the cops try to figure it out. I always have a Plan B."

Nicky shuffled over to the chair that Dr. Evers sat in and released the bonds that held her. Her eyes stared into his, and he felt the defiance in her motionless body. He wanted to do something, but his slow mind could not think what. Her eyes caught his, and she moved her gaze toward Nicky's oxygen tank.

"You know, Nicky, I am glad this opportunity arose. I have always hated you for your 'Provenzano Privilege.' I worked twice as hard as you. I was twice as mean...hell, I was twice the man. But do you think I ever got looked at with the same respect that you did?"

Nicky took a look at the metal lighter held in Joey's hand—the one engraved with the letters NT. Nicky knew well. He had used it for decades to fuel his nicotine addiction. The day the doctors put him on oxygen, he left it on the bar at the gang's hangout. Joey Pasco had scooped it up. The lighter had a history. Nicky had almost used it to start the fire at Rothstein's before chickening out. That would have been a mistake because the initials would have been found at the scene when Nicky dropped it into the gasoline. Now that was precisely what Pasco intended to do—perfect evidence of the clown's ineptitude.

"Nicky, come over here and grab this gas can." Pasco waved the Glock maliciously in Nicky's direction. Dr. Evers tried to speak, but nothing came out; the paralysis still gripped her body. Her eyes tried to catch Nicky's attention to get him to stop. She failed. Thinking he was doing something good, he moved the gas can away from Dr. Evers and toward the middle of the room.

"You're such a goddamn fool," chuckled Pasco, "Now I have your fingerprints on the handle."

Joey ignited and held the lighter over his head, and, almost simultaneously, kicked the gas can onto its side. He had previously left the top loose, so now it fell off, spilling flammable fluid in a nearly perfect line that split the room in half, with Maggie and Nicky on one side and Pasco on the other. The rug became stained in a pattern that left Joey with the only access to the front door. Nicky and Maggie were on the wrong side of the line.

Nicky again surged toward Pasco. However, he was slowed by the encumbrance of his oxygen tank and again fell short. This time, each of them stood on a different side of the gasoline line. Joey Pasco, the Back Door Man... Scarface Joey smiled...and dropped the lighter onto the gasoline, and it ignited quickly.

"This is so perfect. My new friend, The Actor, will be so proud of me. Your fingerprints on the can...your documented and admitted history as an arsonist...your sheer stupidity causing you to get caught up in the fire."

Nicky Toto, alias Nicky Glue, alias "Little Nicky Glue," was filled with rage. Once in his youth, he could have strangled Joey with one hand. Now still in his forties, he was an invalid, chained to his life-saving oxygen tank. Yes, trapped for life with the weight of...

Nicky looked down at the flames licking at his knees, but then a smile spread across his face, incomprehensible under the circumstances. He stared across the burgeoning wall of fire that separated the two of them. Joey stared back at him, never noticing that Nicky lowered his right arm and embraced the top of the metal canister that kept him alive. He released a valve that now allowed the oxygen to escape from its container.

In one motion, he swung the tank in an arc that caught both the Glock and Joey's jaw. The oxygen accelerated the flames around Joey, and he soon found himself battling to put them out. Nicky paid little heed to the wall of fire and crossed over to Joey's side, throwing punches with a brutality he had forgotten long ago he possessed. His onslaught only stopped when he realized that he could no longer breathe. The lack of his tank and the rapidly growing presence of toxic smoke were sapping the life out of him. But before he died, he knew he had one thing that had to be done.

He dragged Joey Pasco back over the wall of flames, using his body to suffocate just enough of the barrier to keep him safe enough to reach Maggie. She had started to regain some movement in her limbs; unfortunately, it was in her upper extremities. Her legs were not working, and Nicky knew he had to carry her out. Yet as he bent down to pick her up, his chest started to heave in convulsive spasms of coughing. He fell to his knees beside Maggie.

Her eyes pleaded for salvation as they stared at the fallen man. When she looked at the broken body beside her, she accepted her fate. She believed Nicky was unconscious or dead but spoke to him anyway.

"Nicky, I forgive you for what you did all those years ago…and I think Bracko would have felt the same way." Her hand caressed the top of Nicky's head with a tender touch. He moved.

"No, Doc, you ain't dying. You don't deserve it even if I do."

His wheezing, coughing bulk rose from his knees and bent over Maggie Evers. With unexplained strength, he threw her over his shoulder and started to look for a way out. Still holding her full weight on his left shoulder, he used his right arm to upend her desk and launch it right onto the flames. A pathway briefly appeared as the desktop smothered the fire below it. Nicky walked across the desk rapidly, just before the ancient wood became consumed.

Nicky heard a sound behind him and turned. Joey was on his knees and trying to decide what to do. One side of his face was badly burned, and he felt as if his jaw might be broken. Yet he had ramped up to survival mode.

If he tried to use the same method of escape that Nicky had taken, he might make it through the fire and out the front door. However, the sirens of both the police and firefighters could already be heard approaching the inferno. If he chose that direction, he would run right into their waiting arms. He had another choice. A lone door stood on the wall behind Dr. Evers' desk—presumably to a rear exit. He chose that direction.

Meanwhile, Nicky peered back over his shoulder and saw his tank lying within his grasp. Oxygen flowed swiftly from the top of the broken canister, and he tried to inhale some of it. His brief relief, however, was at the cost of Maggie's labored breathing. He decided to continue Maggie's rescue without risking her life any further.

He heard Joey Pasco's tortured scream as he opened up what he had assumed was a hallway to a rear exit, but in reality, was a closet door. With the wall of flames in front of him now almost reaching the ceiling, there would be no escape.

Nicky kicked the leaking oxygen tank toward Joey, igniting the back part of the room into an even larger firestorm around the shrieking man.

"Who's stupid now, Mr. Back Door Man? There is no back door."

With Maggie over his shoulder, Nicky exited.

KNOCKIN' ON HEAVEN'S DOOR

"That cold black cloud is comin'
Feels like I'm knockin' on Heaven's door."
- Bob Dylan

Astoria Park

*A*storia Park was an unusual place—the grassy fields were surrounded by concrete on *five* sides. In addition to four streets forming its perimeter, the overhead sky above was blocked from sunlight by the Triborough Bridge. That thoroughfare began its ascent to lofty heights in Queens on its way over the East River to the Bronx directly above the park.

Dr. Maggie McAvoy-Evers' office faced the park, and the grassy fields under the bridge became Nicky Toto's destination. The police and fire contingents had not arrived yet, and so it was only a group of kids playing soccer who witnessed his excruciatingly painful trek across the pavement and his collapse onto the grass. He had been careful to lay Maggie gently down before allowing his body to surrender to its fate.

He lay gasping for air that his damaged lungs could not properly circulate. He had spent every last ounce of his resources to save Maggie from the burning house. Was it his imagination, or could he still hear the last desperate screams of Joey Pasco?

He felt the palm of Maggie's hand on his face. She still felt numbness in her legs from the paralytic drug, and so she could do no more than crawl to the dying man's side.

"I did good...right?"

"Yes, you did great, Nicky."

"You think maybe I did good enough for Him," he gasped for air and pointed upward.

At first, Maggie was confused because Nicky was pointing to the bridge above. She was still trying to gain full consciousness and her wits.

"You know...Him. Is it enough in God's eyes?"

Maggie was going to say, *I am just a simple therapist, and that decision is above my pay grade.* However, the human being in her realized that Nicky was looking for comfort and a confirmation of his redemption in his final moments.

"Yeah, Nicky, I think you're good with Him."

Nicky started to gasp for air and choke on the smoke that had filled his damaged lungs. His eyes rolled in his head, and he seemed in the final throes of a death swoon. Yet suddenly his right hand gripped Maggie's arm, and he stared into her eyes.

"Tell my son that I loved him."

"What the hell, Nicky. In all our talks through these months, you never mentioned having a son."

"A man's got to have some secrets," he faintly whispered as a small smile came over his face...and he was gone.

64

DEATH OF A CLOWN

"Let's all drink to the death of a clown."
- The Kinks

Maggie's Memos and Memories

I had put this little notebook away when Nicky agreed to testify. Its purpose had always been to keep a record of our progress—both his and mine. With Nicky's tragic end and my newfound relationship with Aylin and DJ, it seemed unnecessary. However, I went to Nicky's funeral today. Somehow, I need to record all that happened. I need to finish our stories—both Nicky's and mine. I need to recount all the events that occurred dispassionately so that I can understand the craziness—the sadness, joy, and confusion that have changed my life forever. Here goes nothing...

I found it interesting that Nicky's funeral mass was held at Sacred Heart Church in Cambria Heights. It seemed a bit improper for a known murderer to use church facilities. Then I realized that it was "Brick House" Maggie who was thinking that. I had received my first communion in this very same church. Young Maggie would understand the concept of forgiveness, and the older Dr. Maggie McAvoy-Evers should have understood that he fully earned his redemption with the final sacrifice he made for me. I thought that over as I got ready for what would prove to be an insane day.

As I was about to leave my home, I noticed a few clouds in the sky, so I retrieved my raincoat from the closet. While putting it on, my right hand instinctively went into the right front pocket. As I pulled out the crinkled napkin, I immediately realized what it was—Nicky's hand-drawn chart of the "Good, the Bad, and the Ugly" of Mad Guy's Dirty Dozen. I'm not sure why, but I felt compelled to update the list he had given me months ago.

"The Good"

Richie Shea
~~Greg "Chinx" Cincotta~~ R.I.P
~~Vinnie "The Cat" Catalano~~ **R.I.P**
~~Jack "Leo" Leonardo~~ **disabled & on the good guy team**

"The Bad"

~~Little Nicky Glue Toto~~ **R.I.P.**
~~Sammy Crespo~~ **R.I.P.**
~~Sal Timpani~~ **(Life in Sing-Sing)**
~~Frankie "The Roach" Resch~~ **R.I.P.**

"The Ugly"
~~Mad Guy Provenzano~~ **R.I.P.**

~~Tony Provenzano~~ **R.I.P.**
~~Joey Pasco R.I.P.~~
The Actor

The list reminded me of why I was going to Nicky's funeral (That is, besides the fact that he was the man who saved my life). I needed information on the Provenzano gang, and I assumed that in the confines of a church, I would be safe.

As I arrived in Cambria Heights for the first time in decades, I drove by Mac and Son Candy Store, which was now boarded up. It was ironic to see the Mac and Son sign, because even after my father had renamed it, it was still commonly referred to as Newcombe's by most people in Cambria. I then thought of all the bad things that had happened there. This had been where my father and brother had died. This was where Aylin was so traumatized that she lost years of her life to insanity. I couldn't stay.

I drove around to other places I remembered vaguely and then made my final stop at Sacred Heart Church, the place where all four of us McAvoy kids had been baptized and received our first communions—more mixed memories. This was also the place where the funeral mass was held for my father and brother. I had promised myself not to think about those events on this day. I would slip into the building a few minutes late and sit in the back, observing — and praying for Nicky's soul. I parked a block away and walked on the same cracked concrete that I had in my youth. However, when I turned the corner, I was surprised to find a large crowd of people outside.

"Geez, those Rouse Funeral Home people…you'd think they would have the casket here and ready by 10 o'clock for a 10 o'clock funeral mass."

This was the gist of the conversations throughout the crowd as I nudged my way through it. I realized that Richie Shea, newly proclaimed "Don" of the organization, would require the attendance of everyone linked to *"La Familia"* at the funeral of his cousin Nicky.

Joey Pasco, on the other hand, would be buried alone in an unmarked grave in a Potter's Field. Richie would make sure of this by posting guards outside the city morgue where his body lay. If any person, relative or not, attempted to retrieve the body, they were calmly "persuaded" not to do so.

It was an extremely hot day in June, and many of those assembled were becoming agitated by the wait.

"What the fuck are we doing here?" complained one young man to the group surrounding him. "Nicky Toto was a shithead. He was a fool. He was a clown, and we're a better organization without him. Yup, a real clown." The other three men in the group looked down at their feet, trying to ignore their friend's rant. "Our gang is a laughingstock, because of that cl..."

He never finished his sentence. A strong right hand grabbed his shoulder and spun him around. That same hand then reeled back and delivered a devastating punch that knocked a few of the loudmouth's teeth loose and sent him plummeting to the ground. If he even thought about getting up and reacting to the blow, one look at his assailant's face discouraged him.

"Richie, I, I didn't mean nuthin'."

In any other organized crime group, often referred to as "La Familia," Richie Shea would have been addressed as a *don*. With Richie possessing his father's Irish last name, this formality was dropped. "Don Shea" just sounded ludicrous. However, that did not mean that Shea did not demand the same respect that all of his predecessors and peers received. He needed to make this clear to the loudmouth who had just called Nicky a clown.

The loudmouth was new to the gang. In reality, if this had been a legitimate business organization, he would have been at the level of an intern. Richie had two of his cohort lift the loudmouth from the floor and face him.

"I am not going to disrespect my cousin by making a scene. But you and I will have another 'meeting' sometime in the future. Get the hell out of here for now...and think about this...

"You never disrespect the dead. You never disrespect anyone in the organization...and certainly, never disrespect anyone in my family." Shea held up his hand to preclude any more comments or apologies. He ended the conversation and ordered his men to "get this asshole out of here."

And so, I finally got to see the famous Richie Shea in action. There was no doubt about who was in charge of the Provenzano gang. I remember thinking that I never wanted to get on his bad side. I also really hoped that he didn't know about my connection to Nicky,

As if on cue, the funeral director announced that the service would begin, and all filed into the church. It was a strange collection of middle-aged men, who obviously had not been told that the "greaser look" was out of style, and young aspiring gangsters wearing their best dress clothes in an attempt to be noticed. The assorted girlfriends, wives, and female relatives also included some middle-aged women who still believed teased, beehive hairdos to be in style, as well as young, fashionably dressed and coiffed girlfriends and trophy wives.

After all these people entered the church, I silently slipped into the back and sat in the last row of pews. I immediately noticed another woman sitting in a different section of the last row. I wondered what her story was as the ceremony began, and then it seemed to drone on for an excessive amount of time. Yet, it was an interesting homily performed by Father Hanratty, the savior of Aylin and still the pastor decades later.

I almost laughed when the priest told stories about Nicky. Unlike many funerals I had attended, he knew and liked the person he was speaking about. He shared stories about the times when Nicky was an altar boy and struggled to understand when to ring the bells correctly. I could see Richie Shea smile and nod when Hanratty told of Nicky flinching and wiping his eyes when the priest swung the holy water sprinkler in his direction, and how Nicky held his nose when the ceremony called for the burning of incense.

In conclusion, Father Hanratty prayed and pronounced that Nicky was happily residing in Heaven. Because he was a priest, I knew that conversations between him and Nicky were even more confidential than those that I had had with him. I had a strong suspicion that former altar boy Nicky Toto had confessed everything to his lifelong pastor.

When the ceremony was concluded, the crowd shuffled out, and I made my way to Father Hanratty, who now stood alone in the nave of the church.

"Little Maggie McAvoy, I would recognize you anywhere. How have you been? And how's…" He stopped abruptly, realizing that he was about to finish the sentence with "the family."

Father Hanratty had presided over the funerals of my father, mother, brother, and sister. All that was left of "the family" were Aylin and me. I saw his discomfort and quickly replied.

"Aylin is doing wonderfully," I interjected. "Her husband, DJ, is lucky that Aylin left the novitiate and then married him. God's loss was DJ's gain." I winked at him. He understood that I was aware of his long-ago intervention and deceit that had allowed Aylin to escape Mad Guy's wrath. We both nodded.

"Our family will never forget your kindness." I hugged him, and when we separated, he made the sign of the cross and mumbled a blessing. He then turned and made his way down the aisle to the room where he would change into the clothes he would wear to the cemetery. As I turned to leave, the door from the outside opened.

"So finally, we meet, Maggie," said Richie Shea.

65

STRANGERS WHEN WE MEET

"We will still be strangers when we meet."
- The Smithereens

Maggie's Memos and Memories

I turned quickly to see if Father Hanratty was still in earshot. Shea realized what I was thinking and calmly said, "Don't worry."

"Am I in trouble?"

"No, not at all. I know exactly why Nicky died saving you, and I hold no grudge against you. I wanted you to know that."

"So, the whole Omerta thing wasn't real?"

"Oh yeah, it was…it is. If the whole story of Nicky's snitching had come out, it would have put me in a difficult situation. I loved my cousin, but my position as "The Don" would have required me to act. It would have been difficult for me."

"So, when did you know of Nicky's actions?"

"Only a few hours before he died. Only I and one other person knew — and it wasn't Joey Pasco. He must have eavesdropped when I spoke to The Actor."

"Again, do I have to worry?" As I spoke those words, I took out the crumpled "Dirty Dozen" list and gave it to him. He smiled, even laughed, as he looked at it. It brought him back to times long gone. He said nothing.

"There are only two names left on that list...You and The Actor."

"As long as the story of Nicky's testimony remains a secret, you have no worries. If it were to come out that you knew all that you know, I would be forced to act. I don't want to do that. So, speak to your people. Don't force my hand."

"And?" I pointed to The Actor's name on the list.

"Oh, he's a mercenary. He acts purely for profit. If no one is paying him to kill, he does not kill,"

"That's good to know," I answered, but I was not entirely sure that it was the truth.

"However, there is one name that you can add to that list. He isn't on it because he wasn't even born when the Dirty Dozen had their heyday. You can worry about Dominick Provenzano, Mad Guy's son in every sense of the word. They call him D-Mon because he is that vicious. I have to watch that someday he doesn't come after me to claim the title of "Don." If he knows about you, nothing will stand in his way."

"That's not good," I mumbled.

"That's another reason that your people can't let it be known that this all happened. Listen, I wouldn't worry. He doesn't know, and he is not finding out from me. So, go about your business, have a good life, and forget about the entire Provenzano family."

"That's easy for you to say. You won't have to look over your shoulder for the rest of your life."

"I can give you some solace in the fact that before D-Mon acts, he has to get my permission. If it comes to that, I will give you ample warning."

"Why are you being so nice to me?"

"In honor of Nicky. For him to give up his life, you must be something special. And…though I didn't take part in it, I know what Mad Guy put your family through all those years ago. No matter what I did, I couldn't stop my cousin. But I'm the boss now, and I believe we owe you peace of mind, at the very least. Now I have to go. Will you be at Montefiore Cemetery?"

"Yeah, again in the background."

"Good."

"One final question, just out of curiosity. Who was the beautiful woman who hid out in the back like I did? Nicky's lover?"

Richie Shea could not contain his laughter. It was so loud that it filled the nave and spilled out into the pews. He only stopped when one of his lackeys opened the door and asked if he was okay.

"Jimmy, tell everyone to line up in their cars. I'll only be a minute more."

"Well?"

"She was in the back because D-Mon would pulverize her if he saw her at the funeral."

"D-Mon would hit a woman. Why, what did she do to him?"

"Because she is not a 'she.' That 'woman' is Mad Guy's other son, Carmine…or Carmen, as he or she now calls himself…or herself. It doesn't bother me at all, but then again, I am not her father or brother. I say live and let live. Nicky took it a bit further. He was kind to her, and he was the only one in the family who treated her with any decency."

I was dumbstruck as Richie Shea exited the church.

———

I slowly walked back to my car, not wanting to follow the long line of mourners to Montefiore Cemetery. I knew how to get there on my own. I had once walked it with Michael to visit Bracko's grave. I had been there for my father's and brother's funerals. I had not been around for my mother and Siobhan's, but knew at some point I would go with Aylin and pay respects. Today, I just wanted to stand in the background and say goodbye to Nicky.

The crowd stood around the open grave in respectful silence. Perhaps they remembered what had happened to the loudmouth at the church. Then again, maybe they were decent enough to comprehend the solemnity of the moment.

I heard footsteps behind me and realized I wasn't alone. I smelled perfume and the unmistakable sound of stockinged legs rubbing together.

"So here we are, relegated to the cheap seats."

I couldn't help thinking of the words to the Kinks' song, "Lola," "I couldn't understand why she walked like a woman but talked like a man." This allowed me to know who was behind even before I turned around.

"Hello, Carmen," I said softly.

"I should have known Richie spotted me and told you."

"Actually, it was me who asked who you were first." I now looked at her as she was beside me. She had a body and face that many women would die for, though I noticed the heavy makeup covering a slight five o'clock shadow. Her clothing was impeccable and must have come from a designer house. She sported long, luxurious blonde hair that I assumed was an expensive wig.

"I just wanted to tell you how much Nicky thought of you. He was the only one in the family who would talk to me. He would come to see me at times to keep me informed. He was a little uncomfortable about me being in drag, but he always told me that it was his problem, and he would try to get over it. He was such a caring person...and he cared about you."

"Wait, he told you about talking to me?"

"Who do you think convinced him to do it? My crazy father belonged in jail...if not the electric chair. You can imagine what he thought of me."

I was speechless but wanted to know more. However, when I tried to speak again, I noticed her hurrying away.

"Wait, I have one last question. Is Nicky's son here?"

"Yeah, he was always a better son than Nicky was a father."

"Okay, which one is he?"

"See the tall, handsome one in the gray suit, next to Richie? That's him."

I strained to see, but the crowd and distance allowed only a profile. However, when the ceremony concluded, I would easily find him by virtue of his wearing the only light suit.

I stepped behind a tree to stay away from the prying eyes of all who were now leaving the gravesite. No one in a gray suit passed me by, and I thought I had missed him.

I ran toward the grave, which was empty except for the men assigned to fill it in. I saw a glimpse of gray in the distance and followed. I would make good on my promise to tell Nicky's son that his father loved him.

66

I KNOW YOU'RE OUT
THERE SOMEWHERE

"I know you're out there somewhere,
Somewhere, somewhere."
- Moody Blues

Montefiore Cemetery

*I*n many other cemeteries, it would be impossible to lose someone. Usually, level flat ground sprinkled with headstones would allow visibility for acres. However, Montefiore Cemetery was a step below a forest, and I therefore had to work hard to find Nicky's son.

As I turned one final corner, I came to a part of Montefiore that I was not familiar with. There, about fifty yards in front of me, Nicky's son stood with his head bowed and his hands seemingly clenched in prayer in front of a headstone. I didn't have to be a genius to realize that this was Nicky's late wife. In our sessions, Nicky had not talked about her with any consistency. They had married young and fought with each other from the very beginning. When Nicky was sent into exile, Lucia did not handle it well. Eventually, she had left him and returned to New York. There was a brief reconciliation that didn't work. Though Nicky had never mentioned his son, I had to assume that he took his mother's side and therefore had minimal contact with his father.

I watched as the dutiful son spent more time merely standing by his mother's grave than he had at his father's actual burial. I could not interrupt him. It seemed like hours that he stood there in motionless prayer and meditation. And then abruptly he left. As I ran to catch up to him, I passed the grave spot where he had stood and looked at the headstone.

Lucia Tomaselli Toto
1945 – 1988

She had died very young. I believe Nicky said it was breast cancer. For some reason, I felt that I, too, needed to pay my respects. After all, this had once been Nicky's wife. She had meant something to him. I wouldn't be surprised if Nicky still loved her even after she left him. My diversion, however, meant that I fell even further behind Nicky's son.

If he were heading to a back exit of the cemetery, I would lose him forever. I did not even know his name. I kicked myself for not asking Carmen. Once out in the streets, perhaps in his car, I would have no method of finding him. I ran down one path that was bordered by six-foot-high hedges, and I followed it. When I reached the end, I realized he had not gone that way. Now panicked and sweating, I backtracked and tried another row. When I emerged from that path, I saw him, and he was not exiting the cemetery. But he also was not standing at a grave like he had at his adopted mother's. No, strangely, I found that he was sitting on the floor with his legs crossed...his hand lay on a stone sunk into the ground. This stone memorialized someone who could not afford an upright stone to mark their demise. All that was there was a one-foot-by-two-foot piece of quarried stone set in the ground.

I approached quietly, hoping not to disturb Nicky's son. He, in turn, seemed to hear nothing, his total concentration placed on the stone and his hand that was placed upon it. I crept close enough to see the engraved name just as something amazing happened. His fingers started to move on the stone that read...

Susan Quinn Powers
1934 - 1967

His fingers danced.
"Michael," I whispered.
He looked up at me and replied, "Hi, Maggie."

67

YESTERDAY

"Yesterday, all my troubles seemed so far away."
- The Beatles
Maggie's Memos and Memories

There were no words between us for quite a while. His fingers danced as I had always seen them do at his mother's bedside. If we were younger, I would have joined his magical finger dance. We had done it so many times at Those Born Free practices. However, this seemed like such a personal and private moment that I said and did nothing until he was done. He rose and looked me in the eyes.

"I'm guessing that you are confused. Let's walk, and I'll tell you the abridged version of my life. I owe you that after disappearing without a trace. I wanted to contact you, but they wouldn't allow it. They said it was better that way. I was so young, what did I know?

"It all started the night of Bracko's death. I came out of my house just as Nicky was exiting Bracko's. The flames were devouring the home, and I pleaded with Nicky to run back into the building to save Bracko...and he did. At least, I thought he did. He was actually going in to clean up evidence of him starting the fire. I wasn't aware of that at the time. I proclaimed to everyone that he was a hero for trying to save Bracko.

"In the months that followed, I had only you...and him for support. My adopted Mom, Lucia, told me the truth when I was older. Looking back at it now, I think her motive was to drive me away from Nicky so that I would choose sides in their ugly divorce. Whatever the reason, she shared the true story with me.

"Guilt had made Nicky take care of my mom and me after Bracko was gone. While planning Bracko's murder, he had seen all that he was doing for us. Nicky soon realized that he had taken away our lifeline with his crime. He knew that my mom and I had no one. And so, Nicky was there whenever we needed food and necessities. He even drove my mom to the hospital until the very end. I was confused when he told me not to mention it to you when you visited. He made up some ridiculous reason why I should keep you in the dark. I don't even remember what it was. I was eight and desperate, so I did what he told me even if it made no sense. When Mom passed away in November, it seemed natural that Nicky and Lucia would take me in.

"Nicky had screwed up badly with the murder of Bracko. He had brought too much publicity to himself...and, in turn, to the family. Guy was furious with him and wanted to have him "taken care of" by this Actor character. My "Uncle Richie" Shea intervened, and instead, the three of us were sent to Las Vegas. That meant that I was taken away from everyone I knew. I was taken away from you.

"Years later, my adopted mom left Nicky because of some nasty things he was involved in while in Vegas. When she left, I went with her. It was then that she revealed the truth about Nicky to me. She was so angry with him that she wanted me to hate him as well. It worked. When Nicky came back into our lives, I left both of them. I ran away to the West Coast. I survived by using the only skill I had— playing the guitar. Eventually, I assembled a group, and we started earning some real money. And I wrote a song..."

"'Dancing with the Lost.' No wonder I thought I knew the words when I heard the song on the radio. I had heard them before—you had spoken them to me at Bracko's grave. I was going through some tough times myself in 1975, and your song gave me solace. I didn't pay attention to the details, only knowing that a group named Powerhouse had recorded the song. How was I to know that Powerhouse was Michael Powers?"

"You couldn't know because I didn't even use my real name then. I didn't want Nicky, or worse yet, Mad Guy, to know who I was. After all, I was still a loose end—a witness to a murder."

"That was smart, but how long did you expect to fly under the radar?"

"I don't know, but it didn't matter; it was my only hit song. But that wasn't a problem. While we were touring, I realized that the whole rock star scene wasn't for me. I came to that conclusion early enough that I socked away all my royalty checks and then left music.

"I got an education and a new career. After Lucia left Nicky for a second time, I took care of her until she passed away. I built a life as a teacher on Long Island, and I left no forwarding address for Nicky to find. That worked for years to keep him from me. However, after I read the details of the story in the paper about how he died saving you, I was forced to rethink how I felt about him. I decided to go to the funeral."

"Nicky never told me about you until the very end. His dying words were, 'Tell my son that I love him.'"

"I guess maybe I shouldn't have cut him totally out of my life. But I couldn't face the man after I knew…"

"That he didn't try to save Bracko."

"Yeah."

"If it helps you to get past what he did, I think he regretted Bracko's death the rest of his life. His final act was to save me. 'Is it enough in God's eyes?' was Nicky's final question. My final question *to you* is…is it enough in *your* eyes?"

"Yeah, maybe it is…because…and only because it was you that he saved."

"Aww, that's sweet of you to say."

We stared at each other for a while.

"Michael, I think we have one more stop in this cemetery before we leave."

"I was thinking the same thing...the same place we last went to together as kids?"

We started off to find Bracko's grave. As we did, he took my hand just as he had done twenty-three years before. It felt so natural. We moved as one, knowing exactly where to go. It was as if the distant memories of our earlier visit had ingrained the location in us. We spoke very little, often turning to each other with silent smiles. Michael broke that silence as we approached Bracko's grave.

"And what about you?"

"It's a long story," I answered.

"How about we catch up after this?"

"Yeah, I'd like that."

Soon, we found ourselves standing over Bracko's resting place for a few minutes. Without a word, we sat down across from each other.

"What was it that you said last time we were here?" I knew because he had made it into a hit song. Yet I wanted to hear his words spoken aloud.

"The end should never be the end..."

I smiled at him, a single tear falling from his eye as he spoke.

"I guess that says it all. We've both lost so many people, but they are still alive in our hearts and memories...and so our feelings...our love...should never end."

"I know," I whispered.

"To remind myself of that love, I use the method my mom taught me."

He smiled at me...and then smiled down at the stone that had been placed there twenty-three years before. Our fingers lay on that stone. We started to move them. Our fingers danced. He slowly spoke the words that meant so much so long ago...and still meant so much today.

The end should never be the end,
That's why I dance with the lost.

EPILOGUE

AFTER THE STORM

"How come I have to explain,
People are worth all the pain.
I just want to see all the love in your eyes,
After the storm has passed you and gone."
- Crosby, Stills, Nash, and Young

Five Years Later
June 1995

EPILOGUE - SCENE 1

LOLA

"I can't understand why she walked like a woman,
But talked like a man."
- The Kinks

Maggie's Memos and Memories
June 11, 1995

J am meeting a new client today; someone I met at Nicky Toto's gravesite five years ago. At that time, she had mentioned that she would seek my services someday. Today is that day. Over the years, I had forgotten about Carmen/Carmine Provenzano and wondered what problem she needed help with.

As she walked in, I noticed her transformation: her figure was model-like, her platinum blonde hair was now her own, and her makeup was flawless. She had perfected her female persona so well that it was hard to believe she was genetically male. Her voice, while slightly deep, was no longer a giveaway. I felt momentarily inadequate as a female in her presence.

As she sat before me, she crossed her legs in a very ladylike manner and handed me the written "homework" that I required from each client before we began. She then gave me a self-confident smile, making me wonder why she needed my help. She had her act together.

"Hi Maggie, long time no see," she said in a breathy, even sultry voice.

"I was wondering when you would show up at my doorstep," I replied, and we both laughed.

Carmen Lola Brigitta's Homework

Many people like me believe they were born into the wrong body, and to be honest, that could be true. However, more importantly, it is with me that I was born into the wrong family.

Yes, Dr. Evers, I am not like most trans people. I believe all my deep-rooted problems come from being born into the Provenzano family rather than being born into the body of a man. I could have been gay or straight. I could have been a closet queen or a drag queen. I could have been just about anything in this world and not have had to seek counseling from you. I could have been anything...but a Provenzano.

I know that this little journal technique you use in your therapy is meant to help us uncover our innermost feelings. But you see, I am different...I know the root of my problems—my family tree. Get it? Family tree... the root of my problem? I think I'll put that in my act.

So, my grandfather, God rest his soul (though I am pretty sure that he is not within the same zip code as God), Dominick Provenzano (The Elder), came from Italy and, with diligent hard work (and a few contract murder assignments), became a big shot in the Gambino crime family. His nickname, the "King of Cambria Heights," said it all. He dreamed of being a "Don," but those dreams were almost crushed when his son and right-hand man (and my father, Gaetano

306

Provenzano alias Mad Guy Provenzano) screwed up one of his business ventures. The result was more than a dozen murders. My Uncle Nicky (God rest his soul, too, and I mean it this time) told me just before his death all of this when he was trying to convince me to see you, Dr. Evers. Okay, I am a bit slow. It took me five years to take his advice.

So, then my father gets whacked by an unknown assailant while on his boat, *Fun Ghoul,* in 1990. My uncle Richie Shea takes over the reins of the kingdom in Southeast Queens. However, there is another problem—my brother Dominick (named for our violent grandfather). Currently, my brother is waiting for Uncle Richie to die so he can reclaim the kingdom for himself.

My brother Dominick is by far the most insane of all the Provenzanos who have ever existed. That says a great deal when considering our father was Mad Guy Provenzano. Just think that my brother's mob name is D-Mon. Get it? Never was there a more fitting name for a complete and total lunatic.

Do you understand my situation now? Grandfather—run-of-the-mill murderer, father—mass murderer, brother—psychotic murderer, and me, a flaming faggot. I know that it is not politically correct to use that word, but I can use that word "faggot" ...you can't.

I know my whole situation drives my brother up the wall. He thinks my being a drag queen is somehow an affront to *his* masculinity. In turn, I believe the inadequacies of a small penis are the cause of his. You have to remember that I saw D-Mon naked as a child! Just kidding, I think that my brother came from the womb a psychotic murderer. He got the murder gene. I got the gay gene.

I don't know why I taunt him so much, consciously and unconsciously. I mean, someday, he may decide to whack me. I have already picked out a gorgeous gold sequined gown for my wake. I make sure my platinum blonde hair is touched up so often that I am unsure if I even have dark roots. All my manicures and pedicures are kept up to date.

All that, and the one action that most offends my brother, is my show. Living my life as a woman, he can ignore—as long as I keep to myself and my lifestyle is safely hidden in the East Village. No, my principal crime is that I mock him every time I take the stage. Carmine Provenzano becomes Carmen Lola Brigitta, the leader of a pseudo-mob of Powder-Puffs known as the "Good-Bellas." Get it, Good-Bellas…Good Fellas. Ha, ha, ha—take that D-mon. You're not the only one who can play with words—Dominick alias D-Mon.

Session #1 with Carmen "Lola Brigitta" Provenzano

Dr. Evers: Let's try to get to the heart of this. Why are you here today? What do you want to change in your life?

Carmen: Nothing!

Dr. Evers: That doesn't make any sense.

Carmen: I love my life, as crazy as that may seem. I just want to keep on living it…without fear. Yeah, that's it. Doc, please teach me to live without fear.

Dr. Evers: Well, is the fear from a real or imagined threat? Do you have a real reason to worry, or is this…?

Carmen: All in my head? Was that what you were going to ask me? No, this is real. I think my brother, that psychopath D-Mon, is going to do something to me. I'm just too much of an affront to his masculinity.

Dr. Evers: If it's real, what do you expect to get from me? I'm not a police officer or any form of security personnel. I think you are in the wrong place.

Carmen: Oh, I don't think I made myself clear. I have taken precautions.

At this point, Carmen curiously makes the sign of the cross and looks at me like I should understand. She smiles and does it again.

Dr. Evers: Okay, you lost me. Are you saying that God is going to protect you?

She lets out a loud, nervous laugh.

Carmen: No, Doc, I am physically protected by the Trinity. I need to learn to relax and trust that they will take care of me. That's why I need you...to teach me to relax.

Dr. Evers: Now I am confused. You make a religious sign and then tell me that you are physically protected from your brother.

Carmen: Oh, the Trinity is very real, and my sign of the cross is to let them know that I am in trouble. However, I sometimes do it when I am nervous, like right now.

Dr. Evers: Carmen, you'd better explain this all to me.

Carmen: Many people regularly hang out at my club. Some are gay. Some are not, and they just enjoy the shows. A while ago, I noticed three men hanging out quite often. At first, I thought this was my brother's hit squad. In a rare show of courage, I confronted them...in the public arena of the club, of course.

Dr. Evers: And?

Carmen: They just liked to drink and watch the show...and none was The Actor.

I hadn't thought of The Actor in five years...since Richie Shea informed me that he was a mercenary and would only come after me if he was hired to do so. However, it now occurred to me that perhaps my meeting with Carmen could also make me a target. I felt a fear that I had not known in a long time.

Carmen: Your expression tells me that you're familiar with The Actor.

Dr. Evers: When Joey Pasco came after Nicky and me...you know... the day Nicky died, he let slip that The Actor had put him on to us... and that the bastard had even lured Nicky to my office by imitating my voice. I have spent many a sleepless night worrying about him. Knowing that he is out there

Carmen: As a little kid, I would eavesdrop on my father's meetings. He would take me to Umberto's Ristorante in Little Italy. He would leave me eating spaghetti while he went into a back room to meet someone for dinner. The confusing part to me was that he would meet with all different kinds of people, yet they all seemed to have the same voice, but only once they were behind the closed door with him. Old men, young men, and women would enter the room, yet the voice was the same once inside. And more importantly, each conversation would end with the mystery person saying, "The Actor will take care of everything." I can hear that voice, that phrase in my dreams. That is the fear that I want you to help me cope with.

Dr. Evers: Unless what you are feeling is real. Carmen, if it is real, you need more help than I can give you.

She made the sign of the cross again.

Carmen: Oh, I got off track with my storytelling. The three individuals, whom I affectionately call "The Trinity," are huge. They offered to help me stay safe in return for almost permanent residence and free drinks at my club. They protect me.

Again, the sign of the cross. I looked at her, confused.

Carmen: Geno Tanza is a huge man who spends many hours bodybuilding. His son Geno Junior is the same size and build. They are wonderful people. When Geno Senior found a young street urchin alone and abandoned, he adopted him and loved him as much as his biological son.

Geraldo is a bit shorter than the father and son but built along the same chiseled format. Unfortunately, he is both deaf and mute, so he is often overlooked in the craziness of my club. He is a sweetheart, yet he is like a spirit, just there. Someone once referred to him as a ghost. After Geno Senior almost killed the guy who commented, Geraldo made it known that he liked the name. It made him feel special. So...

She made the sign of the cross again.

Carmen: Yup, we laughed the first time I realized I was being protected by a father, a son, and a *holy* ghost...my Trinity. We developed a code that if I made the sign of the cross, they would know that I was in trouble.

Dr. Evers: I think that I have now heard everything. You...You...

Carmen: What did you want to say? You Italians? You gang families?

Dr. Evers: Well, you've got to admit the nicknaming is obsessive.

Carmen: It all goes back to the fact that we are required by tradition to name children after grandparents. I once knew a guy named Frank who had five sons. Each of the sons named their first son Frank. Can you imagine the confusion at large extended family dinners? This is the reason you get nicknames like "Frankie No-Knees," "Frankie, The Nose," or the less physical description variations like "Sonny" or "Junior."

I laughed. Carmen could tell a story or talk about any topic with ease. However, I needed to get back to the session's main discussion.

Dr. Evers: As a therapist, I can only recommend increased vigilance. As a friend, I can make some recommendations. Go to your Uncle Richie. Tell him your fears. Wouldn't your brother need his permission to...ah...

Carmen: Kill me! You would think so! But D-Mon is that crazy, and The Actor is so secretive that Richie might not know. It could be an "accident." Still, it's not a bad idea to approach him with my fears.

Dr. Evers: And I would suggest that you keep the Trinity close at all times. You know, as a psychologist, not a psychiatrist, I can't prescribe medications. However, would you like me to get a colleague to give you some Xanax?

Carmen: Now you're talking, Doc.

Post-Interview Conclusions

1. Carmen's problem isn't something that can be solved with therapy. However, I like Carmen, and there is a bond between us that began five years ago.

2. I will try reaching out to sources I have (I won't mention here) who have some inside knowledge of the Provenzano gang. I can find out if the threat is real.

3. I will see Carmen again next week. I will check her progress.

EPILOGUE - SCENE 2

DEVIL IN DISGUISE (REPRISE)

"You're the devil in disguise,
Oh yes, you are."
- Elvis Presley

The Actor's Script

So, Carmen Prima Donna, or whatever he calls himself, went to see my old friend Dr. Evers. Isn't that interesting? I know she likes her patients to write a little story before they see her. I remember having to do that in my persona of Josef Stern, the old Holocaust victim... one of my better roles. It will be fun to pretend I'm seeing her again...as a different character. I think she figured out I was Josef Stern.

I will write my little love note in the identity of my new role, Lizzie Boobin. Okay, that's a silly name, but all those drag names are. I, at least, thought mine out. I always felt a kinship with Lizzie Borden, a New England folk anti-hero to some, but to me an actual hero and my personal idol. Therefore, when I auditioned for the Carmen Lola Brigitta Show two weeks ago, I devised a bloody but sexy act that impressed the boss (my future victim).

What? Have you never heard of Lizzie Borden, the model for my Lizzie Boobin character? Then, I will have to include the famous nursery rhyme that chilled the hearts of many…but was so beautifully heart-warming to me.

Lizzie Borden took an axe,
She gave her mother forty whacks,
When she saw what she had done,
She gave her father forty-one.

Such majestic poetry. Such depth of character. The first time I heard it, I wanted to marry Lizzie…or be her. Who knows? My sexual identity has been a work in progress my entire life. All I know is that I am enjoying being my Lizzie character right now.

My audition earned me a part in the review and, more importantly, a spot close to my target. I have noticed three guys are hovering over her, protecting her. My "boss," Carmen, calls these guys "The Trinity." I must bide my time and figure out how to do this correctly and secretly. My new employer, D-Mon, doesn't want any blowback on him.

And then I will give myself the pleasure of "taking care of" the illustrious Dr. Evers. I have not allowed myself the thrill of the kill just for the sake of enjoyment in quite a while. But she has been a thorn in my side going back to my Nicky Toto days. First, I will earn my keep with the demise of Carmen blah, blah blah, what's-her-name…and then take care of the dear Dr. Evers.

The Actor will take care of everything.

EPILOGUE - SCENE 3

RUNNIN' WITH THE DEVIL

"I'm runnin' with the devil,
I'll tell you all about it."
\- Van Halen

Interview Transcript – Carmen "Lola Brigitta" Provenzano

armen walked into the office with a paper in hand and a smile as wide as the Grand Canyon on her face. I offered her a seat and was prepared to review this week's "homework assignment." She just laughed, holding the paper close to her chest.

Dr. Evers: What's going on?
Carmen: I didn't write anything this week. I didn't need to.
Dr. Evers: Then what are you holding in your hand?
Carmen: A document that closes my case and ensures I will no longer have to worry.

Dr. Evers: Explain.

Carmen: You see, a few years ago, a reporter tried to infiltrate my show to do an exposé on the "Provenzano in Drag," as the article called me. I caught her red-handed and made her an offer she couldn't refuse to squash the article. She had seen all the "Godfather" movies, and I was, after all, still a Provenzano.

Dr. Evers: What's this got to do with anything?

Carmen: Since that day, I have every inch of my theater checked for anything that might harm me physically, emotionally, or professionally. And yesterday, this was found.

She handed me the paper she had clutched in her hands...a paper with the title "The Actor's Script." I read it in its entirety and knew that the final line, "The Actor will take care of everything," was as good as a signature.

Dr. Evers: So now you know what he is going to try and do to you... and me.

Carmen: What he *was going...to try* to do to me...and you. And yes, that's past tense. I repeat, what *he was going to try to do?*

I just looked at her in disbelief.

Carmen: Doc, I may be a drag queen, a fairy, a faggot...whatever people want to call me to put me down. But I am proud of who I am. I don't care. But don't let anyone ever forget that I am also a Provenzano. There is no getting away from the blood that runs in my veins.

I was afraid of what I would hear next — and rightly so.

Carmen: The Trinity took The Actor to Staten Island, where all the other garbage is dumped. They then removed a specific...er...piece of his anatomy that would have made him fit just a little better in with my show...if you catch my meaning. The body part in question was sent to D-Mon with a note that read, "The Actor has played his final scene. Now leave me the fuck alone."

I had to try desperately to keep from vomiting.

I failed.

Carmen: The good news is that you and I never have to worry about him again. He bled to death. If his body is found in the dump dressed as he was, it will be assumed that he was not mentally stable and tried a do-it-yourself sex change operation. You can say, "Thank you" to me whenever you want.

I vomited again.

Carmen: I guess you're not ready to appreciate everything I've done. No hard feelings. I'm guessing this is goodbye. See you around.

As she closed the door behind her, I thought—No, you won't. I am destroying these notes and hope never to hear the name Provenzano again.

EPILOGUE - SCENE 4

TURN THE PAGE

"There I go again,
Turn the page."
- Bob Seger and the Silver Bullet Band

Two months later - September 5, 1995

Maggie's Memories

*I*n 1972, I ran away from home and the horrible situation that existed there. Yet, in the years that followed, I matured. I became self-confident. And somewhere along the line, I decided I would never run *away* from anything in this world again. When I made a move, it would always be *towards* something.

I only mention this to clarify why I changed careers. I was not running away from those final moments with Carmen or my work as a therapist, but rather towards a better lifestyle. It was a change I had long been considering; Carmen made the decision so much easier.

Tomorrow, I will start my life as a professor of psychology at Stony Brook University. Though I liked helping people with my therapy sessions, it has taken its toll on me. I took too many problems to heart and internalized them. More and more, I couldn't leave all that I had heard at the office. Now, I begin my work to create the next generation of therapists who will someday take my place.

I look forward to teaching. It will be the next chapter of my life outside that "brick house" I had built. Yes, I have fully dismantled it, brick by brick, mainly due to family.

With full disclosure, I will immensely enjoy my new schedule—a full load of classes from 8 a.m. to 4 p.m., Monday through Thursday. However, the nights and long weekends are mine...to spend with my growing family. Yes, *my* family.

After a very short courtship that began that day in the cemetery, I married Michael. There had always been something special between us. All those years ago, we were just too young to know what it meant. Now, as adults, we understand that it had always been love. Our lives together unfolded with a sense of both urgency and inevitability. It was as if every twist and turn of our lives had been quietly guiding us to this point. Our journey was one filled with laughter, warmth, and the gentle reassurance that comes from truly knowing and being known by another.

Because DJ and Aylin are older, they remember much of our youth. They often allude to those days during band practice, when we playfully performed with our dancing fingers. They often tease us about those times and can't help but mention that at eleven, I guided the much younger Michael, who was eight at the time. Even today, the kidding never stops about me being older. When we married, I was 35 and Michael was 32. Aylin has a new nickname for me. She calls me "Cougar."

Our wedding was a small ceremony attended only by Aylin and DJ, presided over by Padre. Padre's schedule determined our wedding date to be early December 1991. He had the least body and soul saving at that time of year, so he flew up for a few days. This "Jack" character has stuck around and helped Padre by holding down the fort in Key West while my old friend officiated our nuptials.

Another advantage of giving up my therapy career for teaching is that I no longer have to commute to the city. We own a lovely three-bedroom house on Lake Panamoka in Ridge. A small beach on the lake lies on our property and a small patch of sand borders the water.

We are not too far from Aylin and DJ. That will be helpful after I give birth to our second child in May. This date conveniently falls just after my first two semesters of teaching are completed.

With the wonders of modern medicine, the sex of the child can now be predicted. Therefore, we have decided to name our daughter Susan Quinn Powers after Michael's mother. We can't wait to welcome "Suzy Q." Obviously, I am still obsessed with sixties music, and the name and nickname worked out because "Quinn" is Michael's mother's maiden name...and we both like the John Fogerty reference.

We will have three months before Michael (teaching music at a local high school) and I head back to our respective positions in September. Aylin and DJ have agreed to help with Suzy Q's care, at least for a while, until we arrange something more permanent.

I noticed that for the first time, I dropped the word "memo" from the title of these short pieces. They are, after all, no longer professional writings, but memories of an extraordinary life. I am about to end *this* short memory piece. I will soon join Michael and our son on our little sandy beach on the lake. As I write, I watch out the window as my two favorite men bond and make their own memories by skipping stones. Our son starts preschool tomorrow, and I'm eager for the phone call that will inevitably come...about our son's name. I can hear the teacher upon meeting our son.

"You should learn to spell your full legal name, not your nickname. So, what does your birth certificate say?"

I can see our confident little boy tell his teacher what he tells everyone else, "Bracko is my legal name. I am Bracko Powers, and I was named after a great person."

And he was. The original Rocco "Bracko" Brackowski was the

kindest, gentlest, most honorable person Michael and I have ever met. If "our" Bracko grows up to be half the person that the original was, then we'll consider ourselves damn good parents.

Now it's time for me to break up my guys' playtime. Bracko's bath, story time, and bedtime await. After we are sure he is down, we have this nightly tradition of re-creating the mood of when we first witnessed real love. We will dance closely on our little beach. Although it was almost a quarter of a century ago, we still remember listening to the band and watching Johnny and Maria dance. As young as we were...and as young as they were, we still saw the look in their eyes and knew that something special was happening. We will never know where Johnny or Maria's paths in life took them, but we hope they are happy now. We are.

Aylin still has tapes of the band's practices. We might someday copy all the songs to listen to, but for now, our tradition only includes dancing to one song...Johnny and Maria's song, and now ours. I can still see and hear the band performing Johnny Rivers' song a cappella while Johnny and Maria danced; I hear my dear departed brother singing lead as our bodies cling to each other, moving rhythmically to the music playing on the tape.

Together...we remember the past...but look forward to a wonderful future. We will never forget to dance with the lost...but now we know it is also pretty damn great dancing with the living.

As we dance together in the dark,
So much love in this heart of mine.
You whisper to me, hold me tight,
You're the one I thought I'd never find.

Now we're slow dancin', swayin' to the music.
Slow dancin', just me and my girl,
Slow dancin', swayin' to the music,
No one else in the whole wide world.

And then the song will hit its climactic bridge...

Hold me, oh, hold me,
No, never let me go.

And I will hold him tightly...and never let go.

AUTHOR'S NOTES

JUST A SONG BEFORE I GO

"Just a song before I go,
To whom it may concern."
- Crosby, Stills, and Nash

#1 – I Was Here
#2 – Last Words
#3 – Live Like You Were Dying

AUTHOR NOTE #1

I WAS HERE

I always incorporate a bit of my real life in every book and short story I write. By the fifth book of my "fictional autobiography series," I am still sprinkling in a bit of my life. Here is the real stuff if you are interested.

- Nicky's tirade about the nuns does have some basis in truth. Though I believe that I got a good education from the nuns and brothers in my twelve years of education in that system, I was physically assaulted many times, and I considered myself a "good kid." "Billy Rossini" was actually Billy Rostron. It was my friend Larry who committed the crime of talking on the stairway...and then ducked out of the way. My "flight" down the stairs was indeed interrupted by one of my best friends at the time, Greg Salata.

- The Shangri-Las did grow up in Cambria Heights and did sing on street corners. I own a copy of a taped basement practice in which the group performs "You Cheated, You Lied" and "She Cried." A mutual friend caught it on a reel-to-reel tape recorder before the girls signed a record contract. It was transferred to a CD in the 1990s.
- The Garden of Eden was a real place though I gave it the fictional name in my books rather than just calling it "the garden in the schoolyard."
- Newcombe's was the candy store that everyone in Cambria went to for their candy, comics, ice cream, and egg creams. This was especially true before a double feature at the Cambria Theater three doors down.
- My dentist, Dr. Irving Shotten, did have his office above the candy store. I never did reconcile that whole situation.
- The nuns really did circulate at the dances in Sacred Heart basement and did consistently use the phrase "Leave room for the Holy Ghost."
- The character of Gio is based on three of my friends. One of them recently passed away. I wrote the true details of life after the Driftwood Club in a short piece I entitled "The Last Chord." The Visible Ink organization made this story into a short film. It may be viewed on my website. www. WilliamJohnRostron.com
- The band *Those Born Free* was based on the band...well... *Those Born Free*. Johnny Cipp was based on Billy Rostron (William John Rostron for purposes of this book). The band really did play in Central Park and Greenwich Village and did audition for a high paying job and record contract. The Driftwood Lounge incident (minus the ensuing death and destruction) did happen and is the basis of *Band in the Wind*.

- The Mellotones really did snitch to the police. (Though I don't think their house was blown up)
- My "Gio" really did sing "Wild Thing, you make my thing ping." (Yes, all of us were young, stupid, and probably a bit overdosed on burgeoning hormones.)
- The character of Tony Provenzano is a fictional character but is based on my childhood remembrances of a certain individual who constantly sniffed glue and as a result suffered mental disabilities in the long run. I just moved up the time frame and made his demise a one-night misadventure.
- Mauro's Ristorante was a high-class restaurant on the very edge of Cambria Heights, near the Cross Island Parkway. In 1969, I took my girlfriend and future wife for the first "fancy" adult dinner of our lives together. (53 years married at present) We were all dressed up and enjoying ourselves until a waiter dropped the entire chicken cacciatore dinner on Marilyn's beautiful dress. Though the restaurant is now defunct and has become the site of a dry cleaner (ironic?), I just figured it would be a well-deserved payback to make it the scene of the horrific murder of Desiderio Gomez.
- Broadway Sherwood was really a diner that lay just over the border from Cambria Heights in Nassau County. When Joey and Nicky went there after the Gomez murder at Mauro's they might have had my mother as their waitress. She worked there for many years to supplement the cost of my private school education.
- Bracko and Michael's houses are as described. I lived in an attic bedroom of one of them for the first twenty years of my life.
- My bad eating habits are documented in my award-winning short piece, "Call Me T-Rex." However, I have never mentioned that for five years of my life I ate nothing but peanut butter and sugar sandwiches for lunch. Why my mother agreed to this is a mystery. Yet, Dr. Irving Shotten

DANCING WITH THE LOST

was extremely happy as I spent a great deal of time (and my parents' money) in his care.

- My friend for over sixty years, James J. Spina (Jimmy to only a few of us) was the basis for the character of DJ Spinelli in all five books. We went to high school and Queens College together. He was the driving force pushing me to write these books. He is now retired after a long career in writing and editing.

- Jimmy actually was shut out of writing for the Queens College newspaper. He really did create his own "Indy" paper. The Queens Undies name was purely my imagination.

- The Vietnam war did end on April 30, 1975. The newspapers that day showed the graphic picture of the last Americans escaping from the roof of the embassy to a waiting helicopter. The last two casualties of the war were suffered protecting that departure. Those marines were named Darwin Judge and Charles McMahon. I do feel guilty co-opting their sacrifice for the story of Danny Boy Evers, and I hope mentioning their names here does hopefully honor them.

- I knew the picture and the story of the fall of Saigon extremely well. I have kept the newspapers printed on the exact day each of my three children were born. My son Justin was born on April 30, 1975.

- The story of Danny Boy's home island of Ocracoke is true. It was at the heart of "Torpedo Alley" during World War II. My wife and I were touched by a visit to the gravesites of the four British sailors from the HMS Bedfordshire. We viewed the tiny bit of soil that holds their graves and is sovereign territory of the United Kingdom

- Astoria Park, site of Nicky's demise is exactly as described. My daughter Brittany lived across the street from it for many years. (Triborough Bridge and all)

- Saint Mary, Star of the Seas, is located off Duval Street in Key West. I have been to church there many times.
- Duval Street is known for its "Duval Crawl."
- Very often the Duval Crawl originates in Mallory Square where the sunset is viewed by thousands of people each night.
- Earnest Hemingway did frequent Sloppy Joe's and it is exactly as described in the book.
- Fort Zachary Taylor Beach is as described and does really back up to a naval base.
- Leonardo, Barlow, and Cooperman Law Firm is not real but rather a prelude to their story in *Brotherhood of Forever*. However, Morganthau was an actual District Attorney who sought to be mayor of New York City
- Michael's final decision to use his musical royalties follows the real-life story of an actual Long Island musician who had one hit and used the money to fund his education and eventual career as a teacher. With his group, he performed at a presidential inauguration.
- At Nicky's funeral, the loudmouth in the crowd complains that "Geez, those Rouse Funeral Home people…you'd think they would have the casket here and ready by 10 o'clock for a 10 o'clock funeral mass." My first Little League team was sponsored by the Rouse Funeral Home in Cambria Heights. We were the Rouse Funeral Home Indians. Modern society has deemed "Indians" as improper. I wonder if anyone would have found a team of eight-year-olds, with a funeral home name plastered in six-inch letters on our backs, also a bit offensive?
- The story of Lizzie Borden (The Actor's Lizzie Boobin) is little known outside of New England. However, my father was born and raised in New Bedford, Massachusetts and therefore knew the story and poem intimately. Why he thought it was a good idea to tell his young son this tale baffles me.

- The song "I Could Love You If You Live" was published in a poetry anthology. The song "Thief of My Forever" has been published three times as a poem. It also was performed as a song in the film "Pretty Flamingo" which can be viewed at www.PrettyFlamingoFilm.com
- Lake Panamoka is one of the two fresh lakes on Long Island that is not polluted. One of my sons lives a block away and we often make use of its beaches. I even picked out the specific house on the lake that I believe Michael and Maggie would have lived in.

AUTHOR NOTE #2

LAST WORDS

"These are the last words I have to say
That's why it took so long to write."
- Billy Joel

For those familiar with my writing, you know that I like to finish off my books with a brief bullshit session about how the book came about, how the ideas progressed, and how the real world slipped into my writing. (It always does!) This is the last time I will do this.

I need to start these notes with an apology for the fact that I have resolutely stated that this series was over on at least four different occasions. After the first two books, I believed I had told the complete story of a band named Those Born Free. I was done and I wrote that very fact. However, a few factors changed my mind. First was the success of the books. *Band in the Wind* has been read on four continents and in all fifty states according to publishing data. (Who knew that I would have readers in India, Australia, and a few European countries?) I would be hard pressed to explain the phenomena of the first two books if I didn't read all the comments that came to me in emails, Facebook, and reviews.

Readers liked *the people* in the books and to be honest so did I. Most of the characters (good and bad) in the books were based on people I had known in my formative years. The fact that I had created them did not make them any less real…to me. Therefore, I yearned to return to that world and immerse myself in our friendship, our jokes, our music, and our lives. But they were dead! (fictionally, most of them). I therefore wrote the third book purely to live in that time with those people. To do that, I concentrated on the peripheral characters of the first two books as the main protagonists. Yet, the main guys, Bracko, Gio, Tinman, Johnny, and Jimmy Mac, were there in the form of conversations on tapes that had been left running too long during band sessions. This brought the spirit of the band back to life. I, as their creator, felt I was back home.

However, this third book of the trilogy also allowed me to create a new cadre of friends (and villains), by bringing the peripheral characters of the first two books to the forefront of the story. (Brother Christian, DJ Spinelli, Aylin McAvoy, Riet Carver, Greg Cincotta, Neil Connaughton, and many more.) Because the original main characters had disappeared from the real world, they had missed a half century of American history and culture. I wanted the reader to "live" vicariously through the Vietnam War, Woodstock, Moon Landing, 9/11, and more, through this cast of characters.

Yet, the underlying theme was that each of the new characters was somehow influenced in their decisions by the words and feelings heard on the tapes of the original band. I had to work those guys, Those Born Free, into the story. Unbelievably, as of this date, Bracko has received three marriage proposals from readers who were so enamored with his goodness.

So now I was done. Right? I thought so. It was then that I came to the realization that there was both an advantage and a disadvantage to writing a trilogy of books. On one hand, if a reader liked *Band in the Wind*, they would probably move on to *Sound of Redemption* and *Brotherhood of Forever*. However, on the other hand, there are so many books in this world, that readers often moved on to something else rather than continue with a trilogy. Many would revisit the books, but not right away. That meant that sales for my second and third books were a bit stunted. This was frustrating because anecdotal and review information firmly convinced me that the third book of the trilogy was indeed the best. Despite it having a 4.8 out of 5 rating on Amazon, a reader could not just read that one book. Maybe time will allow the latter books of the trilogy to catch up. Who knows?

Again, I was done. I moved on to short stories. Indeed, to date forty-three of my stories have been published in various anthologies, magazines, and newspapers. Five that I submitted have won awards and six have been presented on stage and film in New York City. I memorialized these successes by publishing two books of short pieces, *A Flamingo Under the Carousel* and *T-Rex Stole My Computer*. Notice I did not say short stories. Some of the pieces fit this category, but some are nonfiction, and some are a combination of fiction and nonfiction. I used the tag line of "Some of this happened, some of it didn't, and some of it *almost* happened." The back cover was more descriptive. Both books include "Thirty stories that will make you laugh, cry, and feel a thousand emotions in between."

So now was I done? No! A harmless comment by my wife, Marilyn, led to a fourth novel. One day, out of the blue, she said to me while we were watching TV, "You know you never told the story of Maria." Perfectly aware that some reading this have not read the trilogy, I will report that yes, I did leave her hanging. I never told the details of her life after Johnny.

In *Sound of Redemption,* I wrote a forty-page subplot telling of her life after the events in 1967. A publisher advised me that this veered too much away from the main action of that book and that I should cut it. I did. Poor Maria's fate went from forty pages to two. She deserved better.

And so, *The Other Side of the Wind*, was created. However, I determined before initiating the project that it would not be book four of the trilogy (which itself would have been an oxymoron). It had to be a stand-alone book that did not require the reading of the other three books. This presented an interesting challenge. I had never written a first-person account from a woman's perspective. My wife dared me to try. *The Other Side of the Wind* (Maria's Memoir) is told from her point of view and has received ratings as high as *Brotherhood of Forever* without the burden of the trilogy label.

Yet there was another problem. How do you write a stand-alone novel without "stepping on the toes" of the thousand pages of the trilogy that existed in the same fictional world? I constantly had to make sure that some event or character did not contradict the other books. I also had to make sure that I did not give away any of the plot from those books—just in case the reader now wanted to go back and pick up the trilogy. These factors required a great deal of time and effort above the usual writing method. Though it took a very long time to write, I think it worked.

Okay, so now I was done. Right? I wanted to revisit that world again but saw no way to do it logically. I mentioned this to a friend whom I have never met in person. Mike Burduck was a Professor of English (recently retired) in Tennessee. What we had in common was that he had grown up in Cambria Heights, the setting for all the Cambria series of books. He is a bit younger and so we had never met in our youth. He had liked my early books and had even written blurbs for the covers. Yet a thousand miles separate us, so though we correspond, we have never met in person. He suggested I write short stories on that theme and immediately thought that a good idea. I would take the few characters who had *not* been developed in the first four books and give them their own short stories. I wrote these tales about the mysterious Padre, inept villain, Nicky "Glue" Toto, and Maggie McAvoy.

I think that I might unconsciously have left Maggie out of all the other books because I was saving her for "bigger things." I remember thinking while was writing *Brotherhood of Forever* that I had not mentioned her. Her two sisters are predominant characters, yet I merely referred to Maggie as being "gone." Did I know I had a more dominant role for her in the future?

After I had worked up the short stories for Maggie, Padre, and Nicky, I decided that the world needed a bit more Bracko. After all, he had his own built in following. I gave him a subplot that included a character (Michael) that had previously not existed in the Cambria series "world." Bracko and Michael's interaction allows many setting and character devices, such as flashbacks of the eight-year-old attending band practices.

I had gone this far—why not tie the stories together? I now realize that this was perhaps one of the most difficult tasks of my entire writing career. I had to tell all their stories, combine all their stories, and meanwhile integrate into the plot of the series at large. Plus, as a stand-alone book, I did not want to reveal any spoilers from the first four books. (If you want to know who killed Mad Guy Provenzano and the identity of Captain Jack Paradise, read *Band in the Wind* and *Sound of Redemption*.)

So that's the story of the five books. I am really done now. (Unless anyone out there has a suggestion?)

AUTHOR NOTE #3

LIVE LIKE YOU WERE DYING

"I asked him when it sank in,
That this might really be the real end.
How's it hit ya when you get that kind of news?"
- Tim McGraw

If you have gotten this far in reading my post-novel ramblings, I give you credit for exceptional patience. This section is reprinted from Author Notes at the end of T-Rex Stole My Computer. It is the one topic from my real life that has never found its way into my novels.

I have recurrent, incurable cancer. At the time of my diagnosis and first surgery, I was informed that life expectancy for cases like mine averaged about eight years. It has now been over fifteen years, and I owe my continued existence to a team of excellent doctors at Memorial Sloan-Kettering Cancer Center. Oh, don't worry. I am not going to pass away before I finish this book. My ongoing goal *now* is to die *with* cancer, not *from* it. However, during that initial traumatic period in 2010, I assumed that the eight-year time frame was firm. Therefore, I had a quite literal **deadline** to complete the book I had always thought about writing.

An event in 1967 had inspired a lifelong quest to create a novel about a certain incident that changed the course of my life. However, though it never was far from my conscious mind, I just never got around to writing that "Great American Novel." As John Lennon once said, "Life is what happens while you are busy making plans." Cancer changed all that.

I started my writing career at almost the exact time that they sent me home from the hospital after my first surgery. At that time, I decided that I wanted to write to escape thinking about my illness. Yet I soon found that my writing and cancer were inexplicably linked together.

My serious novel writing began with my rehabilitation. I found my storylines while obsessively walking and listening to music. The songs and their meanings fueled my creative juices and led to five novels and two short story books, but the synchronicity of my writing and my cancer did not end there.

From 2010 to 2013, I was both writing my novel and temporarily cancer-free. Though the doctors had hopes that they had contained and removed all cancer cells from my body, they consistently informed me that the odds were against that being the case. Life became a waiting game—with testing every three months to measure whether the nefarious cells were still roaming free in my body. Each test proved negative. Meanwhile, I wrote.

My writing was initially meant as therapy. My stories were filled with nostalgia. The culture and music of the 1960s were used as the setting for a humorous and tragic tale that was fictional but based on real-life experiences. It was fun...and that was all it was meant to be. I assumed my audience would eventually be those who shared those times with me. With that in mind, I sent the first copy to a high school and college friend with a decades-long writing career. At that time, he was editor-in-chief of a magazine. I thought he would be part of a

limited audience that would enjoy my tale of coming of age (including some fictional murder and mayhem) solely because of the nostalgia of our times.

On August 21, 2013, I received a phone call from him. His first words will remain with me forever, "You've got to publish this." I know the exact date of his call because one hour after hanging up, my oncologist called. The first recurrent cancer cells had been confirmed in my system. How can I explain that day? Some of the joy of my friend's call got me through the nightmare that my life became. My wife and family were very supportive, and I put negative thoughts aside.

My wife and I continued our RV travels, which took us to every contiguous state and every major league baseball stadium. We wintered in Key West, spent the summer on Long Island beaches, and enjoyed the Fall in South Carolina. There were close family holidays, events, and vacations. All the while, I lived with the specter of what the future held but was determined to live life to the fullest. And I wrote.

For the next five years, I edited and re-edited the book (eventually determining that it was too long and splitting it into two books). I researched traditional, self-publishing, and hybrid publishing options. Yet I couldn't pull the trigger. Despite my friend's continued insistence, I lacked the confidence to put it out there. Then there was that whole synchronicity thing I mentioned before.

In the summer of 2017, my cancer treatments and writing efforts crossed paths again. I was made aware that the nationally renowned cancer center, Memorial Sloan-Kettering, offered a writing program. My first thoughts were that this was a cute little benefit of having a life-threatening disease. I was then informed that this was an organization almost a thousand strong. They published an anthology of members' works each year, picking the best eighty pieces from over five hundred submissions for the book. I reworked one of the more amusing chapters of my book into a short story and submitted it. This entry was to be my personal litmus test. If they liked my short story, perhaps...just perhaps, I would put my book out there.

On December 18, 2017, I received notification that my short story, "Pretty Flamingo," was not only going to be in the anthology but was picked to be one of twelve that would be read and performed on a New York stage by actors from Broadway and film. This final push persuaded me to publish *Band in the Wind.*

On November 28, 2018, the first copies of that book arrived at my doorstep. I know the date because it was also the date that my oncologist informed me that my numbers were up, and I would begin chemical treatments within a few weeks. It seemed too much of a coincidence. However, I used the time of my confinement to finalize a sequel to *Band in the Wind* titled *Sound of Redemption.* I received my first copy in late April 2019—the same week I completed my treatments.

My health situation was good in 2020. Unfortunately, this was not true for the rest of the country...indeed, the rest of the world. *Brotherhood of Forever* (Book 3) was published in the darkest days of the Covid pandemic. Although I was cloistered due to being immunosuppressed, the most significant effect was on my inability to get out and publicize the third book. No one was going anywhere—especially a bookstore signing.

With the considerable time I was cooped up, I looked for other activities. I retaught myself the guitar, read a great deal, and started writing more short stories. Those short pieces that were accepted by various publishers were later published in my two books, *A Flamingo Under the Carousel* and *T-Rex Stole My Computer.* I realized that despite the success of the novels, I lacked self-confidence. Therefore, only stories that were accepted for publication by someone else were included in *my* books.

In the fall of 2021, my condition required very aggressive chemotherapy which physically took away six months of my life. I described this battle, in a short story ("Senseless") that won recognition from Writers Digest Awards. To be honest I wish I hadn't had the experience to write about.

When all the short stories were written, all the books read, and the guitar mastered (lol), I still had free time in my forced imprisonment.

My wife, Marilyn, suggested that I write another novel… this time about the character of Maria. Thus, was born *The Other Side of the Wind*. This fourth book was completed while I was in the throes of chemo. When I arrived home from my second to last excruciating treatment, there was the first copy of the book waiting for me.

Writing had always taken away some of the pain and brightened my mood. Sometimes, real life is stranger than fiction. My cancer and my writing are inextricably tied together…and that doesn't bother me.

At one time, you must remember that I thought I was writing with what I considered a **literal dead-line**. However, due to the miracles of modern medicine, I no longer contemplate that. For now, I will keep writing, traveling, and playing the guitar poorly. My wife and I will continue to jump in the RV and seek the sand and serenity of that perfect beach…whether it is in South Carolina, Key West, or Montauk.

And I am still listening to music while I walk. In fact, a certain song by Tim McGraw that I heard today inspired me to write this very author's note.

"And I loved deeper, and I spoke sweeter.
And I gave forgiveness I'd been denying.
Someday, I hope you get the chance,
To live like you were dying."

www.ingramcontent.com/pod-product-compliance
Lightning Source LLC
Chambersburg PA
CBHW020658110726
47901CB00001B/236